PRAISE FOR
THE EVOLUTION OF CALPURNIA TATE

"*The Evolution of Calpurnia Tate* is the most delightful historical novel for tweens in many, many years. . . . Callie's struggles to find a place in the world where she'll be encouraged in the gawky joys of intellectual curiosity are fresh, funny, and poignant today."—*The New Yorker*

"In her debut novel, Jacqueline Kelly brings to vivid life a boisterous small-town family at the dawn of a new century. And she especially shines in her depiction of the natural world that so intrigues Callie. . . . Readers will want to crank up the A.C. before cracking the cover, though. That first chapter packs a lot of summer heat."—*The Washington Post*

"Each chapter of this winning . . . novel opens with a quotation from 'On the Origin of Species'—a forbidden book that her own grandfather turns out to have hidden away. Together they study Darwin's masterpiece, leading to a revolution in Callie's ideas of what she might accomplish on her own."—*New York Times Book Review*

★ "Callie's transformation into an adult and her unexpected bravery make for an exciting and enjoyable read. Kelly's rich images and setting, believable relationships and a touch of magic take this story far."
—*Publishers Weekly*, Starred Review

★ "Interwoven with the scientific theme are threads of daily life in a large family . . . all told with wry humor and a sharp eye for details that bring the characters and the setting to life. The eye-catching jacket art, which silhouettes Callie and images from nature against a yellow background, is true to the period and the story. Many readers will hope for a sequel to this engaging, satisfying first novel."—*Booklist*, Starred Review

JACQUELINE KELLY

THE EVOLUTION OF CALPURNIA TATE

SQUARE
FISH

HENRY HOLT AND COMPANY

NEW YORK

The epigraphs at the beginning of each chapter are from
The Origin of Species by Charles Darwin.

SQUARE
FISH

An Imprint of Macmillan

THE EVOLUTION OF CALPURNIA TATE. Copyright © 2009
by Jacqueline Kelly. All rights reserved. Printed in the
United States of America by LSC Communications,
Harrisonburg, Virginia. For information, address Square Fish,
175 Fifth Avenue, New York, NY 10010.

Square Fish and the Square Fish logo are trademarks of Macmillan and are
used by Henry Holt and Company under license from Macmillan.

Library of Congress Cataloging-in-Publication Data
Kelly, Jacqueline.
The evolution of Calpurnia Tate / Jacqueline Kelly.
p.   cm.
Summary: In central Texas in 1899, eleven-year-old Callie Vee Tate is
instructed to be a lady by her mother, learns about love from the older three
of her six brothers, and studies the natural world with her grandfather,
the latter of which leads to an important discovery.
ISBN 978-0-312-65930-1
[1. Nature—Fiction.   2. Family life—Texas—Fiction.
3. Grandfathers—Fiction.   4. Naturalists—Fiction.   5. Texas—
History—19th century—Fiction.]   I. Title.
PZ7.K296184Evo 2009
[Fic]—dc22
2008040595

Originally published in the United States by Henry Holt and Company
First Square Fish Edition: January 2011
Square Fish logo designed by Filomena Tuosto
Book designed by April Ward
mackids.com

15   17   19   20   18   16

LEXILE 830L

For my mother, Noeline Kelly
For my father, Brian Kelly
For my husband, Robert Duncan

CHAPTER 1

THE ORIGIN OF SPECIES

When a young naturalist commences the study of a group of organisms quite unknown to him, he is at first much perplexed to determine what differences to consider ... for he knows nothing of the amount and kind of variation to which the group is subject. ...

BY 1899, WE HAD LEARNED to tame the darkness but not the Texas heat. We arose in the dark, hours before sunrise, when there was barely a smudge of indigo along the eastern sky and the rest of the horizon was still pure pitch. We lit our kerosene lamps and carried them before us in the dark like our own tiny wavering suns. There was a full day's work to be done before noon, when the deadly heat drove everyone back into our big shuttered house and we lay down in the dim high-ceilinged rooms like sweating victims. Mother's usual summer remedy of sprinkling the sheets with refreshing cologne lasted only a minute. At three o'clock in the afternoon, when it was time to get up again, the temperature was still killing.

The heat was a misery for all of us in Fentress, but it was the women who suffered the most in their corsets and petticoats. (I was still a few years too young for this uniquely feminine form of torture.) They loosened their stays and sighed the hours away and cursed the heat and their husbands, too, for dragging them to Caldwell County to plant cotton and acres of pecan trees. Mother temporarily gave up her hairpieces, a crimped false fringe and a rolled horsehair rat, platforms on which she daily constructed an elaborate mountain of her own hair. On those days when we had no company, she even took to sticking her head under the kitchen pump and letting Viola, our quadroon cook, pump away until she was soaked through. We were forbidden by sharp orders to laugh at this astounding entertainment. As Mother gradually surrendered her dignity to the heat, we discovered (as did Father) that it was best to keep out of her way.

My name is Calpurnia Virginia Tate, but back then every-body called me Callie Vee. That summer, I was eleven years old and the only girl out of seven children. Can you imagine a worse situation? I was spliced midway between three older brothers—Harry, Sam Houston, and Lamar—and three younger brothers—Travis, Sul Ross, and the baby, Jim Bowie, whom we called J.B. The little boys actually managed to sleep at midday, sometimes even piled atop one another like damp, steaming puppies. The men who came in from the fields and my father, back from his office at the cotton gin, slept too, first dousing themselves with tin buckets of tepid well water on the sleeping porch before falling down on their rope beds as if poleaxed.

Yes, the heat was a misery, but it also brought me my freedom. While the rest of the family tossed and dozed, I secretly made my way to the San Marcos River bank and enjoyed a daily interlude of no school, no pestiferous brothers, and no Mother. I didn't have permission to do this, exactly, but no one said I couldn't. I got away with it because I had my own room at the far end of the hall, whereas my brothers all had to share, and they would have tattled in a red-hot second. As far as I could tell, this was the sole decent thing about being the only girl.

Our house was separated from the river by a crescent-shaped parcel of five acres of wild, uncleared growth. It would have been an ordeal to push my way through it except that the regular river patrons—dogs, deer, brothers—kept a narrow path beaten down through the treacherous sticker burrs that rose as high as my head and snatched at my hair and pinafore as I folded myself narrow to slide by. When I reached the river, I stripped down to my chemise, floating on my back with my shimmy gently billowing around me in the mild currents, luxuriating in the coolness of the water flowing around me. I was a river cloud, turning gently in the eddies. I looked up at the filmy bags of webworms high above me in the lush canopy of oaks bending over the river. The webworms seemed to mirror me, floating in their own balloons of gauze in the pale turquoise sky.

That summer, all the men except for my grandfather Walter Tate cut their hair close and shaved off their thick beards and mustaches. They looked as naked as blind salamanders for the few days it took to get over the shock of their pale, weak chins. Strangely, Grandfather felt no distress from the heat, even with his full white beard tumbling down his chest. He claimed it was because he was a man of regular and moderate habits who never took whiskey before noon. His smelly old swallowtail coat was hopelessly outdated by then, but he wouldn't hear of parting with it. Despite regular spongings with benzene at the hands of our maid SanJuanna, the coat always kept its musty smell and strange color, which was neither black nor green.

Grandfather lived under the same roof with us but was something of a shadowy figure. He had long since turned over the running of the family business to his only son, my father, Alfred Tate, and spent his days engaged in "experiments" in his "laboratory" out back. The laboratory was just an old shed that had once been part of the slave quarters. When he wasn't in the laboratory, he was either out hunting specimens or holed up with his moldering books in a dim corner of the library, where no one dared disturb him.

I asked Mother if I could cut off my hair, which hung in a dense swelter all the way down my back. She said no, she wouldn't have me running about like a shorn savage. I found this manifestly unfair, to say nothing of *hot*. So I devised a plan: Every week I would cut off an inch of hair—just one stealthy inch—so that Mother wouldn't notice. She wouldn't notice because I would camouflage myself with good manners. When I took on the disguise of a polite young lady, I could often escape her closer scrutiny. She was usually swamped by the constant demands of the household and the ceaseless uproar of my brothers. You wouldn't believe the amount of chaos and commotion six brothers could create. Plus, the heat aggravated her crippling sick headaches, and she had to resort to a big spoonful of Lydia Pinkham's Vegetable Compound, known to be the Best Blood Purifier for Women.

That night I took a pair of embroidery scissors and, with great exhilaration and a pounding heart, cut off the first inch. I looked at the soft haystack of hair cupped in my palm. I was striding forth to greet my future in the shiny New Century, a few short months away. It seemed to me a great moment indeed. I slept poorly that night in fear of the morning.

The next day I held my breath coming down the stairs to breakfast. The pecan flapjacks tasted like cardboard. And do you know what happened? Absolutely nothing. No one noticed in the slightest. I was mightily relieved but also thought, *Well, isn't that just like this family*. In fact, no one noticed anything until four weeks and four inches went by and our cook, Viola, gave me a hard look one morning. But she didn't say a word.

It was so hot that for the first time in history Mother left the candles of the chandelier unlit at dinnertime. She even let Harry and me skip our piano lessons for two weeks. Which was just as well. Harry sweated on the keys so that they turned hazy along the pattern of the Minuet in G. Nothing Mother or SanJuanna tried could bring the sheen back to the ivory. Besides, our music teacher, Miss Brown, was ancient, and her decrepit horse had to pull her gig three miles from Prairie Lea. They would both likely collapse on the trip and have to be put down. On consideration, not such a bad idea.

Father, on learning that we would miss our lessons, said, "A good thing, too. A boy needs piano like a snake needs a hoopskirt."

Mother didn't want to hear it. She wanted seventeen-year-old Harry, her oldest, to become a gentleman. She had plans to send him off to the university in Austin fifty miles away when he turned eighteen. According to the newspaper, there were five hundred students at the university, seventeen of them well-chaperoned young ladies in the School of Liberal Arts (with a choice of music, English, or Latin). Father's plan was different; he wanted Harry to be a businessman and one day take over the cotton gin and the pecan orchards and join the Freemasons, as he had. Father apparently didn't think piano lessons were a bad idea for me though, if he considered the matter at all.

In late June, the *Fentress Indicator* reported that the temperature was 106 degrees in the middle of the street outside the newspaper office. The paper did not mention the temperature in the shade. I wondered why not, as no one in his right mind spent more than a second in the sun, except to make smartly for the next patch of shadow, whether it be cast by tree or barn or plow horse. It seemed to me that the temperature in the shade would be a lot more useful to the citizens of our town. I labored over A Letter To The Editor pointing this out, and to my great amazement, the paper published my letter the following week. To my family's greater amazement, it began to publish the temperature in the shade as well. Reading that it was only 98 in the shade somehow made us all feel a bit cooler.

There was a sudden surge in insect activity both inside the house and out. Grasshoppers rose in flocks beneath the horses' hooves. The fireflies came out in such great numbers that no one could remember a summer with a more spectacular show. Every evening, my brothers and I gathered on the front porch and held a contest to see who could spot the first flicker. There was considerable excitement and honor in winning, especially after Mother took a scrap of blue silk from her sewing basket and cut out a fine medallion, complete with long streamers. In between headaches she embroidered FENTRESS FIREFLY PRIZE on it in gold floss. It was an elegant and much-coveted prize. The winner kept it until the following night.

Ants invaded the kitchen as never before. They marched in military formation through minute cracks around the baseboards and windows and headed straight for the sink. They were desperate for water and would not be stopped. Viola took up arms against them to no avail. We deemed the fireflies a bounty and the ants a plague, but it occurred to me for the first time to question why there should be such a distinction. They were all just creatures trying to survive the drought, as we were. I thought Viola should give up and leave them alone, but I reconsidered after discovering that the black pepper in the egg salad was not pepper at all.

While certain insects overran us, some of the other normal inhabitants of our property, such as earthworms, disappeared. My brothers complained about the lack of worms for fishing and the difficulty of digging for them in the hard, parched ground. Perhaps you've wondered, Can earthworms be trained? I'm here to tell you that they can. The solution seemed obvious to me: The worms always came when it rained, and it was easy enough to make some rain for them. I carried a tin bucket of water to a shaded area in the five acres of scrub and dumped it on the ground in the same place a couple of times a day. After four days, I only had to show up with my bucket, and the worms, drawn by my footsteps and the promise of water, crawled to the surface. I scooped them up and sold them to Lamar for a penny a dozen. Lamar nagged me to tell him where I'd found them, but I wouldn't. However, I did confess my method to Harry, my favorite, from whom I could keep nothing. (Well, almost nothing.)

"Callie Vee," he said, "I've got something for you." He went to his bureau and took out a pocket-sized red leather notebook with SOUVENIR OF AUSTIN stamped on the front.

"Look here," he said. "I've never used it. You can use it to write down your scientific observations. You're a regular naturalist in the making."

What, exactly, was a naturalist? I wasn't sure, but I decided to spend the rest of my summer being one. If all it meant was writing about what you saw around you, I could do that.

Besides, now that I had my own place to write things down, I saw things I'd never noticed before.

My first recorded notes were of the dogs. Due to the heat, they lay so still in the dirt as to look dead. Even when my younger brothers chivvied them with sticks out of boredom, they wouldn't bother to raise their heads. They got up long enough to slurp at the water trough and then flopped down again, raising puffs of dust in their shallow hollows. You couldn't have rousted Ajax, Father's prize bird dog, with a shotgun let off a foot in front of his muzzle. He lay with his mouth lolling open and let me count his teeth. In this way, I discovered that the roof of a dog's mouth is deeply ridged in a backwards direction down his gullet, in order no doubt to encourage the passage of struggling prey in one direction only, namely that of DINNER. I wrote this in my Notebook.

I observed that the expressions of a dog's face are mainly manifested by the movement of its eyebrows. I wrote, Why do dogs have eyebrows? Why do dogs *need* eyebrows?

I asked Harry, but he didn't know. He said, "Go ask Grandfather. He knows that sort of thing."

But I wouldn't. The old man had fierce tufty eyebrows of his own, rather like a dragon's, and he was altogether too imposing a figure for me to have clambered on as an infant. He had never spoken to me directly that I remembered, and I wasn't entirely convinced he knew my name.

Next I turned my attention to the birds. For some reason,

we had a great number of cardinals about the place that year. Harry tickled me when he said we had a fine crop of them, as if we had something to do with their number, as if we had labored to harvest their bright, cheerful bodies and place them in the trees along our gravel drive like Christmas ornaments. But because there were so many and the drought had cut down on their normal diet of seeds and berries, the males squabbled furiously over possession of each hackberry tree. I found a mutilated dead male in the brush, a startling and sad sight. Then one morning a female came to perch on the back of the wicker chair next to me on the porch. I froze. I could have reached out and touched her with my finger. A lump of gray-brown matter dangled from her pale-apricot beak. It looked like a tiny baby mouse, thimble-sized, dead or dying.

When I related this at dinner, Father said, "Calpurnia, cardinals do not eat mice. They live on vegetation. Sam Houston, please pass the potatoes."

"Yes, well, I'm just telling you, sir," I said lamely, and then felt furious with myself for not having defended what I'd seen with my own eyes. The thought of the cardinals driven to such unnatural behavior repelled me. The next step would be cannibalism. Before I went to bed that night, I took a can full of oats from the stable and dribbled them along the drive. I wrote in the Notebook, How many cardinals will we have next year, with not enough to eat? Remember to count.

I next wrote in my Notebook that we had two very different kinds of grasshoppers that summer. We had the usual quick little emerald ones decorated all over with black speckles. And then there were huge bright yellow ones, twice as big, and torpid, so waxy and fat that they bowed down the grasses when they landed. I had never seen these before. I polled everyone in the house (except Grandfather) to find out where these odd yellow specimens had come from, but nobody could tell me. None of them was the slightest bit interested.

As a last resort, I rounded up my courage and went out to my grandfather's laboratory. I pushed back the burlap flap that served as a door and stood quaking on the threshold. He looked up in surprise from the counter where he was pouring a foul-looking brown liquid into various beakers and retorts. He didn't invite me in. I stumbled through my grasshopper conundrum while he stared at me as if he was having trouble placing me.

"Oh," he said mildly, "I suspect that a smart young whip like you can figure it out. Come back and tell me when you have." He turned away from me and began to write in his ledger.

So, that was that. My audience with the dragon. I counted it a wash. On the one hand, he hadn't breathed fire at me, but on the other, he'd been no help at all. Perhaps if I'd made Harry go with me, Grandfather would have accorded me more attention. Maybe he was peeved that I'd interrupted his work, although he had spoken to me in polite tones. I knew what he was working on. For some reason, he had gotten it in his head to figure out a way to distill pecans into whiskey. He apparently reasoned that if you could make fine spirits from common corn and the lowly potato, why not the princely pecan? And, Lord knows, we were drowning in pecans—sixty acres of them.

I went back to my room and contemplated the grasshopper puzzle. I had one of the small green grasshoppers in a jar on my vanity, and I stared at it for inspiration. I had been unable to catch one of the big yellow ones, even though they were much slower.

"Why are you different?" I asked, but it refused to answer.

The next morning, I awoke as usual to a scuffling in the wall next to my bed. It was a possum, returning to his lair at his normal time. Shortly after this, I heard the slap and slam of sash weights as SanJuanna threw open the parlor windows beneath my room. I sat up in my high brass bed, and suddenly it came to me that the fat yellow grasshoppers had to be *an entirely new species,* separate and apart from the green ones, and that I— Calpurnia Virginia Tate—had discovered them. And didn't the discoverer of a brand-new species get to put her name on it? I was going to be famous! My name would be heralded far and wide; the governor would shake my hand; the university would award me a diploma.

But what did I do now? How did I stake my claim on the natural world? I had a vague idea that I had to write to someone to register my find, some official in Washington.

I had heard debates at the dinner table between my grandfather and our minister, Mr. Barker, concerning Mr. Charles Darwin's book *The Origin of Species* and the dinosaurs they were unearthing in Colorado and what this meant to the Book of Genesis. They talked about how Nature weeded out the weak and left the hardy to carry on. Our schoolteacher, Miss Harbottle, had glossed over Mr. Darwin, looking discomfited as she did so. Surely such a book addressing the origin of species would tell me what to do. But how on earth could I get my hands on it when controversy still raged about such matters in our corner of the world? There was even an active chapter of the Flat Earth Society in San Antonio.

Then I remembered that Harry was due to take the long-bed wagon into Lockhart for supplies. Lockhart was the seat of Caldwell County. The county library was there. Books were there. All I had to do was beg a ride from Harry, the one brother who could deny me nothing.

IN LOCKHART, after conducting our business, Harry loitered on the corner so he could admire the figures of the ladies strolling by, exhibiting the latest finery from the local milliner. I mumbled excuses and slipped across the courthouse square. The library was cool and dark. I walked up to the counter where the elderly lady librarian was handing some books to a fat man in a white linen suit. Then it was my turn. Just at that moment, a woman with a little boy came up. It was Mrs. Ogletree and her six-year-old, Georgie. Georgie and I shared the same piano teacher, and his mother knew my mother.

Oh, no. The last thing I wanted was a witness.

"Good afternoon, Callie," she said. "Is your mother here today?"

"She's at home, Mrs. Ogletree. Hello, Georgie."

"Hi, Callie," he said. "What are you doing here?"

"Um . . . just looking at books. Here, you've got yours, you go ahead of me. Please."

I stepped back and grandly waved them forward.

"Why, thank you, Callie," she said. "Such lovely manners. I shall have to mention it to your mother next time I see her."

After an eternity, they left. I kept glancing around to see if anyone else was about to come up. The librarian frowned at me. I stepped up to the counter and whispered, "Please, ma'am, do you have a copy of Mr. Darwin's book?"

She leaned over the counter and said, "What was that?"

"Mr. Darwin's book. You know, *The Origin of Species*."

She frowned and cupped a hand behind her ear. "You have to speak up."

I spoke up in a shaking voice. "Mr. Darwin's book. That one. Please."

She pinioned me with a sour look and said, "I most certainly do not. I wouldn't keep such a thing in my library. They keep a copy at the Austin library, but I would have to order it by post. That's fifty cents. Do you *have* fifty cents?"

"No, ma'am." I could feel myself turning pink. I'd never had fifty cents in my life.

"And," she added, "I would need a letter from your mother

permitting you to read that particular book. Do you *have* such a letter?"

"No, ma'am," I said, mortified. My neck was starting to itch, the telltale precursor to an outbreak of hives.

She sniffed. "I thought not. Now, I have books to be shelved. You must excuse me."

I wanted to weep with rage and humiliation, but I refused to cry in front of the old bat. I left the library in a purple froth and found Harry lounging in front of the general store. He looked at me with concern.

I scratched the welts that had popped up on my neck and yelled, "What is the point of a library if they won't give you a book?"

Harry glanced around. "What are you talking about?"

"Some people aren't fit to be librarians," I said. "I want to go home now."

On the long, hot, silent trip back in the wagon piled high with goods, Harry looked over at me. "What's the matter, my own pet?"

"Nothing," I snapped. Oh, absolutely nothing, except that I was strangling on bitterness and gall and was in no mood to talk about it. For once I was glad of the privacy of the deep sunbonnet that Mother made me wear to prevent freckling.

"Do you know what's in that crate?" Harry said. "The one right behind you?" I didn't bother to reply. I didn't know and I didn't care. I hated the world.

"It's a wind machine," he said, "for Mother."

If it had been any of my other brothers, I would have snarled at him, Don't be ridiculous—there's no such thing.

"Really, it is," he said. "You'll see."

When we got home, I couldn't stand the noisy excitement at the unloading of the wagon. I bolted for the river. I ripped off my bonnet and pinafore and dress and threw myself into the water, casting terror into the hearts of the local tadpoles and turtles. Good. That lady librarian had ruined my day, and I was determined to ruin someone—or something—else's day. I ducked my head underwater and let out a long, loud scream, the sound burbling in my ears. I came up for air and did it again. And one more time, just to be thorough. The cooling water gradually soothed me. After all, what was one book to me? Really, it didn't matter. One day I would have all the books in the world, shelves and shelves of them. I would live my life in a tower of books. I would read all day long and eat peaches. And if any young knights in armor dared to come calling on their white chargers and plead with me to let down my hair, I would pelt them with peach pits until they went home.

I lay on my back and watched a pair of swallows racing up and down the river, tumbling like acrobats in pursuit of invisible bugs. Despite my hours of freedom, the summer was not proceeding as I'd envisaged. Nobody was interested in the Questions that I wrote in my Notebook. Nobody was interested in helping me figure out the Answers. The heat sapped the life out of everybody and everything.

I thought of our beloved, big old house and how sad it looked in the middle of the yellow dried-out lawn. Usually the grass was soft and cool and green, inviting you to take off your boots and run across it barefoot and play Statues, but now it was a scorched bright gold and as menacing to the feet as straw stubble. The yellow grass made it hard to see my brand-new species of big yellow grasshopper. You couldn't find them until you practically stepped on them. Then they would zing upward and fly ponderously on clacking wings for a few feet and disappear in the grass again. Catching them was difficult, despite their being fat and slow. Funny how the smaller and quicker emerald ones were such a snap to catch. They were just too easy to spot. The birds spent their days gobbling them up while the yellow ones hid nearby and taunted their less-fortunate brothers.

And then I understood. There was no new species. They were all one kind of grasshopper. The ones that were born a bit yellower to begin with lived to an old age in the drought; the birds couldn't see them in the parched grass. The greener ones, the ones the birds picked off, didn't last long enough to grow big. Only the yellower ones survived because they were more fit to survive the torrid weather. Mr. Charles Darwin was right. The proof lay in my own front yard.

I lay in shock in the water thinking about this, staring at the sky, looking for some flaw in my reasoning, some crack in my conclusion. I could find none. Then I splashed my way to the bank. I hauled myself out by some handy elephant ears, dried off with my pinafore, dressed as fast as I could, and ran home.

When I got back to the house, I found the whole family clustered around a busted-open crate in the hallway. In the middle of the excelsior nest sat a squat, black metal machine with four blades on the front and a glass reservoir on the back into which my father poured kerosene. In the middle of the blades, a round brass boss proclaimed in curly script, *Chicago's Finest Wind Machine*.

Father said, "Stand back." He struck a match and set the thing alight. It filled the room with a mineral stink and a great *whoosh* of air. My brothers all cheered. I cheered too but for a different reason.

Life in our house got somewhat easier after that. Mother retired at midday with her wind machine, and all our lives got better, especially Father's, whom she sometimes invited to retire with her.

It took me a week to get up the nerve to visit Grandfather again. He was sitting in his laboratory on a dilapidated armchair, the oozing stuffing mined by mice.

I said, "I know why the big grasshoppers are yellow and why the little ones are green." I told him my discovery and how I'd figured it out. I shifted from foot to foot as he looked at me and listened in silence. After a while he said, "Did you come up with this on your own? With no help?"

"Yes," I said, then told him about my humiliating trip to the Lockhart library. He stared at me for a moment with an odd expression on his face—perhaps surprise, perhaps consternation—as if I were a species he'd never seen before. He said, "Come with me."

He didn't speak a word as we walked to the house. Oh, dear. I had done the unthinkable, not once, but twice, by interrupting him at his work. Was he going to turn me over to Mother for yet another lecture on good manners? He led me into the library, where we children were not supposed to go. So he was going to deliver the lecture himself. Perhaps he would berate me for my clumsy theory. Or perhaps he would switch me across the hands. My dread grew. Who was I—Callie Vee Tate of Fentress, Texas—to think I could even contemplate such matters? A nobody from nowhere.

Despite my fear, I took a good look around the room, since I knew I'd never have the chance again. The library was dim, even with the heavy bottle-green velvet drapes drawn back from the tall double window. Right by the window sat a huge leather armchair and a spool table holding a lamp for reading. There were books on the floor by the chair and more books stacked in tall wooden shelves made from our failed pecan trees (you couldn't escape the enduring fact of pecans in our lives). There was a large oak desk covered in intriguing oddities: a blown ostrich egg on a carved wooden stand, a microscope nesting in a shagreen leather case, a carved whale's tooth etched with a bosomy lady not exactly contained by her corset. The family Bible and a huge dictionary with its own magnifying glass lay side by side next to a red plush album full of cramped formal portraits of my ancestors. So. Would I be getting the Bible lecture or the Letting-Down-My-Ancestors lecture? I waited while he made up his mind. I glanced around the walls, which were covered with shallow boxes displaying alarming stick insects and bright multicolored butterflies. Below each gay scrap of color was a scientific name in my grandfather's careful copperplate script. I forgot myself and went over to peer at them.

"Bear," said Grandfather.

Huh? I thought.

"Watch the bear," he said, just as I tripped on the open sneering mouth of a black bearskin rug, its fangs a trap in the gloom for the unwary.

"Right. Bear. Sir."

Grandfather unthreaded his watch chain to remove a tiny key. He unlocked a tall glass cabinet crammed with more books, preserved birds, bottled beasts, and other curios. I sidled over to get a better look at this irresistible display. A misshapen armadillo caught my eye, warped and buckled and lumpy, obviously stuffed by the most inept amateur. Why did he have that? I could have done better. Next to it was a five-gallon specimen bottle of thick glass containing the strangest beast I had ever seen. A thick, blobby form, multiple arms, two big glaring eyes distorted by the glass into huge saucer orbs, the stuff of nightmares. What on earth was it? I drew closer.

Grandfather reached into the stack of books. I saw *Dante's Inferno* next to *The Science of Hot Air Ballooning*. There was *A*

Study of Mammalian Reproduction and *A Treatise on Drawing the Female Nude*. He extracted a book covered in rich green morocco leather handsomely tipped with gold. He polished it with his sleeve, although I could see no dust on it. Ceremoniously, he bowed and offered it to me. I looked at it. *The Origin of Species*. Here, in my own house. I received it in both my hands. He smiled.

Thus began my relationship with Granddaddy.

CHAPTER 2

THE MEASURE OF
THE MORNING

The laws governing inheritance are quite unknown;
no one can say why . . . the child often reverts in certain characters to its grandfather. . . .

THREE DAYS LATER, I crept downstairs and went out onto the
front porch very early before the daily avalanche of my brothers could crack open the peace of the morning. I scattered a
handful of sunflower seeds thirty paces down the drive to draw
the birds and then I sat down on the steps on a ratty old cushion
I'd scavenged from the trunk room. I made a list in my red
leather Notebook of everything that moved. Isn't that what
naturalists do?

One of the sunflower seeds hopped across the slate tiles
of the front walk. Odd, that. On inspection it turned out to be
a tiny toad, a quarter of an inch long, hopping mightily
after an escaping millipede, itself no bigger than a thread, both
going for all they were worth until they disappeared in the
grass. Then a wolf spider, startling in size and hairiness,
streaked over the gravel, either chasing something smaller or

being chased by something bigger, I couldn't tell which. I reckoned there must be a million minor dramas playing out around the place without ceasing. Oh, but they were hardly minor to the chaser and the chasee who were dealing in the coin of life and death. I was a mere bystander, an idler. They were playing for keeps.

Then a hummingbird careened around the corner of the house and plunged into the trumpet of the nearest lily drooping in the heat. Not finding it to his liking, he abruptly backed out and explored the next one. I sat a few feet away, entranced, close enough to hear the angry low-pitched buzzing of his wings, so at odds with his jewel-like appearance and jaunty attitude. The bird paused at the lip of a flower and then turned and caught sight of me. He hovered in midair for a second and then rushed at me. I froze. The bird stopped four inches shy of my face and hung there, I swear. I felt the tiny rush of wind from his wings against my forehead and, reflexively, my eyes squeezed shut of their own accord. How I wish I'd been able to keep them open, but it was a natural reaction and I couldn't stop myself. The second I opened them, the bird flew off. He was the size of a winged pecan. Fueled by rage or curiosity—who could tell—he cared not at all that I could have crushed him with the lightest swat.

I had once seen Ajax, Father's best dog, get into a fight with a hummingbird and lose. The hummingbird had dived at him and spooked him until he'd trotted back to the front porch, looking very embarrassed. (It is possible for a dog to look embarrassed, you know. He'd whipped around and started licking his nether parts, a sure sign a dog is trying to hide his true feelings.)

The front door opened, and Granddaddy came out onto the porch, an ancient leather satchel strapped over his shoulder, a butterfly net in one hand, and a malacca walking stick in the other.

"Good morning, Calpurnia," he said. So he knew my name after all.

"Good morning, Granddaddy."

"What have you got there, if I may ask?"

I jumped to my feet. "It's my Scientific Notebook," I said grandly. "Harry gave it to me. I write down everything I observe in it. Look, here's my list for this morning."

Observe was not a word I normally used in conversation, but I wanted to prove my seriousness to him. He put down his satchel, and it made interesting clinking noises. He took out his spectacles and looked at my list. It read:

cardinals, male and female
a hummingbird, some other birds (?)
rabbits, a few
cats, some
lizard, green
insects, various
C. V. Tate's grasshoppers, big/yellow and
    small/green (these are the same species)

He took off his spectacles and tapped the page. "A fair start," he said.

"A start?" I said, hurt. "I thought it was finished."

"How old are you, Calpurnia?"

"Twelve," I said.

He looked at me.

"Eleven and three quarters," I blurted. "I'm practically twelve. Really. You can hardly tell the difference."

"And how are you coming along with Mr. Darwin and his conclusions?"

"Oh, it's marvelous. Yes. Marvelous. Of course, I haven't read the whole thing yet. I'm taking my time." Truthfully, I had read the first chapter several times and found it to be heavy weather. I had then jumped ahead to the section on "Natural Selection" but still struggled with the language.

Granddaddy looked at me gravely. "Mr. Darwin did not write for an audience of eleven-and-three-quarters-practically-twelve-year-olds. Perhaps we can discuss his ideas sometime. Would you care to do that?"

"Yes," I said. "Yessir, yes."

"I am going to collect specimens at the river. Order Odonata today, I think. Dragonflies and damselflies. Would you like to accompany me?"

"Yes, please."

"We shall have to take your Notebook." He opened the satchel, and in it I saw some glass jars and *A Field Guide to the Insects,* his lunch packet, and a miniature silver flask. He tucked

my red Notebook and pencil in beside it. I picked up his butterfly net and slung it over my shoulder.

"Shall we?" he said, and offered me his arm in the manner
of a gentleman taking a lady in to dinner. I linked my arm
through his. He was so much taller than I that we jostled each
other down the steps, so I let go of his arm and slipped my hand
into his. The palm was calloused and weathered, the nails
thick and curved, a miraculous construction of leather and
horn. My grandfather looked startled, then pleased, I think,
although I couldn't tell for sure. Nevertheless, his hand closed
on mine.

We picked our way across the wild field to the river. Granddaddy stopped every now and then to peer at a leaf, a rock, a
mound of dirt, things I didn't find terribly interesting. What
was interesting was how he stooped over and scrutinized each
object before extending a slow, deliberate hand. He was careful
with everything he touched, putting each bug back where
he found it, nudging each pile of dirt back into place. I stood
holding the butterfly net at the ready, itching to pounce on
something.

"Do you know, Calpurnia, that the class Insecta comprises
the largest number of living organisms known to man?"

"Granddaddy, nobody calls me Calpurnia except Mother,
and then only when I'm in lots of trouble."

"Why on earth not? It's a lovely name. Pliny the Younger's
fourth wife, the one he married for love, was named Calpurnia,

and we have been left by him some of the great love letters of all time. There's also the natal acacia tree, genus *Calpurnia*, a useful laburnum mainly confined to the African continent. Then there's Julius Caesar's wife, mentioned in Shakespeare. I could go on."

"Oh. I didn't know that." Why hadn't anyone ever told me these things? All my brothers except for Harry bore the names of proud Texas heroes, many of whom had laid down their lives at the Alamo. (Harry had been named after a bachelor great-uncle with lots of money and no heirs.) I had been named after my mother's older sister. I guess it could have been worse: Her younger sisters were Agatha, Sophronia, and Vonzetta. Actually, it could have been *much* worse—like Governor Hogg's daughter, Ima. Gad, Ima Hogg! Can you imagine? I wondered if her great beauty and massive fortune were enough to protect her from a lifetime of torture? Perhaps if you had enough money, no one laughed at you for anything. And me, Calpurnia, with a name I'd hated all my life, why . . . why, it was a *fine* name, it was *music*, it was *poetry*. It was . . . it was incredibly *annoying* that no one in my family had bothered to tell me any of this.

So, then. Calpurnia would do.

We pushed on through the woods and the scrub. For all his age and his spectacles, Granddaddy's eyes were a lot keener than mine. Where I saw nothing but leaf mold and dried twigs, he saw camouflaged beetles, motionless lizards, invisible spiders.

"Look there," he said. "It's Scarabaeidae, probably *Cotinus texana*. The fig beetle. Quite unusual to find one in a drought. Take it in the net, gently now."

I swished the net, and the bug was mine. He extracted it and held it in his hand and we examined it together. It was an inch long, middling green, and otherwise unexceptional in appearance. Granddaddy flipped it over, and I saw that its underside shone a startling greeny-blue, iridescent and shot through with purple. The colors changed as it squirmed in dismay. It reminded me of my mother's abalone brooch, lovely and rare.

"It's beautiful," I said.

"It's related to the scarab beetle, which the ancient Egyptians worshipped as a symbol of the morning sun and the afterlife. Sometimes they wore it as jewelry."

"They did?" I wondered how you'd get a beetle to stay on your dress. I had visions of sticking it on with a hatpin or perhaps wallpaper paste, neither of which seemed like a particularly good idea.

"Here," he said, and held it out to me.

He tipped it into my palm, and I'm proud to say I didn't flinch. The beetle tickled as it wandered over my hand.

"Should we keep him, sir?" I asked.

"I have one in my collection in the library. We can let this one go."

I put my hand to the ground, and the bug or, rather, *Cotinus texana* stumbled off and wandered away unconcerned.

"What can you tell me about the Scientific Method,

Calpurnia?" The way he said these words, I knew they had capital letters.

"Um, not much."

"What are you studying in school? You do go to school, don't you?"

"Of course I do. We're studying Reading, Spelling, Arithmetic, and Penmanship. Oh, and Deportment. I got an 'acceptable' for Posture but an 'unsatisfactory' for Use of Hankie and Thimble. Mother was kind of unhappy about that."

"Good God," he said. "It's worse than I thought."

This was an intriguing statement, although I didn't understand it.

"And is there no science? No physics?" he said.

"We did have botany one day. What's physics?"

"Have you never heard of Sir Isaac Newton? Sir Francis Bacon?"

"No." I wanted to laugh at this ridiculous name, but there was something about Granddaddy's expression that told me we were discussing mighty serious business and he would be disappointed in me if I didn't take it seriously, too.

"And I suppose they teach you that the world is flat and that there are dragons gobbling up the ships that fall over the edge." He peered at me. "There are many things to talk about. I hope it's not too late. Let us find a place to sit."

We resumed our walk to the riverbank and found shade under a hospitable tree in the pecan bottom. Then he told me some stupefying things. He told me about ways in which you could get to the truth of any matter, not merely sitting around thinking about it like Aristotle (a smart but confused Grecian gentleman), but going out and looking with your own eyes; about making your Hypothesis and devising your Experiment, and testing by Observation, and coming to a Conclusion. And then testing the strength of your Conclusion, over and over. He told me about Occam's razor, about Ptolemy and the music of the spheres, and how everyone had been all wrong about the sun and the planets for so many centuries. He told me about Linnaeus and his system for naming all living things in Nature and how we still followed this system whenever we named a new species. He told me about Copernicus and Kepler and why Newton's apple fell down instead of up. About how the moon is always falling in a circle around our Earth. About the difference between deductive and inductive reasoning and how Sir Francis Bacon of the peculiar name got it right. Granddaddy told me how he had traveled to Washington in 1888 to join a new organization of gentlemen who called themselves the National Geographic Society. They had banded together to fill in the bare spots on the globe and to pull the country out of the morass of superstition and backward thinking in which it floundered after the War Between the States. All of this was heady news of a world far removed from hankies and thimbles, patiently delivered to me under a tree amidst the drowsing bees and nodding wildflowers.

The hours passed, and the sun moved overhead (or to be

correct, we moved below it, rotating slowly away from the day and toward the night). We shared a thick cheese-and-onion sandwich and a wedge of pecan pie and a canteen of water. Then he took a couple of nips from his silver flask, and we napped awhile as the insects buzzed and ticked and the dappled shade shifted around us.

We awoke and dipped our handkerchiefs in the river to refresh ourselves, then poked our way along the bank. I caught various crawling and swimming and flying oddities at his direction, and we examined them all, but he kept only one insect, putting it in a Mason canning jar with holes poked in the lid, which I knew had come from our kitchen. (Viola constantly complained to Mother that her jars were disappearing, and Mother in turn always blamed my brothers, who were—as it turned out for the first time in recorded history—blameless.) There was a small, neat paper label pasted on the jar. I penciled the date and time of collection on it as instructed, but I didn't know what to put for the location.

"Think about where we are," Granddaddy said. "Can you describe it concisely so that you can find this spot again if you have to?"

I looked at the angle of the sun through the trees and thought about how far we had walked. "Can I put one half mile west of the Tate house, near the three-forked oak?"

Yes, that was fine. We wandered on and found one of the regular deer paths dotted with droppings. We sat down and waited in silence. A white-tailed doe came by, making no sound. I could almost reach out and touch her. How could such a large creature move so silently through the snapping underbrush? She turned her long neck and looked right at me, and for the first time I understood the expression "doe-eyed." Her deep brown eyes were huge, her gaze gentle and melting. Her large ears flicked in all directions, independent of each other. A shaft of sunlight caught the blood-rich ears and turned them a brilliant pink. I thought she was the most gorgeous creature I'd ever seen, until a few seconds later her spotted fawn meandered into view. Oh, the fawn broke my heart with its sweet, dished face, its absurdly fragile legs, its still-fuzzy coat. I wanted to scoop it up in my arms and protect it from its inevitable future of coyotes, starvation, hunters. How could anybody shoot such a beauty? And then the fawn did this miraculous thing: It folded up its front legs, then its hind legs, and sank to the ground where it . . . *disappeared*. The white spots scattered over its brown back mimicked the dappled light so that one second a fawn lay there, and the next second there was nothing but undergrowth.

Granddaddy and I sat motionless for a good five minutes and then quietly collected our things and moved on. We followed the river until the shadows grew long and then we arced through the scrub and made for home. On the way back, he spotted the rarest and most delicate object in the wild, an old hummingbird's nest, fragile and expertly woven, smaller than an eggcup.

"What extraordinary good luck!" Granddaddy said. "Treasure this, Calpurnia. You may go through your whole life and never see another one."

The nest was the most intricately constructed thing, like something built by the fairies in my childhood tales. I almost said so aloud but caught myself in time. Members of the scientific community did not say such things.

"How can we carry it home?" I said. I was afraid to touch it.

"Let's slide it into a jar for now. I have a glass box in the library that will be the right size. You can keep it on display in your room. It would be a shame to hide it away in a drawer."

The library was so much Granddaddy's territory that even my parents seldom went in there. SanJuanna was allowed to dust once a quarter. Granddaddy usually kept it locked. What he didn't know was that on those rare occasions when there were no adults around, my brothers would sometimes boost each other over the transom. My second-oldest brother, Sam Houston, once got a long look at Mathew Brady's book of battlefield photographs and breathlessly reported to us the butchered horses lying in the mud and the shoeless dead men staring at the sky.

We got back to the house around five o'clock. Jim Bowie and Ajax ran out to greet us as soon as they saw us coming up the drive.

"You're in trouble, Callie," J.B. puffed. "Mama's really mad." He ignored Granddaddy. "Mama says you missed your piano practice today."

This was true. Our lessons had started again, and I knew I'd have to make up the practice, plus an additional half hour as punishment. That was the rule, but I didn't care. The day had been worth it. The day had been worth a thousand extra hours at the piano.

We went into the house, and Granddaddy put the hummingbird's nest in a tiny glass box and gave it to me. Then I left him pottering about in the library and went off to plead my case before Mother, to no avail.

I managed to cram my piano punishment in before dinner, playing with a light heart and a sure, spirited touch, if I do say so myself. I went to bed that night exhausted and exhilarated, the hummingbird nest in its neat glass box on my dresser next to my hairpins and ribbons.

A week later, my morning list looked like this:

5:15 a.m., clear and fine, winds from the south
8 rabbits (7 cottontail, 1 jack)
1 skunk (juvenile, appears lost)
1 possum (notched left ear)
5 cats (3 ours, 2 feral)
1 snake (grass-type, harmless)
1 lizard (green, same color as lily stems, vy
   hard to spot)
2 red-tailed hawks
1 buzzard

3 toads
2 hummingbirds (Rufous?)
assorted untallied Odonata, Hymenoptera, Arachnidae

I showed it to Granddaddy, who nodded his approval. "It's amazing what you can see when you just sit quietly and look."

CHAPTER 3

THE POSSUM WARS

Seedlings from the same fruit, and the young of the same litter, sometimes differ considerably from each other, though both the young and the parents . . . have apparently been exposed to exactly the same conditions of life. . . .

THE POSSUM WARS had started up and were, once again, raging around the back porch. That is, as much as a war of passiveness and inaction could be said to rage. This presented me with an excellent field of study, since every night the battle always played out exactly like this: A portly, dusty possum emerged from under the house to forage for his nocturnal breakfast of kitchen scraps and whatnot. He was inevitably surprised by one of the Outside Cats that patrolled the back porch as part of her domain. The cat and the possum stared at each other with big, round eyes of mutual shock, and then the possum groaned and slumped to the ground. He lay there on his side, motionless and stiff, his grimacing mouth exhibiting tiny needle teeth. His eyes were fixed, his whiskers frozen. He presented the very picture of Possum Death.

The cat, always freshly amazed by this display, looked on in wonder. She approached the corpse with caution and tentatively sniffed the ground around him. She then folded herself up into that loaf shape peculiar to cats and regarded her vanquished foe with enormous feline satisfaction, her duty done. After a while, she got bored and wandered off to the kitchen door, hoping to cadge a handout from Viola. The corpse lay in state for another five minutes and then, without warning or ceremony, lurched to his feet and casually strolled off in search of his own meal.

This scene played night after night, all summer long. Neither I nor the adversaries ever fatigued of it. How satisfying to have a bloodless war in which each side was equally convinced of its own triumph.

Every morning, the possum returned at five o'clock sharp. He made his way back under the house and climbed up into the wall beside my bed. His scuffling woke me as dependably as any alarm clock, my five o'clock possum. I didn't tell anyone about him because if Mother found out she would send SanJuanna's husband, Alberto, under the house to stop up the hole and set a trap. But I didn't begrudge the possum his home in ours. (Question for the Notebook: How is it that the possum knows the exact time?)

I asked Granddaddy about this. He said seriously, "Maybe he carries a watch in his pouch like Alice's rabbit."

"Oh, yes," I said, trying not to smile and failing. I wrote

this in my Notebook so that I'd remember to tell my best friend, Lula Gates.

ONE EVENING while Granddaddy fiddled with his formula for making liquor from pecans, I sat on a tall stool at his elbow and watched him work. He had hung a dozen or so kerosene lamps from the ceiling at various heights around the old slave quarters, and you had to watch your head. The lamps filled the small space with a dancing yellow light. Mother was terrified the place would go up in flames, and she made Alberto keep big buckets of damp river sand in each corner. The windows had no glass, just flaps of gunnysack strung up in a futile attempt to keep out the insects. It was a paradise for moths.

Granddaddy had been working for years on a way to distill pecans into liquor. The experiment itself didn't interest me, but his company was never boring. We talked as he worked. I handed him things, and I sharpened his pencils, which he kept in a shaving mug.

He tended to hum cheery scraps of Vivaldi when his work was going well; when it was not going well, he hissed softly through the thicket of his mustache. I picked a moment when he was humming in a major key and said, "Granddaddy, have you always been a naturalist?"

"What was that?" he said. He held a beaker of muddy brown liquid up to the warm, wavering light and put on his spectacles to peer at the thick sediment that settled to the bottom like river sludge. "Oh. No. Not always."

"Was *your* grandfather a naturalist, sir?" I said.

"I don't know," he said. "I can't say I knew him. He died when I was a young boy." He took a sip of the murky liquid and made a face. Distill, sip, grimace. Then he would usually swear. This was his pattern.

"Damn," he said, "that's ghastly stuff."

Progress had not, apparently, been made.

"How old were you when he died?" I said.

"Oh, about five or so, I reckon." And then, anticipating my next question, he said, "He died of wounds he sustained in a battle against the Comanche in the Oklahoma Territories."

"Well," I said, "was he interested in science?"

"Not that I know of. He traded in beaver and buff, but I don't believe he had anything other than a pure business interest in them. Strain this for me, won't you? Then put it in one of those bottles and label it with today's date. Perhaps it will improve with time. It couldn't possibly get any worse."

I took the beaker from him and poured the contents through a gauze sieve into one of Mother's empty Lydia Pinkham's bottles. Sometimes she could really go through that stuff, especially when my brothers got on her nerves (which was a lot of the time). I stoppered the bottle and marked it with a red grease pencil: JULY 1, 1899. I placed it on a shelf next to its many unsuccessful fellows.

"Then how did you come to be interested in science, sir?" I asked.

He stopped what he was doing and appeared to stare out the

window, except that I knew you couldn't see out through the burlap at night, only in.

After a long moment, he said, "It happened at twilight. Eighteen sixty-five. I remember it as if it were yesterday. Matter of fact, I remember it *better* than I remember yesterday. Old age is a terrible thing, Calpurnia." He looked at me and said, "Don't let it happen to you."

"Nosir," I said. "I won't."

"I was the commanding officer of a troop of boys dragooned from all over Texas. They were fine horsemen, every one of them raised on horseback. They thought they were going for the cavalry, but it turned out they were meant for the infantry. To spend their days marching. My God, the endless complaining when they found out! You never heard such creative profanity. They despised walking, let alone marching. But despite their protestations, a tougher bunch of boys you never saw.

"The sun was setting. It was April on the Sabine River and we had made a cold camp. Our scout was returning, and I threw my arm in the air in silent signal to him and then, the most astounding thing, something flew—*thunk!*—into my hand. In my shock, my hand closed around the thing tight, and I was amazed to feel warm fur against my palm. It was a young bat, quite small, lying stunned in my grasp."

"No," I breathed. "No."

"Yes," said Granddaddy. "I was almost as stunned as the poor animal."

"What did you do?"

"The creature and I regarded each other for a few minutes. It had an intelligent eye and soft, tender fur. It looked like a miniature fox. The wing was leathery, yes, but not cool or repulsive; instead, it was as supple and fine as a kid glove warmed by a lady's hand."

I wondered what I would do if a bat flew into my hand. Probably shriek and drop it. Maybe even faint. I considered this. I'd never fainted in my life, but I thought it sounded like an interesting experience.

"I wrapped it up in my last remaining handkerchief and tucked it inside my shirt to keep it warm. It made no protest to any of these attentions. I took it to my tent. Before I prepared for bed, I took it from its wrapping and turned it upside down and touched its feet to a length of rope I had strung up inside my tent to dry my clothes. Although it still seemed only partly sensible to its surroundings, its feet gripped the twine in what I supposed to be a kind of primitive reflex, and it folded itself with particularity and hung there as if in nature, presenting a compact parcel surprisingly tidy and pleasing to the eye.

"I left the flap of my tent open, and at some point during that long, cold night, I awoke to the air around me *quivering*, if you will—I cannot describe it any better—as the bat flew around my head and then out into the night. I wished him God-speed."

Listening to Granddaddy, I had the strangest feeling. I didn't know whether to cheer or cry.

"But that's not the end of the tale," he said. "Hand me that length of rubber tubing, won't you? I awoke before dawn. Since we had no fire, my man brought me a basin of cold water for my morning toilet. I had dressed and prepared to leave my tent, when the air whirred around me. My friend was back, settling himself on my clothesline."

"He came back?" I cried.

"My very own bat," he said, "or I must assume so. One bat looks much like another to the untutored human eye. He hung there regarding me placidly enough, then went to sleep. I refer to it as he, but, of course, I had no basis in fact for this assumption. As it turns out, sexing the young bat is not a difficult proposition, but I did not know it then."

"Did you keep him?" I said. "Did you keep him?"

"He slept in my tent as my guest all that day." Granddaddy smiled, illuminated by the flickering yellow light of the lamps, steeped in delightful memory. Then his face changed.

"I'll never forget that day," he said. "The Federals fell upon us two hours after sunrise and kept after us until the sun went down. They had hauled in a couple of twelve-pounders and they hammered the hell out of us until we could not hear for the cannon noise or see for the smoke. The minié balls took a terrible toll. We were hemmed in.

"All day long, I sortied up and down the line, exhorting our boys and offering what cheer I could. I sent first one boy off, then another, to carry a message downstream to Major

Duncan. I never saw either of those boys again." He rubbed his forehead.

"With each pass along the line, I couldn't help looking into my tent. I worried, you see, about the bat. I worried that the noise and the smoke would panic him and send him blundering into the cross fire. He was *my* bat by then, you see."

I nodded. I did see.

"The powder smoke filled the air until the sun was blotted out. You couldn't see more than five yards to either hand.

"At sunset the onslaught eased up, I suppose so the Federals could partake of some dinner. My boys stayed in their holes and ate cold biscuit. Those that had pen and paper wrote their last letters to their families and pressed them on me and begged me, if I survived, to see them delivered. Many of them clasped my hand and told me good-bye and bid me to pray for their souls and their families at home. One unlettered boy followed me back to my tent and begged me to write his letter for him. I opened the flap with great apprehension, sure that my bat had panicked and flown away."

I held my breath and sat like a statue.

"But there he was. Fast asleep. As far as I could tell, he had not stirred from his upside-down perch all day. If the boy noted the strange small parcel hanging there, he did not remark upon it. His thoughts were far away with his family.

"I wrote his letter for him to his mother and sisters in Elgin. He told them not to cry overly long for him and to make sure they got the corn in by June. He told me there was no man left on the place, and he did not think they could manage without him. Tears came to his eyes at the thought of their situation. He had no thought of himself. I took his hand and pledged that I would do my best to see his family through all right. He embraced me and called me Cap. He thanked me and said I had relieved his mind and he could die without worry that day. Then he left me and returned to his place in the line."

Granddaddy pulled his big white handkerchief from his pocket and wiped his face.

"I looked at my bat," he said. "I pulled up my chair and studied him from inches away. He was perfect in every way. *Perfect*. He must have felt my presence because he opened his eyes and blinked at me. He was exceedingly calm. The noise and vibrations outside seemed not to bother him at all. He stretched his wings wide for a moment and yawned and then refolded himself and fell fast asleep again. I never wanted to leave that tent.

"But the firing started up again. I stayed there studying him until I was sent for. I didn't want to go."

We sat in silence. Then I said, "Did he die?"

Granddaddy looked at me.

"That boy," I said. "The one from Elgin."

"He didn't die that day." After a moment he said, "He took a ball in the knee. He lay in a field of the dead and dying, all calling out for water, for mother, for mercy. We listened to their terrible cries growing weaker until the middle of the night, when it was safe to crawl out and drag them back. Our surgeon worked all through the night while we held rushlights overhead. If a soldier was not badly wounded, he would keep. If a soldier was too badly wounded, he was put aside and given a canteen and a grain or two of morphia and any comfort he could take from the chaplain. The ones with the shattered arms and legs required urgent amputation before they bled to death, or before the dry gangrene or the wet pus set in.

"Then, as the sun came up, it was the boy from Elgin's turn. He was pitiably weak. We lifted him onto the table. It was thick and warm with blood. I gave him the chloroform. As I put the funnel over his face, he looked right at me and smiled and said, 'Don't mind about me, Cap. I'm all right.'

"Then I pulled on his leg as hard as I could while the surgeon sawed and made his flap. Suddenly the leg came off in my arms, and I stood there cradling it as if it were a child. It's a surprising thing, you know—how heavy a man's leg is. I stood there and held it. I didn't want to throw it on the pile with all the others. But in the end, that's what I did."

"You saved him," I said. "Didn't you?"

After a while, Granddaddy said, "He never woke up." He stared into the corner for a long time and then said, "Two days later, we got word that the war was over. They told us to go home, to take all the provisions and equipment we could carry, but there was little enough left. A handful of cartridges, a pound or two of beans, a moldy blanket; there would be no more pension than that. I knew that I might be in desperate need of my tent. But my bat was still there. I didn't know how I could leave him or how I could take him. Finally, I went to the surgeon's tent and stole the Yellow Jack from his trunk. Do you know the Yellow Jack?"

"No, sir," I whispered.

"It is the flag that signifies yellow fever—a sign to stay away. Yellow fever carried off thousands, whole regiments, maybe as many as Federal fire. I tied the jack to my tent with a leather cord. Then I slashed a hole in the roof. I knew my bat would be safe and undisturbed for a while. I could do no more than this.

"I was overcome with sadness as I bid good-bye to my bat. Yet earlier I had set fire to a mountain of arms and legs and felt nothing. I had thrown the boy from Elgin into a trench with all the others. And I felt nothing.

"It took me eighteen days to make Elgin. I gave the news to his mother and sisters in their front parlor. I told them their boy had died a hero. I didn't tell them that his death meant nothing in the end. They told me they were honored I had come. I stayed with them for three months to get the corn in and make the place right. I sent word to your grandmother that I would be home later—I don't think she ever forgave me for not coming to her directly. But we got the crops in, each taking a turn behind the mule, even down to the youngest."

My grandfather looked at me in surprise. "Why, you are the same age she was."

I thought of walking behind the mule like our field hands. They were grown men with thick forearms and huge, cracked hands; depending on the season, they were covered in gray dust or black mud. I couldn't imagine it.

"I shouldn't be telling you this." He wiped his face and looked so old it scared me. "You are too young to hear it."

I came up and leaned against him, and he put his arm around me. We stood that way for a minute. He kissed me on the forehead.

After a few minutes, he said, "Where were we? Ah, yes. Fetch me that filter, won't you?"

I got him his filter, and we worked on with no more talk.

I THOUGHT OF THE DODDERING old war veterans who sat along the gallery in front of the cotton gin and spat their tobacco and bored everybody with the same stories they'd been telling for decades. Their grandchildren had stopped listening to them years ago. I passed them every day.

Feverish moths of various sizes batted against us before launching themselves at the lamps again and again. One of the fuzzy ones got tangled in my fringe and tickled me unbearably. I plucked it from my hair, pulled back the burlap curtain, and chucked it out into the night. It promptly and enthusiastically flew back in my face, as if gusting in on a high wind. I sighed. One thing I had learned for sure: You could not win when it came to class Insecta, order Lepidoptera.

We would have to make a study of it, my grandfather and I.

CHAPTER 4

VIOLA

We may conclude ... that any change in the numerical proportions of some of the inhabitants, independently of the change of climate itself, would most seriously affect many of the others.

IF I'D BEEN PAYING attention, I might have noticed that Viola gave me a funny look whenever I headed out the back door to Granddaddy's laboratory. Viola had been with us forever—since even before Harry was born—ringing her handbell at the back door to signal to those working outside to come to dinner and then banging a small brass gong at the foot of the stairs (which Mother thought more genteel inside) to signal those of us upstairs in our rooms. Mother would have liked her to use the gong outside as well, but with my brothers and me scattered from the gin to the river, we would never have heard it. And we were expected to be on time for dinner, washed and brushed, or else.

I had never thought about where Viola came from; she had always simply been there, punching down dough, peeling apples, preparing huge roasts in winter and frying up mountains of chicken in summer. No one, not even Mother, crossed her in the duchy of her kitchen. In between meals, she could be found inspecting the hens or the hogs or the vegetable patch to see what was next on the menu, or sitting at the kitchen table with a chipped mug of coffee at her elbow, resting up before the next mammoth meal.

She must have been somewhere in her forties. She was handsome, wiry, always wearing a wash-print dress and long apron, a clean kerchief binding her hair. She was slender but had a surprisingly powerful grip when she grabbed your arm to force your attention. She lived by herself in the old slave quarters out past Granddaddy's laboratory, and though it had once housed a dozen or so slaves, it was the perfect size for one person. At some point a bare plank floor had been installed over the packed dirt. She had a woodstove for winter and a zinc sink with her own pump.

Viola's skin was no darker than mine at the end of summer, although she was careful to stay out of the sun, while I didn't care. She was only one fourth Negro, but that made her the same as full-blooded. I guess she could have "passed" in Austin, but that was a terribly risky business. If the passer was unmasked, it could result in a beating or jail or even worse. An octoroon woman in Bastrop had passed and married a white farmer. Three years later, he discovered her birth certificate in a trunk and pitch-forked her to death. He only served ten months in the county jail.

Viola and my mother had an easy relationship, and I never

saw any high-handedness between them. I think Mother truly did appreciate the enormity of cooking three times a day for so many hungry boys and knew that our family ship would sink without her services. The swinging door between the kitchen and dining room was left open, except when we had dinner guests. Passing by, you could gauge the progress of the next meal—and Viola's temper—by the level of pot noise.

Sometimes the two of them sat together in the kitchen to discuss meals and go over the household accounts. Mother made sure that Viola got nice new lengths of cotton in the summer and flannel in the winter, along with her weekly wages. Mother also shared old copies of *Ladies' Home Journal* with her, and although Viola couldn't read, she enjoyed paging through them and exclaiming over the latest outrageous fashions from Paris. For her birthday, she got a silver dollar; at Christmas, she got a gift of snuff. Viola didn't take snuff often, but she needed a generous dip before making her magnificent lemon meringue pie, a marvel of tart lemon custard and towering egg whites that she whipped into existence with her metal whisk in an agonizing ten-minute exercise that left her panting and exhausted. Every time I saw her taking snuff, she said to me, "Girl, it's a filthy habit. You take it up, and I'll have your hide." It's the only time she ever threatened me, and generally we got along fine, but not as well as she and Harry. Harry had always been her special boy, what with him being so handsome and charming and all.

Her other preferred companion was Idabelle, the one Inside

Cat, whose tour of duty included the kitchen, the pantry, and the laundry, and whose commission it was to keep mice out of the flour bin. Viola doted on her, which was odd since she barely tolerated the other cats—the Outside Cats—and sometimes swept them off the back porch with her broom. Idabelle was a fat, calm tabby who was good at her job, and although she had her own basket in a corner next to the stove, she sometimes wandered upstairs to sleep on your pillow and curled around your head like a purring fur hat. This was wonderful in winter but unbearable in summer. She often got chucked outdoors in summer, much to the smirking satisfaction of the Outside Cats.

The Outside Dogs could usually be found either sprawled on the front porch or else penned up next to the barn, depending on how great a nuisance they were making of themselves on any given day. Ajax, their leader, always pleasantly exhausted with his lot, dozed his days away on the porch, occasionally stirring himself from his dreams to nibble a flea before flopping back down again with a heavy sigh of happiness. I liked to think that he dreamed of ducks and doves, waiting for hunting season, when he would spring into action and work hard for a couple of weeks like, well, a dog.

Ajax had another reason to be happy with his lot. Of all the dogs, he was the only Inside Dog. The others, Homer, Hero, and Zeus, were strictly Outside Dogs. They all knew this, but it didn't stop them from good-naturedly crowding the front door every time it opened, every single time, despite the fact that they were never—*ever*—let into the house. I loved this particularly fine thing about the dogs: Despite a lifetime of denied entrance, hope never died in their hearts.

No doubt the Outside Dogs thought Ajax lived the life of a pampered lapdog once he made it through the magic door. They didn't understand that on those infrequent occasions when he was deemed clean enough, dry enough, and flea-free enough to come into the house, he was confined to a corner of the front hall and was forbidden to enter the parlor or go upstairs. Still, there was a clear pecking order based on this accommodation, and he lorded it over the others. The dogs were all a peaceful and tolerant bunch (Father wouldn't have kept them about the place if they were not), and my younger brothers could crawl all over them as long as they didn't pull their ears too hard. When that did happen, they—the dogs—sheepishly excused themselves from the scene and slunk out of reach under the porch. Sometimes they nosed around the laboratory, and although Granddaddy seemed fond of them, he never let them in. Come to think of it, he didn't let any humans in either, except for me.

CHAPTER 5

DISTILLATIONS

We have seen that man by selection can certainly produce great results, and can adapt organic beings to his
own uses.... But Natural Selection ... is a power
incessantly ready for action, and is as immeasurably
superior to man's feeble efforts, as the works of
Nature are to those of Art.

ONE NIGHT WHEN I JOINED Granddaddy in the laboratory, I
found that he had had a breakthrough of sorts with his liquor.
He held a small vial up to the light and looked at it speculatively.

"Calpurnia," he said, "I think we may have something
that's approaching drinkable here. I'm not saying it's good,
mind you, but I am saying that it's no longer nauseating. That
other stuff"—he waved at the rows of small stoppered
bottles—"is only good, as far as I can tell, for scouring fouled
barge bottoms. Now this isn't exactly good, not yet, but—"

"Why is it better?" I asked.

"I filtered the fourth distillation through a mixture of char-
coal, eggshells, pecan husks, and coffee grounds. I think I'll put
it up in oak for a while and see what happens."

Since none of the other runs had been deemed suitable for preservation this way, this was a big step. He poured it into a baby oak barrel about the size of a loaf of bread.

"Pardon me," he said, turning to me, "I forgot to offer you some. Do you care to try it and tell me what you think?"

He handed me a tiny measure, a thimbleful. I sniffed it cautiously. It smelled strongly of pecans, which reassured me, and faintly of something else rather like kerosene, which did not. I think he had forgotten that I was just a practically-twelve-year-old.

Granddaddy said, "It's easier if you hold your nose and down it in one go."

I pinched my nose and threw the stuff down my throat.

Now, let me tell you, there is a reason why they call it fire-water. I exploded into the world's worst coughing fit as the stuff burned a hole in my gullet. I felt like I'd spontaneously combusted. I think I may have fallen to the ground, but I don't really remember because I was coughing so hard. I do remember Granddaddy setting me on the arm of his chair and thumping me on the back for several minutes until I could breathe again. He looked at me with consternation as my coughing subsided to spluttering and then, finally, to painful wrenching hiccups.

He studied me. "Are you all right? I suppose you haven't learned to hold your liquor yet. Here," he said, pulling a peppermint from his waistcoat pocket, "this will make you feel better."

I nodded and hiccupped and sucked hard on the peppermint while the tears streamed down my face and my nose ran uncontrollably.

"Oh, dear," he said. He pulled a huge white handkerchief out of his pocket and applied it to my nose. "Blow." I honked away and felt somewhat better. He poured me a glass of water from the carafe he kept handy to rinse away the taste of his experiments.

"There, there." He patted me on the back.

"Well," he said, "I have to note my observations in the log. And you, as my collaborator, may also make a note on this red-letter day."

He pulled a lamp close and wrote in the ruled accounts book, his steel nib skritching on the page. The book was filled with the minutiae of his many failed runs. Then he handed me the pen. "Here, note the date and time, your observations in this column, and then place your signature below."

In my penmanship class at school, we had recently graduated from pencil to ink. I worried about making a blot, but I wrote, not too badly, considering my recent trauma:

Run #437: 21 July 1899. It was very good.
Calpurnia Virginia Tate.

Granddaddy looked at my comment. I hiccupped.

"Calpurnia," he said, looking at me, "as a scientist, you must be truthful about your observations."

He handed me the pen again. I wrote on the next line:

Might cause some coffing.

Not an inspired or inspiring comment, I admit. In truth it had nearly killed me, but I could hardly write that down. Granddaddy swiveled the ledger to look at this and smiled.

"Indeed," he said, "and I am to blame. I think it's best we agree not to tell Margaret or Alfred about this. Unfortunately, they do not understand the principles of scientific inquiry or the sacrifices one must be prepared to make."

I gawped at him, thinking, *Tell my parents? Are you crazy? I'd sooner drink a hogshead of the stuff.*

Then we heard Viola ring her bell at the back door. It was time to wash up for dinner. I felt a bit swirly in the head. I *hicced* again, and we looked at each other.

"Here," he said. "Better have another peppermint."

We went into the house, and I managed to wash my hands and change into a clean pinafore without notice. We filed into the dining room. Father held Mother's chair, and we all sat down. SanJuanna came in and waited by the sideboard to serve. My father began the blessing, and we all bowed our heads.

"Heavenly Father, we thank thee for—"

Hic.

This was a quiet one, and it might have escaped notice except for my rotten brothers. Travis and Lamar rustled and stirred, and Jim Bowie peeked at me over the steeple of his hands. Mother flashed them a look, and they subsided.

"—for the bounty of thy worldly harvest and for this food, which—"

Hic.

My brothers tittered.

"Calpurnia. Boys. Stop it," hissed Mother.

"I'm sorry, Mother," I said in a small voice. I knew another one was aborning deep within me, and there wasn't much I could do about it, but nevertheless, I held my breath and struggled mightily.

"—which nourishes us through the grace of Our Lord—"

Up it came, a giant one this time.

HIC.

Oh, how my brothers fell about the place. Granddaddy stared at the ceiling with interest.

"—Jesus Christ!" said Father, in confusion.

Mother threw her napkin on the table. "That's it!" she cried. "What on earth has gotten into you? Were you raised in a barn? Go to your room at once. And the rest of you will control yourselves, or you will follow her upstairs. I've never *heard* of such dreadful behavior during grace. And in my own family yet!"

I wanted to explain that I couldn't help it, I hadn't done it on purpose, but that would mean revealing Granddaddy's and my secret, and I would die broken and twisted on the rack before telling. As I got up from the table, Granddaddy studied the chandelier and smoothed his mustache with his forefinger.

I passed behind Mother's chair, and she said, "What *is* that smell?"

"Peppermint," I mumbled and kept moving. I felt funny and in sudden need of a nap. I trudged up the stairs and could hear Father starting the blessing again from scratch. I shut myself in my room and climbed into my tall brass bed.

I must have fallen asleep because I woke myself up some time later with a loud snore. The sun had set, and I could hear my younger brothers preparing for bed, so I reckoned it to be eight o'clock or so. The fire in my gut had eased somewhat. I sat up and realized I was starving. I had one more hour until my bedtime. Could I make it to the larder without being seen by Mother? It would be tricky.

A soft tap at the door interrupted my planning. Was it Mother come to berate me, or Harry come to rescue me? Neither. It was Travis, the ten-year-old, clutching one of his new litter of kittens, all of which he'd named after gunslingers, outlaws, and others of low repute. "Look," he whispered as he shoved the furry creature into my hands, "I brought you Jesse James. He's my best one. He'll be good company for you." Then he skedaddled down the hall, not wanting to be caught talking to the condemned prisoner.

Jesse James was some comfort, at least. I took him back to bed, and he purred under my chin and kneaded my shoulder.

Just as I dozed off, there was another knock. This time it was Granddaddy, looking solemn. He stood in the doorway, holding a couple of thick books.

"A little something for you to read," he said, "in your exile."

"Thank you," I said, and shut the door as he headed off to his own room. Why was he bringing me books at a time like this? I was too hungry and vexed to read, although the first one, *Great Expectations*, looked promising. The second one, *Principles of Southern Agrarian Economy*, did not. But it felt strangely unbooklike in my hands. It turned out to be not a book at all but a wooden box trickily carved and painted to look like a calf-bound volume. Strange. I fiddled with it and found the catch and the box opened. Inside was a waxed paper parcel containing a thick roast beef sandwich. I took the sandwich and *Great Expectations* and sank into my bed with the utmost feeling of luxuriousness. Ahhh. Bed, book, kitten, sandwich. All one needed in life, really.

Half an hour later, Father tapped on the door, calling quietly, "Callie?" I wanted to be left alone with Pip, so I shoved the book under the covers with Jesse James, who mewed in protest. I turned to the wall and pretended to be asleep. Father came in. After a moment, he left, but not before blowing out my lamp, which irritated me no end, as I was not allowed to keep matches in our bedrooms. There was nothing else to do but go to sleep. Besides, the next day brought my piano lesson, and it was always a good idea to be rested and in top form so as not to provoke Miss Brown.

I lay there contemplating my day as I drifted off. My throat still burned, but I was filled with gratification that with all those brothers, I was the first to imbibe. I think. Later I found out that Mother's health tonic, her Lydia Pinkham's Vegetable Compound for Women, was nearly 20 percent alcohol.

CHAPTER 6

MUSIC LESSONS

It is most difficult always to remember that the increase of every living being is constantly being checked by unperceived injurious agencies. . . .

THE SUMMER WORE ON, and I found respite in the coolness of the river and the dimness of Granddaddy's laboratory. My Notebook progressed nicely, each page filled with many Questions, an occasional Answer, and clumsy illustrations of various plants and animals. But despite my pressing new activities, I was not excused from my music lessons.

Our piano teacher, Miss Brown, looked like a thin, dry stick, but she could swing her ruler with plenty of juice when she thought no one was looking. Sometimes she would smack my knuckles so hard that my hands crashed into the keys, causing an ugly dissonant chord to detonate in the middle of the piece. I wonder if my mother, sitting on the other side of the closed pocket doors with her sewing basket, ever puzzled over these frightful noises. For some reason, I didn't tell her about Miss Brown's assaults. Why didn't I? I guess I had the sense that something shameful on my part—I don't know what—invited these pedagogic outrages. And it's true that Miss Brown did not attack me at random. Her violence boiled over when I got lost picking my way through the thicket of notes I'd been traversing without mistake all week long. (Of course, the hovering ruler didn't help.) I was the worst kind of coward; I seethed in silence and never said anything to anybody. And why did only Harry and I have to suffer through this wretched weekly imposition of culture? My other brothers were free and clear.

I learned to play Mr. Stephen Foster for Father and Vivaldi for Granddaddy, who was also partial to Mozart. He would sit in the parlor, sometimes reading, sometimes sitting with his eyes closed, for as long as I would play. Mother was partial to Chopin. Miss Brown was partial to scales.

Later there were Mr. Scott Joplin's rags, which I learned for myself. They set Mother's teeth on edge, but I didn't care. It was the best music my brothers and I had ever heard, with gorgeous cascading chords and an electrifying ragged timing, which compelled the audience to get up and dance. All of my brothers came running when I struck up the opening bars to "The Maple Leaf Rag." They lurched so wildly around the parlor that Mother feared for the very pictures on the wall. Later we got a gramophone and then I could dance, too. My younger brothers adored running the machine and begged to take a turn, but you had to watch them—they were murder on the crank.

Jim Bowie's favorite tune was "Kitten on the Keys." He'd manhandle one of the beleaguered cats up onto the keyboard and coax it with a scrap of ham to walk back and forth. J.B. thought it was a terrific joke. When you're five years old, I guess it is. It predictably drove Mother up the wall (and me too, though I'd never admit it), which of course added to J.B.'s pleasure. Mother frequently had to resort to a couple of tablespoons of her Lydia Pinkham's. Sul Ross once asked Mother if I would also get to drink Lydia Pinkham's when I grew up to be a lady, and she replied mysteriously, "I hope Callie won't need it."

Viola would sing alto with me in the kitchen to "Hard Times Come Again No More," but she refused to listen to Mr. Scott Joplin.

"Music for savages," she sniffed, which perplexed me.

IT CAME TIME for Miss Brown to present her piano students at a recital held every year at the Confederate Heroes Hall in Lockhart. For the first time, Miss Brown deemed me accomplished enough to be included on the program. To be truthful, it's just that I couldn't talk my way out of it for another year. Harry had performed for six years in a row and told me it was a snap. All you had to do was avoid staring into the gas footlights, since the light might blind you and you could pitch off the stage. Also, I had to memorize a piece of music. Miss Brown gave me Beethoven's Ecossaise in G, which, strangely, had chords not unlike the Joplin rags. Oh, how the ruler twitched with aggravation. "Wrists down! Fingers up! Tempo, tempo, tempo!" *Crack*. I learned that piece in record time, and soon I was playing it in my sleep. It goes without saying I grew to hate it. My best friend, Lula Gates, had to memorize a piece that was twice as long as mine, but she was ten times a better player than I.

For the great occasion, Mother made me a new white broderie-anglaise dress with many layers of stiff, scratchy petticoats. This was no corset but it definitely ranked as a form of torture. I complained at length and clawed savagely at my legs. I also had a brand-new pair of pale cream kid boots. They took forever to close with the hook, but, once on, they were fine-looking, and I secretly admired them.

Miss Brown taught me how to curtsy, holding my dress out sideways and dipping at the knees.

"No, no," she said, "don't grab your skirt like some clod-hopper. Think of making wings, like an angel. Like this. Now sink. Slowly! Don't *plummet*, child—you're not a rock." She made me practice many times before she was satisfied.

Then we had to deal with The Matter of My Hair. Mother had finally noticed that I seemed to have less hair than expected, but I explained that it had snarled so badly over the summer, what with the terrible sticker burrs, that I had been forced to chop out the rats' nests and then cut a smidgen more to even everything up. Mother's expression grew beady at this but she didn't say anything to me. She called for Viola to help. Together they spent a good hour brushing and twisting and parleying as if I weren't even in the room. I didn't know you could spend so much time on hairstyles. Of course, I couldn't protest too much because we all understood that this was my punishment for hacking away at it, and only fitting, too.

Then they slathered me with Peabody's Finest Hair Food, Guaranteed to Produce Lustrous Locks, and set me out in the sun to bake for yet another hour with this revolting sulfur grease on my head. *This*, I thought, *this is what ladies go through?*

The one thing that made it bearable was that Granddaddy took pity on my wretched state and brought me one of his books, *Fascinating Flora and Fauna of the Antipodes*. The picture of the kangaroo showed a baby peeking out of its pouch. (Question for the Notebook: Why don't people have pouches? Such a convenient way to keep a baby at hand. I tried to picture Mother with J.B. in a pouch. Answer: He'd never fit under her corset.) I yearned to see a kangaroo. And a platypus, a mammal that looked like a bizarre cross between, oh, say, an otter and a duck. Since I'd been lucky enough to see a hippopotamus in a touring circus in Austin, maybe my wishes weren't so outlandish. I contemplated my chances and fanned a dim ember of hope in my heart as I sat in the sun, reeking like a giant match.

Finally, they put me in the hip bath and took turns pouring buckets of water over me. Then they scoured my head clean and tied up my hair in ringlets with cotton rags that stuck out all over like a frightful job of bandaging. I smelled like brimstone and looked like a casualty from the War. I was an apparition from H–ll.

Poor Jim Bowie burst into tears when he saw me, and I had to take him on my knee and convince him that I was not mortally wounded. Sul Ross called me Old Golliwog until I caught him and sat on him. Lamar snickered, and even Harry smiled.

There was nothing I enjoyed more than being a source of amusement to my brothers.

I didn't sleep well that night on my lumpy rags. I woke up sluggish and cranky the next morning. Mother decided it was pointless to finish my hair before we got to Lockhart, so I suffered the further indignity of having to wear an enormous ruffled cap over the rags all the way there in the wagon. My head was huge. I looked deformed; I looked like Lula Gates's brother, poor old feeble-minded Toddy Gates, who had water on the brain. (Questions for the Notebook: Where did the water on Toddy's brain come from? Did Mrs. Gates drink too much while carrying him?) I prayed that we wouldn't meet anyone I knew and then felt guilty for drawing God's attention away from serious matters to what was, after all, only an item of vanity. I admit I got more nervous the closer we got to Lockhart, but Harry kept telling me it would be a cakewalk.

We pulled up to the hall, and as the horses came to a stop, I leaped from the wagon and ran around to the back door before I could draw a crowd. Mother and Viola followed behind with a basket filled with hairpins and ribbons and tongs. They parked me on a stool and set to work on me, yanking the rags from my head. There were several other girls being tortured in the same way, so it wasn't as bad as I had feared. Mrs. Ogletree even primped her boy Georgie, whom she'd gadded up in a green velvet Little Lord Fauntleroy suit. He churned with excitement on his stool, his blond sausage curls bouncing on his cambric collar.

Lula trembled and clutched a tin bucket to her chest and looked like she was going to be sick at any moment. The identical twins, Hazel and Hanna Dauncey, were an interesting and identical shade of grayish green. The sight of all this obvious distress in the others perked me up.

Miss Brown swept in wearing a new and unbecoming chartreuse gown and clapped her hands for attention. "Children! Mothers! *Attention, s'il vous plaît.*"

Instantly, there was complete silence. There was not a peep, a squeak, a rustle, not even from the squirmy Georgie. I realized that Miss Brown had the same threatening hold over all her other pupils as she had over me. *Why,* I thought, *I bet she smacks all of us. Probably not Harry, but everybody else. So it's not just me. Well, how about that.*

"In ten minutes you will line up," Miss Brown said, "from youngest to oldest, and then you will file into the auditorium behind me in an orderly—an *orderly*—fashion. You will then sit in the row of chairs along the back of the stage until it is your turn to play. There will be no talking. There will be no fidgeting. And there will *especially* be no pushing. Do I make myself clear?" Mute nods all around.

"Do *not* forget to bow or curtsy after your selection. Mothers, ten minutes." And she turned and swept out, kicking her train behind her in one practiced motion. Viola and Mother both fell on me again with a vengeance, beating and thrashing my hair with brushes and tongs. Finally they stepped back to admire their work.

"There," said Mother, "don't you look a picture? I wouldn't have recognized you. Look." She handed me a mirror.

I wouldn't have recognized me, either, what with the elaborate structural pile teetering on my head. Above my forehead rose a steep cliff of hair, which then swooped into an intricate pointy arrangement at the crown, all massed above triple pontoons of hair along each temple; bringing up the rear was a trailing cascade of fat curls down my back. This magnificence was topped off with the world's largest pink satin bow. Mother and Viola looked well pleased. They didn't bother to ask me what I thought, so I didn't have to say that I thought I looked . . . appalling.

"See how pretty you look?" said Mother.

My hand drifted up to my hair.

"Don't you touch that," said Viola. "Don't you dare." She gathered up their tools while Mother struck up a conversation with Mrs. Gates.

I sidled over to Lula and whispered, "Hey, Lula, are you all right?"

She looked at me with her enormous hazel eyes and nodded but didn't—couldn't—speak. I noticed with envy that she had escaped drastic coiffuric ministrations; her pale, silvery-blond hair hung down her back in two neat braids. I tried to jolly her out of her panic. I nudged her and whispered, "Lula, look at what they did to my hair. It's the worst, isn't it?" Lula's lips were clamped together. She responded with a long, quivering breath through her nose. I had the feeling she didn't remember how to speak English.

"Lula," I said, "you'll be all right. You've played that piece a million times. Take some more deep breaths. And if that doesn't work, well, you've always got your bucket."

I looked around. Harry stood before a mirror in the corner, dousing himself with lavender pomade and painstakingly parting his hair with a comb, over and over. I had never known him to take such care with his appearance before. As the oldest student, he would play last, but he would have to sit onstage and suffer through the rest of us until it was his turn.

Miss Brown returned, and we received final admonishments from our mothers before they hurried out. My last whispered instructions were from Viola: "Don't touch that hair. I mean it." We lined up in silence. No one talked or fidgeted or pushed. Harry winked at me from the back of the line. Lula quaked in front of me, shivering all the way to the tips of her braids.

"Lula," said Miss Brown, frowning, "you have to put that bucket down." Lula didn't move. "Calpurnia, take that bucket from her." I tapped Lula on the shoulder and said, "Give it over, Lula. It's time." She stared at me in mute appeal. I ended up prying it from her damp hands.

Miss Brown said, "Children, this is the time for your very best deportment. Chins *up*. Chests *out*."

She opened the side door to the auditorium, and we marched in behind her to what sounded like hard rain on a tin roof. It was applause, and Lula flinched like a startled fawn. For a moment, I thought she would bolt. I did a rapid and complex series of mental calculations about the range of possible blame that could be assigned to me if she got away, but good old Lula stuck it out and stayed in line.

Then I saw Miss Brown floating majestically upward at the front of the line. Why? How? What was happening? It took me a second to remember that there were a dozen or so steps up to the stage and she was walking up them.

Steps! I had forgotten there were steps. Hundreds and hundreds of steps. I had seen them before, but they were not part of my mental practice; I hadn't practiced them in my mind's eye. My ankles went wobbly, and I felt hot and cold all over. Lula glided upward in front of me without any apparent problem. I followed in terror and somehow made it to the top without falling on my face, and then stopped myself just in time from staring into the dazzling limelights that marked the edge of the precipice. We made it to our chairs, and the applause died down like a passing storm.

Miss Brown walked to the edge of the stage and curtsied to the audience. She gave a small speech about this splendid occasion, about Culture making inroads in Caldwell County, oh yes, and how young minds and fingers benefited from exposure to the Great Composers, and how she hoped the parents there would appreciate her hard work in molding their children to value the Finer Things in Life, since we were still living, after all, almost on the edge of the Wild Frontier. She sat down to more applause, and then we got up, one by one, in varying states of misplaced confidence or paralyzing terror.

Do I need to tell you what happened? It was a massacre. Do I have to tell you that Georgie fell backward off the piano stool before he played a single note and had to be hustled off, wailing, in his mother's arms; that Lula played flawlessly and then got violently sick the second she finished; that Hazel Dauncey's foot slipped off the pedal in the dead silence before she began, filling the auditorium with a deep reverberating *sprrroiiinnnnggg*; that Harry played well but kept looking out at a certain part of the audience for no good reason that I could tell; that I played like a windup clockworks with wooden fingers and forgot to curtsy until Miss Brown hissed at me?

I DON'T REMEMBER much more about the day. I managed to blot it out. But I do remember vowing in the wagon on the way home that I would never do it again. I told Mother and Father this, and there must have been something in my voice because, the next year, despite Miss Brown's formidable efforts, I handed out the programs, along with Lula, who was barred for life from playing in the recital.

CHAPTER 7

HARRY GETS
A GIRLFRIEND

Domestic races of the same species . . . often have a somewhat monstrous character. . . . They often differ in an extreme degree in some one part. . . .

SHORTLY AFTER THE PIANO RECITAL, danger entered our lives and stalked my family.

I must have dimly realized that Harry would marry one day and have a family of his own, but I reckoned it wouldn't happen for decades, at least. After all, Harry already had a family, and we were it. I, especially, was it. His own pet.

For some days after the debacle in Lockhart, he'd been acting odd. He stared off into space with a dumb mooncalf look on his face that made you want to slap him. He didn't answer when spoken to; in fact, he seemed barely present. I had no idea what was going on, but this was not my dear, clever Harry. No, this was some dilute, watery version of him.

I cornered him on the porch and said, "Harry."

"Hmm?"

"*Harry!* What's wrong with you? Are you sick? What's the matter with you?"

"Hmm," he said, and smiled.

"Do you feel all right? Should you see the doctor?"

"Don't worry about me. I'm fine. In fact, I feel grand," he said.

"Then what is it?"

He smiled mysteriously and pulled a much-handled *carte de visite* from his pocket. It was one of the new kind with a photographic portrait on it. ("The height of vulgarity," according to Mother.)

And there She was. A young woman (certainly no longer a girl) with big, protuberant eyes; a fashionably small, squinchy mouth; a long, slender stalk of a neck; and such a great quantity of hair massed above it that she looked like a dandelion puff before the wind decapitated it.

"Isn't she a corker?" he said, in a congested voice I'd never heard before and hated instantly. I hated *her* instantly too, for I saw her plain for what She was: a hag, a stooping harpy, a feaster on the flesh of beloved brothers. The Destroyer of My Family's Happiness. Of *my* happiness. I stared at this apparition.

"A corker?" I said, reeling. My brother was evaporating before my eyes, and I had to find a way of stopping this dreadful abduction. My thoughts scattered in all directions like undisciplined troops facing their first fire, and it took me a moment to marshal them. But before my first skirmish, I needed some intelligence.

"Where did you meet her, Harry?" I said, innocent as any spy.

For a second, the glaze passed from his eyes and he faltered. I'd struck some tender tissue, but I didn't understand its import.

"Why, uh, I stopped off at the supper on the grounds in Prairie Lea the other night. They saw me on the road and invited me to visit for a piece."

Ah. Now, there were two churches in Prairie Lea: the Baptist church, which was acceptable, and the Independent Church of Prairie Lea, which was not. The local Leapers were considered a low and trashy lot by many people. These included my parents, who were both robust Methodists. (Granddaddy had declared he'd had enough sermons to last a lifetime and now chose to spend his Sunday mornings tramping across the fields. Reverend Barker, who enjoyed Granddaddy's company, seemed to take it in stride. It was only Mother who was embarrassed.) And although Mother had once or twice entertained Leapers in the house, she tended to lump them all together, fairly or not, with snake handlers, fallers, foamers, and other fringe examples of the henhouse sects.

A part of my mind I had no idea I possessed until that moment took over and, like a great general, called all to order. I primed my weapons, surveyed the terrain, picked my target. I could see the battle ahead in time and space. I was the Great Stonewall. I was General Lee himself!

"The Baptist church, Harry?" I asked, sweet as pie.

"No." He hesitated. "She belongs to the Independent Church of Prairie Lea."

Blessed relief flooded through me. The enemy was mine. "Oh, Harry," I said, all sisterly concern. "She's a *Leaper*?"

"That's right. So what?" he said mulishly. "And don't call them that. They're Independents."

"Have you told Mother and Father?" I said.

"Um. No." He looked edgy. My opening salvo had hit its mark. Then he looked down at the picture, and I watched him go all sappy again.

"How old is she?" I asked, forging ahead. "She looks kind of old."

"She's not old," he said with indignation. "She only came out five years ago."

I added five to eighteen, the typical age for coming out, and came up with the usual result. "She's *twenty-three*," I said, aghast—and secretly jubilant. "She's practically an old maid. Besides, you're only *seventeen*."

"That makes no difference," he said. He plucked the card from my hand and huffed off.

At dinner that night, Harry mentioned that he might hitch Ulysses to the gig and take him out for exercise.

"Why don't you ride him?" said Father. "You don't need the gig."

"He hasn't been in harness for a while. It would do him good," said Harry.

Time to fire off my next round. In a loud voice, I said, "Are you going to see *her*?"

The table thought this an interesting inquiry and grew still. Everyone except Granddaddy stopped eating and stared at Harry with interest, even the boys who were too young to understand what was going on. Mother swiveled her head, looking first at me and then at Harry. Granddaddy went on placidly addressing his beefsteak.

Harry flushed and cut me a look to let me know he'd settle with me later. He'd never glared at me like that before. There was something close to hatred in that look. Fear shot through me. I broke out all over in hot prickles.

"And who is *her*?" said Mother.

Granddaddy's knife *skreeked* against his plate. He patted his mustache with the big white linen napkin that flowed down his chest. He said mildly to his only daughter-in-law, "Good God, Margaret. That's 'who is she,' not 'who is her.' The verb *to be* never takes an object. Surely you know that by now?"

He peered at her and said, "Why, how old are you, Margaret? I reckon you must be close to thirty. Old enough to know better, I should think," he said, and turned his attention back to his dinner. My mother, aged forty-one, ignored this.

"Harry?" she said. She gave him the gimlet eye. The prickles racing across my skin coalesced into itching pink welts. Our family's future hung by a thread.

"There's a girl—a young lady—at the Prairie Lea picnic

tonight that I'd like to take for a short drive, ma'am," Harry stammered. "Only a short one."

"And," said Mother, in a frosty voice, "exactly who is this young lady? Have we met her? Have we met her people?"

"Her name is Miss Minerva Goodacre. Her people are in Austin. She's spending the month with her aunt and uncle in Prairie Lea."

"And *they* are . . . ?" said Mother.

The thread pulled taut.

"Reverend and Mrs. Goodacre," said Harry.

"And are you referring to Reverend Goodacre of the Independent Church of Prairie Lea?" said Mother.

The thread creaked and frayed.

"Yes," said Harry, flushing deeper. He pushed himself away from the table and bolted from the room, calling over his shoulder with false cheer, "So it's all right, then. I won't be late."

Father looked at Mother and said, "What was all that about?"

Mother noticed the rest of us sitting openmouthed and snapped, "You are so obtuse sometimes, Alfred. We'll discuss it later."

Sitting next to me, Sul Ross, who was swift for his age, broke into a chant: "Harry's got a gur-ull, Harry's got a gur—"

At this point Mother looked volcanic. I hissed, "Shut *up*, Sully," and elbowed him viciously in the short ribs.

Out of the blue, Granddaddy said, "About damned time,

too. That boy was starting to worry me. What's for dessert?" One of the interesting things about Granddaddy was that you couldn't always tell if he was present or not.

Dinner dragged on forever. Whatever we had for dessert, it was ashes in my mouth. When SanJuanna came in to clear the table, Mother said, "You are all excused. Except for Calpurnia."

The others trooped out while I hunkered down at my place. Father lit a cigar and poured himself a larger-than-usual glass of port. Mother looked like she badly wanted one and rubbed her temples.

"Now, Calpurnia," she said, "what is it you know about this . . . this . . . young lady?"

I thought of the way that Harry had glared at me. "Nothing, ma'am," I said, sounding the retreat and recalling my battalions as fast as I could.

"Come, come. Surely he must have told you something about her."

"I don't know anything," I said.

"Stop this, Calpurnia. How did you find out about her? And what is happening to your face? You look all blotchy."

"Harry showed me her visiting card, that's all," I said.

"Her card?" My mother's voice rose. "She has a *card*? How *old* is she?"

"I don't know anything," I said.

Mother looked at Father and said, "Alfred, she has a card." My father looked interested but not alarmed. Clearly the significance of this fact escaped him.

My mother got up and started pacing. "She is of an age to have a card, and my son has been calling on her without telling us. He has been courting her, and we've never even met her. She's a *Leap*—she's an Independent, Alfred."

Mother wheeled on me. "She is an Independent, isn't she? Tell me, Calpurnia."

"I don't know anything."

"Ack, you useless child! Go to your room and don't say a word of this to anyone. Are you breaking out in hives? Did you fall in the nettles again? Get some baking soda and make a compress."

I slipped from my chair and hurried to the kitchen. Viola sat at her table, taking a short rest while SanJuanna pumped water in preparation to start on the mountain of dishes on the counter.

"Mother sent me for baking soda," I mumbled.

"Good Lord," said Viola when she saw my complexion. "How'd you get like that?"

"Nettles," I lied. "I just need a compress."

Viola squinted at me and opened her mouth to speak, then shut it again. She got up and sprinkled soda on a damp rag and handed it to me without saying a word. SanJuanna eyed me as if I might be contagious.

As I went up the stairs, I could hear my parents' voices in the dining room, my mother's raised in outrage, my father's rumbling in placation.

Sul Ross and Lamar were lying in wait for me on the landing and followed me to my room.

"What's going on? What happened to Harry? What's wrong with your face? Tell us."

I ran past them to my room and slapped the cooling rag on my tingling cheek. What had I set in motion? Something I could no longer control. I was a novice commander, shocked by the destruction my troops had wrought.

I lay awake in bed that night waiting for Harry to come home. The half-moon was up before I heard the creaking of the harness and the crunching of the gig on the gravel drive. I held my breath and listened. The house was suspiciously silent. I imagined Mother and Father lying in their big mahogany bed with its heavy carvings of cherubs and fruit. They would be wide awake, or at least Mother would be.

I got out of bed, put on my slippers, and slid around the perimeter of the room, careful to avoid the floorboard in the middle that cracked like a pistol shot. The stairs were also notoriously loud, so I pleated up my white cotton nightgown and slid down the banister as I'd done my whole life. It was fast and quiet transportation, but I misjudged in the dark and braked late and hit the square newel post hard enough to earn myself a nice blue bruise on my behind, a two-weeker, at least.

The moon lit my way to the stable. I crept to the door and looked inside. Harry curried Ulysses in the lantern light and hummed a song that I recognized with a lurch as "I Love You Truly." He looked so happy, happy in a way I'd never seen him look before.

"Harry," I whispered.

He turned and his face grew hard. "What are *you* doing here?" he said. "Go away. Go to bed." He went on brushing the horse.

Oh, that look.

There had been times in the past when I'd been in some kind of mild trouble with him and, uncomfortable as those times had been, they had always passed. I had basked safe in the knowledge that I was forever his favorite; I took his love on faith and wrapped it around me like a blanket. But this was different. I had fundamentally injured him while trying to protect us, to protect him. No. If I were being honest, to protect myself. And I felt the first icy grip of grief around my heart.

Stunned, I backed out of the circle of light and stood alone under the moon. A hiccup—or sob—escaped me. I turned and stumbled back to the house on rubbery legs. I made it through the front door but then foundered on the bottom stairs. That's where Harry found me half an hour later, a huddled heap of misery in a white nightgown, sniffling in the dark, too upset to move, with only Idabelle, who had padded out from the kitchen, for company. I could just see him, standing with his hands on his hips.

"I'm sorry, Harry," I whispered.

"There are some matters in this world that are not for children. They are for grown-ups," he said.

I had never thought of Harry as a grown-up before. My brothers and I had always been children together. But the way he said the word, I knew that at that moment he had crossed some invisible border into a different land, and he would not be returning to our childish band again.

"I didn't mean to get you in trouble," I moaned.

"Yes, you did. I don't understand why you would do this to me."

I wanted to cry out, For the family! For you! But I knew deep down that it was for me, and I was ashamed.

The grandfather clock chimed three times in the dark.

"You should go to bed," he said, in a flat voice.

I clung to the fact that these words were, despite their coldness, less harsh than the words he had spoken to me in the barn. Surely it would be all right. He would put his arm around me and take me upstairs and tuck me in.

But he did not. Instead, he whispered, "I wish you hadn't done that," and walked past me up the stairs, leaving me to contemplate the carnage of my brief command. My campaign had been successful, and it had cost me my brother. It wasn't until the clock bonged four that I could make myself creep up to bed.

The next morning, I was so exhausted that I stayed in bed, feigning illness and dozing fitfully. It wasn't difficult to convince Mother that I was ill, what with my listlessness and lingering hives. She and Viola sent a steady stream of beef tea and baking soda poultices to my room. Late in the afternoon there was talk of tonics and purgatives and cod-liver oil, but at that point I managed to rally and take some plain boiled chicken, averting such drastic management. Any child who stayed in bed for more than one day in our house was dosed with cod-liver oil. The mere prospect of it often wrought a near-miraculous recovery.

Travis came in to lend me his kitten Doc Holliday to cheer me up (Jesse James was indisposed). J.B. climbed up on the bed and cuddled with me awhile to make me feel better. Sul Ross brought me a bouquet of straggly wildflowers for my nightstand and proudly showed me the mark on his trunk where I'd elbowed him. I didn't show him my own much more impressive bruise on account of its indiscreet location.

Harry didn't visit.

The following morning, I staggered down to breakfast. I was relieved to see that Harry at least glanced at me. Before we left the table and scattered for the day, Mother said, "We will be having guests Friday evening, so you will all be ready for inspection at quarter past six."

"Drat," said Granddaddy. "Who is it this time?"

"Grandfather," said Mother, "we wouldn't dream of imposing on you if you have a prior engagement."

Mother knew Granddaddy didn't have a prior engagement, but there was always the siren song of his laboratory or the library. My mother could only hope. I noticed that she never exactly encouraged Granddaddy's presence at her evening entertainments, or "soirees" as she called them. He was always the model of old-fashioned manners, of course, but he could go off on strange and interesting tangents of conversation that I think Mother didn't always find suitable in polite company. Fossils, for example, and whether their existence disproved the Book of Genesis; Brother Mendel's experiments on the sexual reproduction of the sweet pea; the fallacy of laudable pus. Once I had seen my mother shudder on overhearing him expound to a group of ladies on the mating posture of order Opiliones, or daddy longlegs. Then there were his predictions for the future, how man would one day build flying machines and travel to the moon, prognostications that were met with the sly indulgence afforded old codgers, although I secretly agreed with him and could imagine it happening a thousand years hence.

"Who's coming, ma'am?" said Sam Houston.

"The Locketts, the Longorias, Miss Brown. Reverend and Mrs. Goodacre. And a Miss Minerva Goodacre," said Mother, examining her butter knife.

Uh-oh. I looked at Harry, who was also interested in his cutlery, studying it as if he'd never seen it before. I swallowed hard. What to do? I consoled myself that I had three more days to think about it, brooding in my tent like Napoleon.

Every time I passed Harry on the stairs for the next few days, I smiled stiffly. He remained impassive. I chose to interpret his not actually scowling at me as a good sign.

Friday came and I still had no plan. Instead I washed and dried my hair. Then I sat at my vanity and glumly counted one hundred strokes of the hairbrush. I put on my best lawn dress and kid boots, the ones I'd worn to the music recital, and tied a sky-blue ribbon in my hair, the color Harry liked best on me. I went downstairs to join the others.

Harry looked handsome and reeked of the competing scents of lavender pomade and bay rum toilet water. A live undercurrent of excitement fizzed in him, and he softened to the point of giving me a grin. We lined up in the hall by age, Sam Houston gagging as he inhaled the fumes coming off Harry. Mother came down to inspect us. She wore her emerald silk with the short train, one of her best, and the train made a faint *whish-whish* sound as she walked. She looked at our boots, our teeth, our fingernails.

"Calpurnia, for heaven's sake," she said. "Stand up straight. What's the matter with you? Jim Bowie, those nails won't do. You look like you've been grubbing in the garden. Calpurnia, take him and fix him."

I led J.B. off to the bathroom, grateful for something to do. As I scrubbed him, he said, "Is Harry getting married?" This startled me so much I dropped the nail brush.

"Wherever did you get that idea?"

"I heard Mother talking about it. Is Harry going away?"

"I hope not, J.B."

"Me too."

I worked on him until the first guests arrived and we had to line up again at the front door. When Miss Brown arrived, I shook her hand and dropped her a deep, ostentatious curtsy. But I must have overdone it because the old bat gave me a hard smile and said, "Why, hello, Calpurnia. Aren't you just *charming* as always?" She squeezed my hand so tightly with her own tendinous claw that I yelped like a trod-upon dog.

Yes, the evening was off to a marvelous start, and Miss Minerva Goodacre hadn't even arrived yet.

I took a silver tray of smoked oysters and offered them around the room, keeping a close count as instructed by Viola on how many my brothers took. This wasn't too difficult, as the younger boys took one look at the shiny, wrinkled gray sacs and turned away in horror; you couldn't have paid them to put one in their mouths. Harry lurked between the parlor and the hall so that he could watch the front door for the great arrival. Granddaddy appeared with his beard trimmed and his hair plastered down. He sported a pinky-red rose in his buttonhole. Except for his moth-eaten coat, he looked almost distinguished.

The Longorias arrived, and Travis took their children out to the stable to show off his kittens.

I looked around at my family and felt a great wave of tenderness for them. They were all innocents playing out their unsuspecting parts. I wanted to preserve the moment and tuck it away, folded and sealed forever in my memory. Any second it was about to end.

Then Harry rushed to check his hair and tie in the hall mirror once again. I looked out the window and saw Mr. Goodacre tethering his horses. Harry dashed out the front door to hand down two women from the buggy, one stout and one slender. He offered his arm to the slender one—the harpy—and they moved up the walk, their heads together, sharing some word, some laugh, some *something* that none of the rest of us would ever share. My parents met them at the door, and I could overhear the bright chatter of introductions before Mother led everyone into the parlor. I have to give my mother credit, she appeared more relaxed and cheerful than I would have expected under the circumstances. Maybe she'd taken some tonic.

And there She was: taller than I expected, and slender, and dressed in a fussy peach dress with too many jet buttons. There was the petulant mouth, the long neck, the buggy eyes, the massy hair. She carried a spangled peach-colored fan that she opened with a theatrical *fwop* as she met the other guests.

I was about to flee to the kitchen when Harry saw me and beckoned me over.

"Miss Goodacre, may I present to you my sister, Calpurnia Virginia Tate. Callie, this is Miss Minerva Goodacre."

The peach fan beat the air like a giant moth. She looked at me with her big, buggy eyes and said with a trilling laugh, "Why, Calpurnia, what a sweet little girl you are. And so talented, too. I heard you play at the music recital." And with this, she furled her fan and tapped me playfully on the cheek with it, a mite too hard. Was I in for such punishment all night long?

"How do you do, Miss Goodacre?" I managed to croak. "I am pleased to make your acquaintance."

"Oh," she said, "I am sure we shall be more than acquaintances; I'm sure we will become fast friends. Now, Harry, where is that *très amusant grand-père* I've heard so much about?"

Gaah, she was spouting French. Harry steered her over to Granddaddy, who bowed low over her hand, brushed it with his whiskers, and said, *"Enchanté, mademoiselle."* I think he might have even clicked his heels. She responded with what I guess was supposed to be a musical laugh, "My goodness, sir, aren't you just too, *too* delightful."

And that, as they say, was that. She ignored me for the rest of the evening. Carrying trays of this and glasses of that, I trailed after her and Harry as they circulated about the room.

She was given to much fan play. She talked about fashions from Paris and fashions from New York, and wasn't it a shame about the perfectly frightful dress Governor Culberson's wife had worn to her husband's inauguration in Austin, and surely, with all their money, she could have afforded better, or at least sought advice from a *modiste* with taste. Taste was exceedingly important, *n'est-ce pas?* And speaking of taste, had anyone else remarked upon that dreadful, dowdy number that so-and-so had worn to the such-and-such ball . . . ?

Mother tried to engage her in conversation about music, but she would have none of it. Father tried to extract her opinion about the telephone line that would soon come to town, but she had none. She simpered and swished and ordered Harry about. She made me positively sick.

The evening wore on. Somehow we got through an interminable dinner, and then for entertainment Miss Brown sat down at the piano and whipped through her stock party piece, "The Minute Waltz," in fifty-two seconds by Father's pocket watch. Then she accompanied Miss Goodacre, who sang "Drink to Me Only with Thine Eyes" in what I considered to be a completely indifferent voice, all the while emoting heavily in Harry's direction.

> *Drink to me only with thine eyes,*
> *And I will pledge, with mine;*
> *Or leave a kiss within the cup,*
> *And I'll not ask for wine.*

I noticed during this nauseating performance that Grand-daddy stared at her as if mesmerized, which depressed me right into the ground. Conquering Harry was not enough—she had to captivate all the men who were important to me.

Then Harry sang "Beautiful Dreamer" while Miss Goodacre made googly eyes at him. The hateful Miss Brown pushed me forward to play my recital piece. I had a splitting headache and a false smile plastered on my face and managed to give a mediocre performance. Then I went to the kitchen to beg a headache pastille from Viola.

"What she like?" said Viola. "She don't look all that pretty from here. And Mister Harry such a nice-looking boy and all."

"She's dreadful, Viola. She can't talk about anything except clothes."

"Well, clothes is interesting," said Viola.

"Not if that's all you can talk about," I said.

"That's true. She ain't much of a singer, neither. How's your mama holding up?"

"Okay, I guess."

"Good," she said. "Here's a pastille. And take these chocolates out there. Keep a count."

I went back to the party and handed around the chocolates, keeping them away from my brothers as best I could. SanJuanna rounded up the younger ones for bed. Reverend Goodacre discussed the vagaries of the cotton market with my father. Granddaddy trapped Harry and Miss Goodacre in a corner and gave them a detailed explanation of the difference between the male and female *Deinacrida*, or giant locust. Miss Goodacre's smile grew fixed.

"Come to the library," Granddaddy said to her. "I have an excellent pair of specimens to demonstrate the difference." He took her by the elbow and steered her out of the room.

"Bring her back to us soon," Harry called out. "Don't deprive us of her company for too long. Ha ha."

Harry radiated bonhomie. I stood there and handed him a chocolate truffle. I wanted my brother to love me again at any price. In a weak voice I—the World's Biggest, Fattest Liar—said, "She seems very nice, Harry." Welts erupted on my neck. This time they were the hives of hypocrisy.

"Yes," he said, "she's a grand girl, isn't she? I knew you'd like her once you had a chance to meet her. Good bonbon. Let's have another."

Blind, I thought. *You're blind.*

At that moment, Miss Goodacre burst into the room looking flushed and tense. She bustled up to Mrs. Goodacre, and they conversed in an agitated whisper. Mrs. Goodacre turned to the gathering and said, "Minerva has a sick headache, and I'm afraid we must get her home. Such a shame, such a lovely party, but her mother has entrusted her to me for safekeeping. I'm sure you all understand."

They collected their wraps and made their abrupt good nights while Mr. Goodacre and Harry prepared the buggy. There were many calls of thanks to my mother but no promises of doing it again soon. They disappeared into the night.

Harry looked pensive. "Grandfather, did Miss Goodacre seem all right in the library?"

"She seemed well enough. She did display some interest in the gossamer-winged butterflies. I wish she had shown more interest in the carrion beetle collection, though. They are, after all, exceptionally fine specimens." He lit up a cigar. "All in all, we had a good talk, I'd say."

The next day my mother received hand-delivered thank-you letters from our guests and left them out on the dining table to serve as a lesson in good manners to us. The notes were flowery and effusive, except for Miss Goodacre's, which, although correct, was terse to the point of rudeness.

Two days later, Harry tried to call on her. Her aunt informed him that she was not at home. Three days after that, Miss Goodacre returned to Austin without any notice. Harry found out when he stopped in again and the Goodacres' maid told him. He came home and took to his room.

There was speculation among my older brothers about

whether he would be dosed with cod-liver oil. If not, exactly how old did one have to be to escape it? Was sixteen the cutoff? Fourteen? It was a question of intense interest.

Harry did not get dosed with the stinking oil. Instead, he was drenched with confusion and sadness when his letters to Miss Goodacre were returned unopened. He stumbled about the house for days like one of the walking wounded. It was pitiful. I tended my own stupendous bruise through its lurid healing colors and vowed to resign my commission as a meddler.

CHAPTER 8

MICROSCOPY

The crust of the earth is a vast museum. . . .

AFTER OUR NARROW BRUSH with the drippy Miss Goodacre, the house stayed discombobulated for weeks as Harry mourned and moped. I did keep my vow not to meddle, too, except for listening at the keyhole when Granddaddy had a talk with Harry in the library a few days later. Something about how the Law of Natural Selection, which always worked in Nature, sometimes inexplicably broke down in Man. Harry did seem a bit better after that, but it still took a while longer to get our old Harry all the way back. I wondered if Harry blamed our grandfather in some part for showing Miss Goodacre his carrion beetle exhibit. If that's all it took to put her off my brother, she wasn't worthy of him.

I could tell that Mother was relieved that the wretched Goodacre had gone. My mother's usual attitude of noncommittal formality toward her father-in-law warmed to something approaching gratitude or maybe even affection. She enquired after his health at dinner and made sure he got the choicest cuts, although I don't think he noticed.

Harry forgave me. After all, I hadn't been able to prevent him from having his main chance with Miss Goodacre. I had put on my best party manners and was above criticism. Whatever happened that night hadn't been my fault; *I* had given her no cause to flee from the house. And I was his long-standing favorite, his own pet, the one he had carried pig-a-back since infancy. I was flooded with relief to find myself his pet again.

THE SUMMER WORE ON. Sometimes my father would seek advice from Granddaddy about some aspect or other of the farm or the cotton gin. Father found it difficult to tear his own father away from his study of the natural world and make him focus on some point of commerce. Granddaddy had started the business and made it a success, but now he couldn't be bothered. I thought it odd that my parents couldn't understand how Granddaddy could have turned his back on his old life. Ever since he'd told me about his bat, it made perfect sense to me.

"I don't have that many days left," he said as we sat together in the library. "Why would I want to spend them on matters of drainage and overdue accounts? I must husband my hours and spend every one of them wisely. I regret that I didn't come to this realization until I reached fifty years of age. Calpurnia, you would do well to adopt such an attitude at an earlier age. Spend each of your allotted hours with care."

"Yessir," I said. "I'll do my best." There was no chair for a guest, so I sat on the slanting footstool, supposedly a camel's saddle. It didn't look like any saddle I had ever seen, but it had a funny smell and was covered in lots of little beige hairs similar to a Chihuahua's, so I guess it was real. I never tired of looking at Granddaddy's things: his brass spyglass from the War; wide, shallow drawers containing rows of desiccated lizards, spiders, and dragonflies; an ornate black cuckoo clock that announced the quarter hours in a droll, cracked voice. A moldering blue rosette with tarnished print that read "Best Fat Stock, Fentress Fair, 1877." Thick, creamy, parchmentlike envelopes from the National Geographic Society affixed with red wax seals. A carved wooden mermaid holding a pipe rack. Even the bearskin, with its gaping mouth. (The number of times I put my foot in that mouth, I can't begin to say.) In the locked cabinet on the shelf above the prize book was the gnarly stuffed armadillo, the worst example of taxidermy I had ever seen. Why did he keep this, when all his other specimens were paragons of their species?

"Granddaddy," I said, "why do you have that armadillo? I bet you could buy a much better one."

"That's true, I could, but I keep it as a reminder. That was the very first mammal I stuffed myself. I learned by correspondence course, which I advise against. If this path interests you, I suggest you apprentice yourself to a master. There are subtleties to the art that cannot be gleaned from merely reading a pamphlet."

"I don't think I want to learn taxidermy." I poked at a shelf crammed with fossils and old bits of bone.

"A wise decision," he said. "The smell alone is enough to discourage most novices from persevering. I have to say in my defense that the next armadillo was much better. So much better, in fact, that I sent it off to the great man himself as a token of the high esteem in which I held him."

I was hefting a trilobite fossil and half listening. I was fascinated by the ordered ridges of stone that had once been the soft body of a sea animal.

"He had made a study of the South American armadillo, so I thought he should have a North American sample as well. After the armadillos, I took on a bobcat, which I'll admit now was far too ambitious. I found the facial features quite difficult. I was trying to reproduce the snarl of the cat when it is disturbed in the wild. The poor creature ended up looking as if it had the mumps."

How many million years old was the stonified creature I held in my hand? What ancient sea had it swum in? I had never even seen the ocean; I could only imagine the waves, the wind, the brine.

"Anyway, as a thank-you, the great man sent me the bottled beast you see on the shelf next to the armadillo. It is my most prized possession."

"Excuse me?" I said, looking up from the trilobite.

"The bottled beast you see there on the shelf."

I looked at the monster in the thick glass carboy, with its freakish eyes and multiple limbs.

"It is a *Sepia officinalis* he collected near the Cape of Good Hope."

"Who collected it?"

"We are speaking of Mr. Darwin."

"We are?" I couldn't believe it. "*He* sent you that?"

"Indeed. Over his lifetime he carried on an extensive correspondence with many naturalists around the world and traded specimens with quite a few of us."

"Granddaddy, you're kidding."

"Calpurnia, I would never 'kid.' And, for once, your mother and I are in agreement on this important point: The use of slang is an indicator of a weak intellect and an impoverished vocabulary."

I couldn't believe it. We had not just his book in our house, but a monster collected by Mr. Darwin himself. I stared at the thing and tried to make sense of its too many arms and legs.

"What is it?"

"What do you think it is?"

I made a face of exasperation. "You sound like Mother telling me to look up a word in the dictionary when I don't know how to spell it."

"Good. Another point of agreement."

I edged up to the jar and tried to read the small paper tag hanging from a string around the neck of the bottle. The writing was old-fashioned and faded. I couldn't read it, but it was a thrill just to know that Mr. Darwin had written it with his own pen in his own hand.

"Can I take it out of the jar? It's hard to see, what with it being all squashed in there."

"It is almost seventy years old and preserved in spirits of wine. I am afraid it will disintegrate if we remove it."

I peered at it. Land? Sea? Or Air? Although there were

many limbs, they looked rubbery and not substantial enough to bear any weight, so it had to be a swimmer. Sea, then. Except that there were no fins. How could it swim without fins? Hmm, a problem. And I couldn't see any gills. Another problem. The eyes were oversized saucers. Why would they need to be so big? Answer: to see in the dark, of course. It had to live in areas of low light, which meant deep water.

I said, "It is some kind of fish, and it lives near the bottom of the ocean. But it's unlike any other kind of fish I have ever seen. I don't see how it locomotes, or how it breathes."

"As far as you go, you are correct. It is unfair to expect you to surmise more, because it is, as you say, squashed in there. It is a cuttlefish. The family is Sepiida, the genus is *Sepia*. It locomotes by pulling water into a cavity in the mantle and squeezing it through a muscular siphon. The mantle also hides the gills. When startled by a predator, it releases a cloud of brownish black ink to obscure its escape. We use the calcified internal shell as an abrasive. Owners of captive birds sometimes give them the shell on which to sharpen their beaks."

The thing fascinated me. It was a piece of history as well as an oddity. I touched a finger to the cool glass.

I LATER MENTIONED to Harry how interesting I found the bottled beast. Startled, he looked up from the book he was reading and said, "You've been in the library?"

"Yes," I said, and added, "Granddaddy invited me."

"Oh, well, in that case. Did you notice the ship in a bottle? I think that's the most interesting thing, although I haven't had a chance to get a good look at all his things. He got it from the Volunteer Fire Department years ago when he gave them money and bought the pump wagon. I'm hoping he'll leave it to me in his will." He looked at me curiously. "You seem to be spending a lot of time with him."

"Sometimes."

"What do you and that old man talk about?"

This made me wary. Harry didn't so much worry me, but what if the younger brothers discovered that Granddaddy was a trove of weird and fascinating facts about Indian fighting, the larger carnivores, hot-air ballooning? I'd never have him to myself again.

"Um, things," I said and flushed. I hated withholding anything from Harry. He turned back to his book, and I kissed his cheek. He stroked my hair absently. "You're still my own pet, right?"

"That's right," I declared. "I am."

It didn't occur to me that others in my family also noticed I spent time with Granddaddy until Jim Bowie said, "How come you play with Granddaddy more than you play with me, Callie?"

"That's not true, J.B. I play with you lots. And besides, Granddaddy and I aren't playing. We're doing Science," I said, realizing as I spoke how pompous I sounded.

"What's that?"

"It's when you study the world around you and you try to figure out how it works."

"Can I do it too?"

"Maybe you can when you get to be my age."

J.B. thought about this and then said, "I don't want to. He's scary, Callie. He hardly ever smiles. And he smells real funny."

It was true. Granddaddy smelled like wool, tobacco, mothballs, and peppermint. And sometimes whiskey.

J.B. went on, "He's not very jolly. My friend Freddy has a jolly grampa. And where's our other grampa? Don't we get two? Freddy has two, so how come we don't have two?"

"The other one died before you came along. He caught typhus and then he died."

"Oh." He thought about this. "Can we get another one?"

"No, J.B. First he was Mother's father, and then later he caught typhus and died." J.B. looked perplexed by the idea that his own mother had once been a child herself.

"Why can't we get another one?"

"It's hard to explain, J.B. One day you'll understand," I said.

"Okay." Whenever I told him this, instead of becoming infuriated like Sul Ross, he always accepted it on faith. He put his arms up for a kiss.

"Who's your favorite sister?" I said.

"You are, Callie Vee." He giggled.

"Oh, J.B.," I breathed into his silky hair, overcome by his sweetness.

"What?"

"Nothing. I'll play with you more often, okay?" I did mean it when I said it.

"'Kay."

But I had so much work to do following that singular day when, floating in the river and looking at the sky, I'd been struck by a thunderbolt of understanding about grasshoppers and—really—the world itself. By the time I'd clambered up the riverbank, I had been transformed into an explorer, and the first thing I'd discovered was another member of my own odd species living at the other end of the hall. There was a living treasure under our roof, and none of my brothers could see him.

"ARE YOU COMING, Calpurnia?" Granddaddy called.

"Yessir, coming!" I galloped down the hall into the library with a fishing creel over my shoulder. It was an old wicker one of Granddaddy's with hardly any fishy smell left. It was full of my Notebook, collecting jars, a cheese sandwich, a corked bottle of lemonade, and a waxed paper twist of pecans.

"I thought we'd use the microscope today," he said, securing it in its case and nestling it in his haversack. "It's an old one, but the lenses are nicely ground, and it's still in good condition. I expect you have newer ones at school."

A microscope was a rare and valuable thing. We had no microscopes at school. I was willing to bet I was looking at the only one between Austin and San Antonio.

"We don't have any at school, Granddaddy."

This gave him pause. "Is that so? I don't understand the modern educational system at all."

"Neither do I. We have to learn sewing and knitting and smocking. In Deportment, they make us walk around the room with a book on our heads."

Granddaddy said, "I find that actually reading the book is a much more effective way of absorbing it." I laughed. I'd have to tell Lula that one.

"What are we going to study today?" I asked.

"Let us examine pond water for algae. Van Leeuwenhoek was the first man to have seen what you will see today. He was a wool merchant, much as I was a cotton merchant." He smiled. "So, you see, there is something to be said for the inspired amateur. What he saw was unimaginable. Ahh, I remember well my first look. It was like falling through the lens into another world. Do you have your Notebook? There will be much to record."

"Got it."

We walked to the river. On the way, we stirred up a herd of deer that crashed away through the underbrush and disappeared in two seconds flat. This of course raised the subject of deer and something Granddaddy called the food chain and each animal's place in the natural order.

We came to a shallow blind inlet ringed by a thick fringe of mossy green growth. The cooler air and stagnant water smelled of mud and rot. Frantic tadpoles zigzagged away from our shadows; some good-sized creature splashed into the water upstream from us, an otter, maybe, or a river rat. A pair of swallows rushed by, skimming for insects a few inches above the water.

We set down our satchels, and Granddaddy unpacked the microscope and assembled the barrel and the lenses, each of which had a cunning nesting place in the velveteen-lined box. He showed me how the pieces fit together. "Here, you do it," he said. The brass cylinder felt cool and heavy in my hands. I knew I was being trusted with something precious. Then he placed the case on a flat rock and balanced the microscope on top of it.

"Now," he said, handing me two thin pieces of glass, "choose your droplet of water."

"Any droplet?" I asked.

"Any one will do."

"There are so many to choose from," I said.

He smiled. "You will see more interesting things the closer your sample is to the green river plants growing here."

I bent and dipped my fingertip into the water, picking my droplet, then let it fall on one piece of glass. He instructed me to put another slip of glass on top.

"Now place it here on the platform," he said. "That's right. The tricky part is to turn this reflector so that it catches the sunlight at the best angle. You want enough light to illuminate your subject but not so much that the details get washed out."

I fumbled with the reflector and put my eye to the barrel, sure that something momentous was about to appear. What I saw could only be described as a field of pale gray fog. It was supremely disappointing.

"Um, Granddaddy . . . there's nothing here."

"Take the focus knob, here"—he took my hand—"and slowly turn it away from you. No, don't look up. Keep looking while you turn."

An awkward exercise.

"Do you have enough light?" he said. "Don't forget your reflector."

Then it happened. A teeming, swirling world of enormous, wriggling creatures burst into my vision, scaring the daylights out of me.

"Ook!" I cried and jumped back, almost overturning the whole apparatus. "Hewww," I said, steadying the microscope. I looked up at Granddaddy.

"I take it you saw your first microscopic creatures," he said, smiling. "Plato said all science begins with astonishment."

"My goodness," I said and looked through the eyepiece again. Something with many tiny hairs rowed past at high speed; something else with a lashing tail whipped by; a tumbling barbed sphere like a medieval mace rolled past; delicate, filmy ghostlike shadows flitted in and out of the field. It was chaotic, it was wild, it was . . . the most amazing thing I'd ever seen.

"This is what I swim in?" I said, wishing I didn't know. "What *are* these things?"

"That's what we'll find out. Perhaps you should sketch a few of them so we can identify them later from the texts."

"Sketch them? But they're moving so fast."

"In truth, it's a challenge. Here's a pencil."

I perched next to the scope and looked and sketched and looked and sketched as best I could. After a while, I noticed that some of the creatures started reappearing, which made drawing them easier. Granddaddy hummed Vivaldi and puttered nearby with his straining net. I chewed my pencil and frowned at my artwork, which consisted of awkward, blobby forms scattered across the page.

"I'm sorry to say that these aren't much good," I said, showing my page to Granddaddy.

"As artwork goes, you are entirely correct in your appraisal. But the more important point is this: Are these representations true enough so that you can match them with the examples in the atlas once we get back to the library? If that is the case, then you have done an acceptable job."

"I think I might be able to tell," I said, "but I'm not sure I can ever swim in the river again."

"All these creatures are completely harmless, Calpurnia, and they have enjoyed the river for many more eons than you. In addition, console yourself with the thought that you swim in the river proper, and these animals are not happy in flowing water."

"All right," I said. But still.

The bushes rustled, and Father's dog Ajax trotted up, pleased with himself for having found us. He had no doubt been out courting Matilda, Mr. Gates's bluetick hound, she of the unique yodeling cry that could be heard all over town. He greeted us in turn, nosing us for a pat, then splashed into the shallows and slurped at the brackish water. A fist-sized turtle plopped off a rotting log and Ajax charged clumsily after it. He enjoyed the game of chasing turtles and other small river creatures, but I'd never seen him actually catch anything aquatic. He was, more properly, a specialist in avian studies. But this time he surprised me by ducking his whole head underwater and coming up, startled, with an equally startled turtle in his mouth.

"Ajax," I said, "what are you doing? Stop it. Put that back where it belongs."

He pranced back to us, pleased with himself, and dutifully laid the turtle at our feet before shaking water all over us. He sat and looked up at me expectantly.

"He thinks he's doing his job," said Granddaddy. "You had better praise him or all your father's training will be for nothing."

"Oh, Ajax. Good boy, I guess." I gave him a pat. "What are we going to do with your turtle? Travis already has one in his room, and I doubt that Mother will tolerate another. Perhaps you should hold his collar while I let this one go."

"I'll walk him up the bank," said Granddaddy. "He shouldn't see you letting it go, or he will come to question the purpose of his work and eventually grow disheartened." He led Ajax away, and when they were both out of sight I inspected the turtle. Why had it allowed itself to be captured by such a large, dumb land creature? Was it old? Was it sick? There was nothing obviously wrong with it. It looked like every other turtle in the river. Maybe it was simply stupid. Maybe it was better that it died so that it wouldn't produce more generations of stupid baby turtles. But too late, I had interfered and thus made myself responsible for its safety. Wondering if I was, in my own small way, promoting the survival of the unfittest, I pushed it into the water, where it disappeared in a wink.

"It's all right," I yelled over my shoulder. "You can let him go."

I climbed up the bank after them, and Ajax met me at the top, sniffing at me for his turtle. "It's gone," I said, showing him my empty hands. "See?" I swear he understood me because his ears drooped and he turned away.

"It's gone, Ajax, I'm sorry. Come here and be a good dog." I ruffled his coat and thumped his sides the way he liked, even though I knew I would stink like a wet dog for the rest of the day. "There's a good boy. You're a good boy." This cheered him up some, and he forgave me enough to walk with me while we caught up to Granddaddy.

Ajax found the biggest burrow I'd seen in a long while. It looked and smelled like a badger's hole, and badgers were getting rare in our part of the world. He amused himself by sticking his muzzle deep inside and sniffing in excitement.

"What do you see there?" I called out to Granddaddy, who peered with interest at a small, uninteresting plant. "Come *on*, Ajax." I hauled on his collar to keep him from losing the end of his nose to a swipe from the burrow's notoriously irritable tenant.

"Vetch," said Granddaddy. "It looks like hairy vetch, but it may be a mutant. Look, it's got this odd dependent leaf at the bottom." He pinched off a couple of inches of stalk and handed it to me. "Let's save that one."

A boring plant, but I put it in a jar and printed HAIRY VETCH (MOOTANT?) on the label.

He said, "I've also got a woolly caterpillar over here. Have you ever raised one of these?" He held up a twig on which squirmed the biggest, fuzziest caterpillar I'd ever seen, a good two inches long. (Or, more properly, five centimeters. Granddaddy had told me that true scientists used the Continental system, which would soon come into widespread use in America.) The caterpillar was covered in dense fur that looked as plush and inviting as a cat's pelt, but I knew better than to stroke it. I'd been told my whole life that woolly caterpillars would sting you badly. I just didn't know if it was a little badly or a whole lot badly.

"What kind is he?" I asked.

"I'm uncertain about the species," he said. "There are several that look alike to the naked eye, and you can't know what you've got until it emerges as the winged imago."

"So how bad is their sting?"

He said, "I suppose you could touch him and find out. Which raises an interesting point: How far are you willing to go in the name of science? This is something for you to ponder."

Well, maybe. Or maybe I could give one of the younger boys a penny to touch it for me. But then I considered the price I'd have to pay later with Mother. Definitely not worth it.

"Let's take him home, and I'll raise him," I said. "I think I'll call him Petey."

"Calpurnia, you will find it a bad idea to give names to your experimental subjects."

"Why?" I said, dropping Petey and his twig into the biggest Mason jar we had, quart-size, with holes punched in the lid.

"It tends to spoil the truly objective observation."

"I'm not sure what that means, Granddaddy."

But he was lost in thought over some animal tracks. "Fox, I think," he murmured. "With a couple of kits, by the look of it. That's encouraging. I thought the coyotes had got them all."

By the time we got back to the house, we found that Sam Houston and Lamar had brought home a startling catfish that weighed forty-five pounds on the gin scale. Its huge, frowning mouth was framed with lashing barbels as thick around as pencils. It was a fright to look upon. The biggest of these fish didn't fight the hook much, so my brothers did not count them good sport. The main challenge was hauling them out of the river and lugging them home without touching the poisonous spines on their fins.

That night we had big chunks of it for dinner, rolled in cornmeal and deep-fried, its white flesh still tanged with the undertaste of mud that didn't seem to bother anybody else. I didn't want to eat it. I didn't even want to see it. It was as big as J.B. I mean, the *size* of that thing. It was big enough to take my whole leg in its mouth, and me swimming in the river every day. I pictured it grabbing me and dragging me down to the bottom, holding me there too long, or maybe long enough, depending on whether you looked at it from my perspective or the fish's.

My family would find me later, my hair swirling about like tragic Ophelia's. Or maybe they wouldn't find enough good-sized pieces to justify the cost of a funeral; maybe they would only find my chemise. Would you have a casket and a ceremony for just a chemise? Probably not. But how about a limb? Hadn't General Jackson's arm been given a full funeral ceremony? Or how about a head? I guessed a head would do it.

With that, I decided that I had analyzed the matter enough and did my best to think no more about it. Still, for months after that, when I stepped into the river, I thought of that Leviathan at one end of the scale waiting to mutilate me and the swarming microscopic creatures at the other end waiting to insinuate themselves. It was too bad, but sometimes a little knowledge could ruin your whole day, or at least take off some of the shine.

CHAPTER 9

PETEY

Peculiarities in the silkworm are known to appear at
the corresponding caterpillar or cocoon stage.

AS THE SUMMER WORE ON, I spent more and more time studying Science and less and less time practicing the piano. This
turned out to be unwise in the long run, since each time I
missed practice I had to make up the time and pay for it with
an extra half hour. On Saturday, after playing for a whole two
hours (!), I made my escape with my Notebook and tapped on
the library door.

"Enter if you must," Granddaddy called out. He was examining some plates in *The Atlas of Microscopic Pond Life*.

"So you have finished with your cultural obligations for the
day?" he said, without looking up, and I realized that with the
transoms open he could, of course, hear me thumping away in
the parlor across the hall. "I do like the 'Water Music,'" he said,
"and I hope you won't grow so tired of learning it that you put
it aside for the rest of your life. That's the great danger of too
much piano practice. I hope Margaret understands that."

"Mother says I can go back to a half hour tomorrow. Oh," I said, looking at the plates over his shoulder, "that's what I drew, isn't it?" I opened my Notebook to the illustrations I'd made of the microscopic river creatures. My ancient mace looked like the one in the text. "*Volvox*," I read, "it's *Volvox*. Is that how you say it?"

"That's correct. Such a satisfying form. I admit I have a special weakness for it amongst all the Chlorophyta."

"Look," I said, "here's another one." My drawings were up to snuff. I was very pleased with myself.

"Go ahead and label each of them in your book," Granddaddy said, "and note the page in the atlas so you can find them again."

I decided to use ink instead of pencil, which made the whole process nerve-racking, but I ended up with only one tiny blot.

Then I said, "Granddaddy, what should I feed Petey?"

"Who?" he said.

"Petey. The caterpillar."

"Calpurnia, must I give you the answer in a spoon like a baby? Surely you can figure it out on your own. Think about the problem. Do you remember where you found him? What sort of tree was he living on?"

"Ah," I said, and went out to find leaves of the same kind we'd abducted Petey from. That made sense. A caterpillar's job was to eat, so naturally he wouldn't be found wasting his time lounging about on something he didn't like. Petey curled into a fuzzy comma when I put the leaves in his jar. I replaced his narrow twig with a larger-branched one for exercise and diversion, should he feel the need. I set his jar on my dresser between the hummingbird's nest and a bowl of tadpoles I was studying. My dresser was getting crowded. A half hour later, when I looked again, Petey was munching on his foliage and seemed happy enough, but with a caterpillar how can you tell for sure?

I checked on him again before bedtime, and he was motionless, stretched full-length along his twig. He appeared to be asleep. At least, I hoped he was only asleep. I looked to see if he had eyes, and if they were closed. Both of his ends looked the same, but when I inspected him with a magnifying glass, I found two shiny black dots buried deep in the fur at one end. Those had to be his eyes, didn't they? He didn't appear to have eyelids.

Question for the Notebook: Why don't caterpillars have eyelids? You would think they would need them, spending their days in the sun as they do.

Travis inspected him the following morning and raised a good point I hadn't considered when he said, "Why did you call him Petey? How do you know he's a boy?"

"I guess I don't," I said. "Maybe we'll find out when he hatches. I don't know what kind of butterfly he's going to be, either."

More Questions for the Notebook: Do caterpillars come as

male and female? Or do they turn into male or female while they're asleep in their cocoons? Granddaddy had told me about the wasp that could opt to be male or female while in a larval stage. An interesting thought. I wondered why human children weren't given that option in their grub stage, say up through age five. With everything I had seen about the lives of boys and girls, I would definitely choose to be a boy grub.

MOTHER DISLIKED Petey's presence but tolerated him because he would eventually turn into something beautiful. Mother yearned for Beauty in her life. She supported the Lockhart Chamber Orchestra and took us once a year to the ballet in Austin. It took us half a day to get there on the train, and we would spend the night at the Driskill Hotel; there we would have ice cream floats at the fountain and afternoon tea in the Crystal Room.

Every month she pored over her magazines that came in the mail—*The Ladies' Home Journal* and *McCall's*. From these she made patterns, cutting and sewing silk flowers that she arranged in the parlor. Although we had fields full of wildflowers blooming in the spring, she never arranged those. Sometimes I would pick a handful of them and put them in a pitcher by my bed. They looked nice but they were good for only a day or two. Then they didn't so much wilt as disappear. You were left with a vase full of smelly water.

Petey disregarded the world around him; in fact, he

disregarded everything except the bundles of leaves I brought him daily. He ate and slept and ate and slept, and in between bouts of eating and sleeping, he ejected many tiny, compacted green bales from his hind end. This meant I had to spend part of each day cleaning up his quarters. I hadn't signed up for this, and I soon grew tired of it, but I kept telling myself it would all be worth it when he turned into a magnificent butterfly. He grew unbelievably fat, as thick as a sausage. One day I brought him the wrong kind of greenery, and he sulked and wouldn't eat it. I was ready to jettison him outside for all the trouble he put me to. Plus, he didn't make a very entertaining pet.

When I mentioned this to Granddaddy, he chastised me by saying, "Remember, Calpurnia, Petey is not your pet. He is a creature in the natural order of things. While it is easy to be more interested in the higher-order animals, and I must confess I myself am guilty of this weakness, it doesn't mean we can neglect our study of the lower orders. To do so indicates a lack of purpose and a shallowness of scholarship."

So, all for Science, I cleaned up caterpillar poop. Then Petey went off his feed again for no good reason. I checked his forage, and it was the right kind, but he wasn't interested. I thought, *You spoiled, sulky caterpillar, I should throw you out on the lawn. You can take your chances with the birds and see how you like that, mister.*

To my surprise, when I woke up the next morning, I found that he had his cocoon well under way. So he hadn't been pouting after all; he'd been resting up and planning for his labors. I had come close to throwing out a blameless caterpillar.

All day long, he squirted a fine gray thread from his front end (I think), and busily tangled it this way and that, fashioning a messy cocoon with odd bits of thread sticking out here and there. It looked like slapdash work. His knitting was no better than mine, which made me feel some sympathy for him. He slowly sealed himself up in his capsule like an Edgar Allan Poe caterpillar.

"Good night, Petey. Sleep well," I bid him. Petey stirred and then settled one last time in his self-made prison. The cocoon didn't move for two whole weeks while Petey went about the slow, magical business of rearranging his parts in his sleep. There was something gorgeous and mysterious about it, but it was also somewhat revolting if you thought about it too closely. It made me think of Life. And Death.

I had never seen a real live dead person. The closest I had come was a daguerreotype of my uncle Crawford Steele, dead at age three of diphtheria, wrapped in swathes of white lace. You could see some of the whites of his sunken eyes, so you knew that he wasn't asleep, that things were not all right. I went to Harry and asked, "Harry, have you ever seen a dead person?"

He said, "Uh, no. Why are you asking?"

"No particular reason."

"Where do you come up with these things? You scare me sometimes."

"Me? Scare you?" The thought of me scaring my biggest, strongest brother was laughable. "I was thinking about Petey moving his parts around, and that made me think of living things, which made me think of dead things. So the next time there's a funeral in town, will you take me?"

"*Callie Vee.*"

"There's nothing creepy about it. It's scientific interest. Backy Medlin looks kind of decrepit to me. How old is he, do you reckon?"

"Why don't you go down the street and inspect his teeth?"

"That's a good one, Harry, but I doubt he has any left. He'll go soon, don't you think?"

I passed Backy Medlin every day on my way to and from school. He sat with the other codgers on the gallery of the gin, rocking and spitting and interrupting each other's stories of the War and griping at each other that, no, it hadn't happened *that* way, it had happened *this* way. And so on. (Backy's name came from his prodigious use of chewing tobacco and his poor aim at the spittoon. He spat frequently, randomly, mightily. A constant foul brown rain pattered down on the dust around him, and you had to keep a sharp lookout.) No one paid the men the slightest attention anymore. Sometimes even they got sick of yakking and turned to dominoes, playing with an old carved set with dots so stained from a million games that they were nearly indecipherable. The tiles clacked pleasingly, and every now and then one of the old men would exclaim *"Ha!"* and you knew he had thrown down a particularly good one.

"So will you take me to Backy's funeral?" I said.

Harry said, "Really, Callie, this isn't very nice talk."

"I'm not *wishing* him to die. I'm just curious. Granddaddy says that a curious mind is a pree . . . is a perk—"

"Prerequisite?"

"Yes—that—to a scientific understanding of the world."

"Fine. But have you done your piano practice yet? Miss Brown comes tomorrow."

"You sound like Mother. *No,* I haven't done it yet, and *yes,* I'll do it. Harry, how many years will we have to take lessons? I'm getting tired of it, aren't you? Why don't some of the others take piano for a while? I have better things to do."

"Better things to do with Grandfather, you mean."

"Uh, yes."

"I asked you once before and you never answered me. So, what do you talk about with him?"

"Golly, Harry, there's everything to talk about. There's bugs and snakes, cats and coyotes; there's trees and butterflies and hummingbirds; there's clouds and weather and wind; there's bears and otters, although they're getting harder to find around here. There's whaling ships, there's—"

"All right."

"The South Seas and the Grand Canyon. The planets and the stars."

"Okay, okay."

"There's the principles of distillation. You do know he's trying to turn pecans into liquor, right? Although it's not going so well, but don't say I said so, okay?"

"Got it," said Harry.

"There's Newton's laws, there's prisms and microscopes, there's—"

"Got it, I said."

"Gravity, friction, lenses—"

"Enough already."

"The food chain, the rain cycle, the natural order. Harry, where are you going? There's tadpoles and toads, lizards and frogs. Don't go away. There's something called microbes, *germs*, you know. I've seen them through the microscope. There's butterflies and caterpillars, which brings us to Petey; let's not forget about him. Harry?"

I AWOKE in the morning to a tiny *skritch-skratch* sound like the noise a mouse makes in the wall, only it was coming from Petey's jar. It was too dark to see, so I pulled back the curtain and set his jar in the windowsill. His cocoon pitched this way and that. As the room grew lighter, he thrashed and chewed away and either didn't notice my face pressed up against his jar or didn't care. Finally, he had a good-sized hole in one end of his cocoon, and what had once been Petey slowly strained its way out with a mighty effort.

And there, instead of the lovely bright creature I'd imagined, crouched an odd-looking thick-bodied butterfly with damp, tightly furled wings. It shook, struggling to uncrimp itself. I could see that it wasn't my Petey anymore. I would have to find a new name for it. Something to reflect its long-awaited splendor. Something like . . . Fleur . . . since it lived on nectar, or maybe Sapphire, or maybe Ruby, depending on the final color of its wings. I left it to its work and went down to breakfast.

At the table I announced, "Petey hatched. He's busy drying off his wings."

"Oh, wonderful," said Mother. "What color is he?"

"I can't tell yet, ma'am. He's still puckered up. But he definitely needs a new name now that he's not Petey the Caterpillar anymore."

"Children?" said Mother, "do you have any suggestions?"

Sul Ross, the seven-year-old, proclaimed, "We should name him . . . we should name him . . . ," he struggled, ". . . Butterfly."

"That's nice, dear," said Mother.

"How about Belle," said Harry, "for beauty."

"That's nice, Harry. Any other suggestions?"

Granddaddy said, "You might want to wait and see what it looks like first."

I thought this an odd statement. But if anybody knew his butterflies, it was Granddaddy, so I figured he had some reason for making it.

"Yes," I said, "let's see what he looks like before we name

him, although Belle is a good idea." Sul Ross looked crestfallen, and I added, "And Butterfly is good, too, Sully. Maybe I'll call him Belle the Butterfly."

"Is it a him or a her, Callie?" said Travis.

"No idea," I said, tucking into the flapjacks.

"Kindly don't talk with your mouth full," said Mother.

After breakfast I ran up to my room with the three younger boys on my heels debating what to christen our new charge. And there in all his glory was Petey, or Belle, stretched wide on his twig, enormous wings filling his jar. He was huge, he was pale, he was fuzzy all over. He was the world's biggest moth.

"That sure is a funny-looking butterfly," said Sul Ross. "What's wrong with him?"

"It's not a butterfly, Sully," said Travis. "It's a *moth*. Callie, did you know it was going to be a moth?"

"Um," I said, taken aback by his size, "not really."

"Gosh, I've never seen one that big," said Travis.

"Me neither. He's kind of creepy," said Sul Ross, "don't you think?"

"Uh. . . ." It's true, he *was* kind of creepy, but I would never admit it. I had no idea moths could get to be that size. And this one was only a newborn.

"What are you going to do with it?" asked Travis.

"I'm going to study it, of course," I said, wondering what on earth I would do with this monster.

"Oh, okay. So what are you going to study?"

"Um, its . . . um, eating habits, that sort of thing. Its mating habits. Right. Yep, there's territory, wingspan, things like that."

"Are you going to have to touch it?" said Sul Ross. "I sure wouldn't want to touch it."

"Maybe not yet," I said. "It's barely born. It needs time to get used to things."

"You better find a bigger jar fast, Callie. It's going to bust out of that one."

"I don't think they come any bigger."

"Maybe you could let him fly around your room," said Travis.

Not likely.

"Eeeuuuw," said Sul Ross, backing up. "I gotta go."

"Me too," said Travis. "Time for school."

"Hey!" I called after them, "It's all right, come back here. I'm not gonna let him out!"

Now what? Petey—or Belle, or whatever it was—fluttered in its jar. The sound was dry, ominous, morbid. I got ready for school, trying not to look at it, flinching every time it flapped. I'd have to let it out of that jar, I could see that, but I didn't want to think about it. I spent most of the hours at school trying not to.

When I got home, I lingered downstairs and put in some extra piano practice, after which Mother ordered me upstairs to change my pinafore. I dragged myself up to my room and had a sudden spasm of anxiety as I put my hand on the doorknob:

What if it had gotten out? Had I tightened the lid on the jar after opening it the last time? What if it was flying loose around the room? Then I caught myself. *Calpurnia Virginia Tate. You're being ridiculous. Are you a Scientist or aren't you? Come on, now. It's. Only. A. Moth.*

All right. That did it. I peered around my door. There it hunkered in the jar, the same as I'd left it, too big to even turn around. It stirred, wings beating against the glass.

"Petey," I said. "What am I going to do with you? I need to figure out what species you are. And I need to find you a bigger home."

I pulled Granddaddy's *Taxonomy of the Insect World* from my bookshelf and turned to the order Lepidoptera. Based on its color and ridiculous size, it had to be a Saturniidae of some kind. Differentiating between the most likely possibilities meant examining the specimen's spread wings, but there wasn't room enough in the jar. There was nothing for it, I'd either have to get it a bigger home or let it loose. I stared at it for a while. It wasn't so bad looking once you got used to its freakish size. It did have cute feathery antennae. I had brought it this far. It was stuck in that jar because of me; I couldn't pretend it didn't exist.

"All right, Petey, let's go visit Granddaddy and see what he has to say." I picked up the jar at arm's length and carried it downstairs with him pulsating all the way.

I ran into Harry in the hall. He took one look at Petey and

said, "Good heavens, is that your butterfly? It looks more like an albatross."

"Ha," I said, "ha."

"Did you know it would turn into this?" he said.

"Oh, sure," I said, breezily.

Harry eyed me and then said, "Let me look at him. He's a prizewinner, isn't he? If they had an entry for moths at the Fentress Fair, you'd take it, easy."

An interesting thought. Along with the classes for hogs and cattle and home preserves, a category for moths. Which naturally led me to remember the pet division for children every year at the fair. Children showed up with their cats and dogs and parakeets, a bunch of boring, everyday pets. Why not something more interesting like, say, a giant moth?

"Say, Harry," I said, "do you think I could enter Petey in the pet show?"

"He's not much of a pet, Callie Vee," he said, laughing.

"So what? Dovie Medlin showed up last year with her goldfish, Bubbles, who wasn't much of a pet, either. And it's not as if they have to perform tricks or anything. All they have to do is sit there, and the judges come by and look at them. He'd get some extra points for being different, don't you think?"

"That he would, but it's months away," he said. "How are you going to keep him alive? You can't keep him in that jar."

"Of course not," I said. "I'm trying to figure out some housing for him. How long do moths live, anyway?"

Harry said, "I don't know. You're the naturalist. I'm guessing a few weeks."

Mother walked out of the kitchen and came to a sudden halt, staring at Petey's jar in disbelief.

"What is that *thing* you've got in there, Calpurnia?" she said, her voice rising.

I sighed. "This is Petey, Mother. Or," I added with false cheer, "you can call him Belle, if you like." As if a beautiful name could somehow cloak this grotesquerie. Petey rippled drily, and my mother took a step back. She couldn't take her eyes off him.

"What happened to your . . . to your beautiful butterfly?" she said.

"He turned out to be not so much a butterfly as a moth, you see," I said, holding the jar out to show her. She took another step back.

"I want you to get it out of here. That's a *moth*, for pity's sake. Imagine what something that size would do to the woollens!" I had forgotten that she and SanJuanna fought a perennial pitched battle with hordes of small brown moths for possession of our blankets and winter clothes, their trifling weapons of cedar shavings and lavender oil no match for the ongoing push of Nature.

"It doesn't eat wool, ma'am," I said. "At least, I don't think it does. It may only eat nectar, or it may eat nothing at all, depending on its species. Some of them don't feed at all in the adult stage. I haven't figured it out yet."

Mother raised her hands. "Do not, under any circumstances, let that thing loose in here. I want it out of the house. Do you hear me?"

"Yes, ma'am."

She pressed a hand to her temple and turned and went upstairs.

Harry said, "Too bad. I'd have liked to see him in the pet show. Step right up, folks, come and see Calpurnia Virginia Tate and her giant pet moth!"

"Very funny. All right, I have to let him go, but I have to show him to Granddaddy first." I went looking for Granddaddy in the library, but he wasn't there. I could go out the front door and around the long way to the laboratory in back, or cut through the kitchen and face more revulsion and more explanations on the way. I tucked the jar under my arm and went through the kitchen. Viola took one look at me and said, "What you got there?"

"Oh, nothing," I said and kept moving out the back door. Petey stirred in his jar. I wished he would keep still. I had grown used to his appearance, but that noise. There was something foreboding and primeval about it; it made the fine hairs on my arms stand up.

Granddaddy was stooped over his ledger book when I found him.

"Hello, Granddaddy, look what I have," I said, holding out the jar to him.

"My, my, that is certainly a hefty specimen you have there.

I've never seen one so sizeable. Have you identified the family it belongs to?"

"I think he must be Saturniidae, or maybe Sphingidae," I said, proud of my pronunciation.

"What do you plan to do with him?"

"I was going to enter him in the pet show at the Fair, but Harry thinks he won't live that long, and you keep telling me he's not a pet. And Mother wants him out of the house. So that means I can kill him and keep him for my collection. Or I can let him go."

Granddaddy looked at me. We both looked at Petey, squashed in his jar. "He's a handsome specimen," Granddaddy said. "You may never see another like him."

"I know." I frowned. "You did warn me not to name him. But I've raised him this far. I don't think I can kill him."

AT DUSK, when we gathered on the lawn to await the first firefly, my brothers stood on the porch while I set Petey's jar in the grass. Granddaddy watched from a rocker and sipped store-bought bourbon. I took the lid off the jar and stood back.

For a minute Petey huddled there without moving. Then he crawled over the lip of the jar and emerged from his glass cocoon. As he wobbled his way onto the grass, Ajax came trotting around the corner of the house. Petey stretched his quivering wings wide. Too late, from the corner of my eye I saw the dog charge, his ears flapping, thrilled with the prospect of a new game of fetch. Petey pulsed feebly into the air and came to rest a couple of feet away, with Ajax closing fast. He was going to swallow my best specimen, my science project, my Petey. Fury boiled within me. Stupid dog! I ran at him and screamed *Ajax!*—so loud that I startled myself. Who knew I had that much wind in me? The birds in the trees took flight, and Ajax hesitated. I lunged at his collar. But he leaped sideways, thinking that it was all a fine new entertainment. He pounced again and Petey rose again, chest-high this time, flapping like an awkward pullet testing its wings.

"No!" I screamed, and this time Ajax heard a word he recognized. Puzzled, he looked at me with Petey between his front paws. This was all fine sport, wasn't it? His job was to retrieve flying things, wasn't it? I rushed at the dog again, when Petey, with a mighty effort, launched himself into the air and in that split second was transformed from an ungainly land-bound dweller into something else, a creature of the wind, a citizen of the air.

I watched in amazement. Petey looked like he'd been flying forever. Ajax huffed and pulled at his collar, and I let him go. There was no catching that moth now.

"Wow!" exclaimed my brothers. "You did well, Callie." "I thought that moth was a goner, for sure."

Granddaddy raised his glass in salute as Petey disappeared into the scrub.

Later that night, I sat on the front porch by myself as it grew dark, delaying bedtime as long as I could, until all I could see was the last of the white lilies along the front walk. They glowed in the dark like pale miniature stars fallen to earth. Then something whizzed past me through the air, making straight for them, where it set up a commotion, thrashing around inside one flower after another. It sounded like a hummingbird, but I couldn't see it. Did hummingbirds fly at night? I didn't think so. Could it be a nectar-eating bat? I didn't know, and even though I couldn't see for sure, I decided that it had to be Petey. At least, I told myself so.

I preferred a happy ending.

CHAPTER 10

LULA STIRS UP TROUBLE (BUT DOESN'T MEAN TO)

The rock-thrush of Guiana, birds of Paradise, and some others, congregate; and successive males display their gorgeous plumage and perform strange antics before the females, which standing by as spectators, at last choose the most attractive partner.

IT TOOK MY FRIEND Lula Gates a long time to live down the ignominy of getting sick in public at the piano recital. For weeks she talked of nothing else. I grew tired of it and told her it could have been worse, that Maestro Frédéric Chopin had once done the same thing at a command performance for the king and queen of Prussia.

"Really?" said Lula, brightening at once.

No. I made that up. But it did make her feel better, and as a consequence she shut up about it.

I guess Lula was beautiful, although I wasn't aware of it at the time. She had a long blond braid of honey and silver threaded together that hung all the way down her back and swayed with a life of its own when she played a vigorous piece on the piano. Her eyes were an odd, pale color somewhere between blue and green, their hue depending on the color of her hair ribbon. There was one strange thing about her that I found fascinating: She always had a delicate mist of perspiration across the bridge of her nose, winter or summer. It was barely enough to moisten a fingertip, but when you wiped it away, it immediately reappeared. This sounds unattractive, but it was entertaining rather than off-putting. As a small child, I would stand there and dab it away and watch it return for as long as she would let me. There seemed to be no explanation for it.

You would think that having Lula as a friend would be a great relief to me after all my brothers, and generally this was so, but sometimes she could be a bit sappy. She wouldn't collect specimens with me at the dam (snakes). She wouldn't walk with me to the old Confederate Training Ground (blisters and snakes). She wouldn't go swimming in the river (undressing and snakes). But we shared a desk at school, and we always had. This is how our friendship had started and why in part, I guess, it persevered. Plus, I believe that her mother might have promoted the friendship. She might have thought it a social plum for Lula to have a friend in the Tate family. And did her mother also harbor hopes that Lula might one day snag one of the Tate boys as a husband? It's possible. I'm guessing we had more money than other families in the county. Lula's own family seemed comfortable enough. Her father owned the stables, and they could afford piano lessons, and they had a maid but no cook. She had only the one brother, feeble-minded Toddy. Toddy didn't go to school but instead spent his days in a corner of his room, clutching the ragged remnant of an old quilt and rocking himself without ceasing. He was peaceful unless you took his scrap of quilt away, and then he became distressed and produced horrible, loud mooing noises until he got it back. His family found it more trouble than it was worth to take it away from him for washing, so as a consequence it smelled disgusting. Apart from this, the Gateses' house seemed quiet compared with mine.

Lula won prizes for her needlework, whereas mine was straggly and pitiful. I couldn't understand her powers of concentration when she rolled a French knot or toiled over a tatted collar in Sewing class at school.

"It's the same as learning a piano piece, Callie," she would say, "and you can do that fine. All you have to do is practice it over and over until you get it right."

I pondered this and decided she was right. So why did I find the music so different from the needlework? When you played the piano, the notes vanished a second later in the air and you were left with nothing. Still, the music brought joy even as the notes evaporated, and playing a rag exhilarated everyone to the point of jumping around the parlor. What did the embroidery bring? Something decorative and permanent and occasionally useful, yes, but I found it dull and quiet work, suitable for a rainy day with only the monotonous ticking of the parlor clock for company. Mouse work.

I did convince Lula to play some Sousa arrangements for four hands with me, and we made a good go of it, pounding out twice as much music in a veritable torrent of strict-tempo chords, which was highly gratifying.

ONE AFTERNOON, my thirteen-year-old brother Lamar sidled up to me on the porch as I sat tallying Lepidoptera.

"Callie. . . ."

"What?"

"Do you think Lula likes me?"

"Sure, Lamar."

"No, what I mean is, do you think she . . . *likes* me?"

This was a surprise. Lamar had never shown any interest in girls before. "Why are you asking me?" I said. "Why don't you ask her?"

He looked aghast. "I couldn't do that."

"Why not?"

"Well . . . I don't know," he said lamely.

"Then I don't know what to tell you." I had a flash of inspiration. "Why don't you talk to Harry about it?"

He looked relieved. "Yes," he said, "that's a good idea. But you won't tell Lula, will you?"

"No."

"And you won't tell any of the others, will you?"

"No."

"Okay. Thanks, Callie."

I didn't think too much about the conversation until a few days later, when Sam Houston, the fourteen-year-old, crept up to me in the hallway and spoke out of the corner of his mouth.

"Callie, say, I need to talk to you. Do you think Lula Gates likes me?"

"*What?*" I said.

He flinched. "Don't jump like that. I only wondered if maybe she likes me, that's all."

"Golly, Sam."

"What?" he said.

I was in a minor panic. "I think maybe you should ask her yourself."

He looked appalled. "I can't do that."

I said, "You better talk to Harry. He knows all about those things." Who said inspiration doesn't strike twice?

"You're right, Callie. I'll talk to him about it. You won't say anything to Lula, will you?"

"No. I never would."

"Promise?"

"Promise."

"Cross-your-heart-and-hope-to-die promise?"

"Cross my heart and hope to die."

"Double-Injun-blood-brothers-swear-to-die promise?"

"Double Injun."

"It doesn't count unless you say the whole thing," he said.

"Saaaam."

"Okay, okay, okay. But say it, huh?"

"Double Injun blood brothers swear to die," I said. "Now leave me alone."

"Shoot, you sure are getting to be an old grouch," he said,

and walked off, no doubt in search of Harry. I rubbed my temples where a headache was setting up camp.

A couple of days later, I was reading by myself in a quiet corner when my ten-year-old brother, Travis, wandered up with an odd expression on his face. I eyed him and snapped, "What do you want?"

He looked hurt. "I want to ask you something."

"You aren't going to ask me if Lula Gates likes you, are you, Travis?"

He gasped, and his face crumbled in panic. "What?" he cried. "No, no, I was only going to ask you if she likes cats, that's all."

"I have no idea if she likes cats, or you, or anybody else. I'm sick of this. Go and get advice from Harry." I collected my books and stumped off muttering, "There's an awful lot of this going around."

"Sick of what? What are you talking about? What's going around?" he called after me.

I ignored him, fairly certain that there were no hordes of boys across town pestering their sister about whether *Callie Vee* liked them or not. And what did it matter, anyway? Did I care? I did not. No. Did not.

Harry came to my room an hour later, laughing. "You have got to stop sending them to me. I can't get a moment's peace. Give them the benefit of your own wise counsel."

"I don't know what to tell them. It's only old Lula. What's come over them?"

"It's an epidemic of crushes. They're getting to that age."

"Well, they can just quit it."

"There's no quitting at this point," he said. "It's going to get worse. Out of curiosity, does she like any of them?"

"Um, not that I can tell, especially. Should I ask her?"

"If you feel like occupying the middle ground at the Third Battle of Manassas. If I were you, I'd keep well out of it."

I decided he was right and said, "Yes, Harry, that's the thing to do. I'll pretend to know nothing."

"That shouldn't be too hard," he said, and he ducked out the door.

"Funny!" I would have thrown something at him, but the nearest item to hand was my precious Notebook, which I'd never fling about.

The next school day, I met up with Lula at the main road as usual, and we walked the last quarter mile to school together, chatting about nothing in particular. I happened to glance back, and there were my three brothers behind us on the road, strung out at regular intervals, their eyes fixed on her. Oh, dear. Things were worse than I thought. This sudden change in them unnerved me. Weren't they too young for this? Couldn't I have a normal family like other girls? Why did it have to happen to all of them at once?

At recess that day, all three of them managed to find an excuse to stand close to the invisible line that, by unspoken agreement, divided the girls' side of the yard from the boys'. They leaned against the trees in the schoolyard, looking like aimless loiterers, except for their eyes, which they fastened on Lula with studied nonchalance, and then cut sideways at each other like assassins.

Lula and I played hopscotch. Her silvery braid flashed in the sunlight like a living thing. Her petticoats flared as high as her knees, producing a strangled gasp from Lamar. I glared at him. A month before, she could have walked through the yard in her chemise and he wouldn't have noticed. Now this. Tough times lay ahead.

"Lula," I said, pitching my pebble.

"What?"

"Nothing. Never mind."

"No, what, Callie?"

"Um. Do you . . ." I had made a hope-to-die promise I wouldn't tell. And while I myself did not know of anyone who *had* died after breaking one, it wasn't worth the risk.

"Do I what?" she said.

I thought fast. "D'you think we should ask Dovie if she wants to play?"

"I thought you didn't like Dovie."

"Well," I said as I hopped, "I never said I didn't *like* Dovie. . . ."

"Yes, you did, Callie. You said so last week. You said exactly those words."

"It's Christian that we invite her, don't you think?"

Lula looked at me curiously. "If you want to."

I didn't want to—I couldn't stand Dovie—but I walked

over to her. I was about to ask her to join us when Miss Harbottle rang the bell. Dovie gave me a funny look. I seemed to be getting lots of funny looks. I didn't deserve a one of them.

We trooped back inside, girls in one queue, boys in the other. I began to dread the walk home after school and tried to think up an excuse to walk by myself. Miss Harbottle homed in on my distracted state and called on me an inordinate number of times with questions on Texas history, which I could not answer, much to the class's amusement.

"Calpurnia Tate, are we interrupting you?" she said.

"Interrupting me, ma'am? I'm not doing anything."

"Exactly. Where is your mind today?"

"I must have left it at home, Miss Harbottle," I said. The class tittered.

"Precisely," she said. "And don't you get pert with me, Calpurnia. Go to the corner. One hour. Any more comments and it'll be the switch for you."

I stood in the Corner of Shame with my face to the wall for a full hour and contemplated my brothers' situation but came up with no answers. Then came lunch.

We took our pails outside and scattered under the trees. Lamar and Sam Houston sat with their respective friends. I felt sorry for Travis, the youngest and most tender of the bunch, who ate alone and cast piteous, moony looks at Lula.

Lula noticed him and said, "What's wrong with Travis? Is he ill?"

"I think he has spring fever," I said.

"But it's not spring," she said and gave me another funny look. "Shouldn't we ask him to eat with us? He looks lonely."

"I'm not sure that's such a good idea, Lula."

"Why not? You sure are being odd, Callie Vee."

Me? Odd? I thought, *If you only knew the half of it.* "Don't worry, Lula, he's fine. I think you should leave him alone."

But it was too late. She walked up to Travis, whose eyes got bigger and whose face got redder and redder as she came toward him. Lamar and Sam Houston, on the other hand, turned all pinched and squinty.

She bent down and spoke to him. I couldn't hear her words, but he leaped to his feet and followed her back to our spot. Lamar and Sam Houston looked like they were about to go into spasms. Travis sat down, and I thought he might pop with happiness.

"Hi, Callie. Lula asked me to sit with you."

"I know, Travis."

"This is a good place to eat lunch, don't you think? You picked a real good place. Lula, do you want half of my sandwich? Viola made us roast beef today, and it's real good. I'll share it with you, if you like. And I have pie. Lula, do you want to share my pie? Or I can give you the whole piece, if you want. It's peach, I think. Wait, let me look. Yep, it's peach all right."

"Thank you, Travis," she said, graciously, "but I have enough lunch of my own."

"Say, Lula," he said, "do you like cats? Mouser, she's our

old barn cat, she had kittens, and I get to look after them all by myself. Mother said so. I named them all by myself, too. Do you want to hear their names?"

I sighed. Do you think it's any fun listening to a ten-year-old pitching woo?

"And then there's Jesse James, and then there's Billy the Kid, and then there's Doc Holliday, and then there's . . ." He droned on, giving the names of all eight. Lula actually looked interested.

"The one I like best is Jesse James," he finished. "He's got stripes all over him except for his toes, which have some white places on them. He looks like he's wearing spats," he giggled. "He's real friendly. He lets me carry him around in my overalls. Say, Lula, would you like to see my kittens sometime?"

"That would be nice, Travis. I like cats. We used to have a cat, but my mother wouldn't let it come inside the house. It disappeared, and it never came back."

I could almost hear the gears meshing in my brother's head. "Say, Lula," he said, slowly, "maybe you could have one of my kittens. If you wanted."

"Gosh, Travis, really?" Her whole face lit up. "That would be so nice." Travis looked stunned by her radiant smile. "Of course," she said, "I'd have to ask my mother first. Maybe I could come after school tomorrow."

"Okay," he gulped.

Egad, my ten-year-old brother had made a date. Then I looked over and saw my older brothers shooting daggers at him.

Uh-oh.

The afternoon dragged by. I was as tense as a cat in a room full of rockers. When school let out, Lula and I met up outside as usual, and there stood Travis, his face a beacon of hope. A few paces behind him, Lamar and Sam Houston hung about looking shifty.

"Hi, Lula," said Travis. "Hi, Callie. Can I walk with you?"

I grunted noncommittally, which Travis chose to interpret as assent; he fell in beside us, and he and Lula chattered on about the kittens. Lamar and Sam Houston followed twenty yards behind, nudging and plotting.

"You're being real quiet, Callie," said Lula.

"Mmm? Oh, I'm thinking about my book report." And how I was going to prevent two of my brothers from killing a third. I would have to seek advice from Harry, although my estimation of him as a counselor in affairs of the heart had received a substantial drubbing at the hands of the wretched Miss Minerva Goodacre. I wanted to run on ahead, leaving Lula and Travis to their inane conversation, but I feared he would be fallen upon by thugs along the road.

"So what's your book report on, Callie?" said Lula.

"Ah. My book report. Yes. Well, I haven't decided yet. Maybe *Kidnapped*. Maybe *Treasure Island*. What are you going to write about?"

"*The Last Rose of Summer*, I think. Or *Love's Old Sweet Song*." I had noticed that Lula's taste in literature had been tending away from the good old ripping yarns and toward the sticky romantic stuff. Travis looked impatient to get back in the discussion, but he'd run out of conversational coin.

He thought hard and then said, "What are those books about, Lula?"—a pretty good gambit on his part. So I feigned interest in flowery descriptions of thwarted romance and complicated sacrifice all the way back to the main road, where Lula turned off to her house while Travis strenuously waved goodbye. We walked on, and he nattered away for a while. One small cloud floated on his otherwise sunny horizon. Thoughtfully, he said, "You don't think I'd have to give her Jesse James, do you, Callie? I like him best of all. Maybe I should have told her she could pick any of them except him. Maybe I should have said that."

"Don't worry, Travis. Lula wouldn't take him."

"Are you sure, Callie? How can you be sure?"

"She wouldn't do that. She's not like that."

He nagged at me for reassurance for a good five minutes, with me turning every few yards to glower at Lamar and Sam Houston to make them keep their distance.

"How come they wouldn't walk with us today?" said Travis as we headed up our drive. A pang shot through me. He didn't understand that his own brothers—older, bigger, stronger, smarter—were rivals for Lula's affection. He was as damp and wobbly and susceptible to damage as a newly hatched chick. How could I possibly protect him from heartbreak?

LAMAR SAT stony-faced at dinner that night, and Sam Houston didn't speak a word. I kept waiting for one of them to pounce on Travis in some way. Travis bubbled over with his news of walking Lula home, which amused Father and alarmed Mother, who no doubt thought he was too young for such matters. Granddaddy was distracted, as usual. Normally he was not much interested in the dinner conversation. I think he would have preferred dining alone in the library, and while I think Mother might have preferred it too, that just wasn't done. We ate *en famille*, as she called it, and everyone (except Granddaddy) had to make some polite contribution to the general conversation, even if it was no more than a brief description of one's day.

"Callie," Mother said, "what did you learn in school today?"

"Not much," I said.

Lamar perked up and said, "Callie got sent to the corner today."

What a pill. Mother put down her fork and looked at me.

"Is this true?" she said.

"Yes, ma'am."

"Miss Harbottle sent you to the corner?"

"Yes, ma'am."

"For what?"

"I'm not exactly sure," I said.

"How can that be?" said Mother, with steel in her voice.

"She wasn't paying attention in class," said Lamar. He was fast turning into my least-favorite brother.

"I'm sorry, Mother," I said. "I was . . . I was thinking about my book report, and I didn't hear her, that's all."

"I don't ever want to hear of you standing in the corner again, Calpurnia. The boys, I can understand at times. But *you*. Your behavior is a blot on the family name."

"Well," I huffed, *"that's no fair."*

There was stunned silence. Whoops. Everybody looked up, even Granddaddy. Then he threw back his head and let loose a laugh, which shocked the room even more. All heads snapped in his direction. It was a surprisingly vigorous bellow, not an old man's wheeze at all. I almost expected the chandelier to start tinkling. I nearly giggled in response.

He said, "She has a point there, Margaret. Pass the gravy, please. Ha!" And with that, he punctured the tension in the room and deflected any punishment I might have called down upon myself. Harry winked at me. Lamar stuck out his tongue at me, but of course the disciplinarians at the table missed it.

After dinner, I asked Travis to show me his kittens again, and we walked to the far stall in the barn, where a weary Mouser kept watch over her furry family in the nest she'd burrowed in the straw. The kittens tumbled over her, batting at each other.

"See, Callie, don't you think Jesse James is the best one? He purrs real loud. You can hear him from way far away." He lifted the kitten from the straw and tucked it into the bib of his overalls, where it looked at home and produced a rumbling bass purr remarkable for something its size. "You're sure Lula won't take him?"

"No, Travis, I told you. She's not like that."

"She is awful nice, isn't she?"

"Travis," I sighed. "Listen, Travis, you know that Lamar and Sam Houston are sweet on her, too?"

"They are?"

"Yes. I wanted to tell you."

"I'll bet lots of fellas are sweet on her."

This stopped me. I sat down in the straw and stroked Mouser, who looked like she could stand a little attention. "Travis," I said, "aren't you sweet on her?"

"I guess so."

"Then how come you're not upset?"

"About what?" he said, tickling Jesse James under the chin.

"About Sam Houston and Lamar."

"Why should I be upset?" He looked at the kittens. "Which one is the next best, do you think, after Jesse James? I think it might be Bat Masterson, don't you?"

"Which one is that?" I said.

"The orange one. His eyes are the same color as Lula's. Kind of green and kind of blue. See?" He handed me a protesting Bat Masterson, and I could see that his—or maybe her—eyes were in fact the same color as Lula's. "Maybe she'll pick him."

"Travis," I said, "you don't like Lula because she has eyes like your cat, right?"

"No, Callie, course not, don't be silly."

"Okay," I said. "So what about Sam Houston? What about Lamar?"

He looked at me, puzzled, and I realized that he had no clue what I was talking about. But he would grow and change and understand soon enough. "Never mind," I said. "Your cats sure are cute."

The next morning I walked to school with Travis, letting my other brothers set off ahead of us. Lula met us at the bridge. She wore a white pinafore and a dark green hair ribbon that made her eyes look exactly the same color as Bat Masterson's. She seemed pleased to see Travis. They talked all the rest of the way about cats, dogs, horses, school, Halloween, Christmas, and so on. You wouldn't think a twelve-year-old girl would have much to say to a ten-year-old boy, but you'd be wrong. To my relief, the others left Travis alone all day.

But the walk home was another story. Travis again latched on to Lula, and so did Lamar. I wanted to run on ahead, but danger hung in the air.

"Hi, Lula," said Lamar, spying an opportunity. "Can I carry your books home for you?"

Both Lula and Travis flushed. "Thank you, Lamar," she said, and handed him her book strap. There was an awkward silence as we walked on. Then Lamar said, "So, Lula, how come you walk home with a *baby* like Travis? Why don't you walk home with a real man like me?" He made a muscle with his arm. "Look, Lula, tough as whang."

Oh, Lamar. You shouldn't have. The look on Travis's face, and Lula's.

Travis cried, "I'm *not* a baby," in a high unsteady voice, which of course made him sound exactly like one.

"I'm *not* a baby," Lamar mimicked him.

"Quit it, Lamar," I said. "You don't have to be so mean."

"What a baby, has to have his sister stand up for him. *Titty*-baby."

This was too much to bear in front of Lula. Travis, the most placid of my brothers, dropped his books, rushed at Lamar, and shoved him with all his might. Lamar staggered and dropped Lula's books and his lunch pail but managed to keep to his feet. I could see that Lamar was startled by this display but not in the least hurt. He yelled, *"Baby!"*

Travis teetered on the verge of tears. He wheeled and raced for home as fast as he could, sending up puffs of dust in the road. "Baby! Coward!" called Lamar. But I knew it wasn't cowardice that sent Travis flying down the road. He didn't want to shame himself and cry in front of Lula. Like a baby.

The three of us stood in the road in an awkward silence. I picked up Travis's books. Lula cleared her throat and said, "I've got to go home. Bye." She scrambled for her own books and had them gathered up before Lamar could reach them, and then she took off, her long braid flopping as she ran.

"Hey, Lula!" Lamar called after her. *"Hey, Lula!"* But she gave no sign she'd heard him and kept on running.

"Lamar," I said, "sometimes you are such an amazing pill."

"What are you talking about? He attacked me. He punched me. He *hurt* me."

"He did not. I'm gonna tell Mother on you."

"You snitch," he said.

"You pill," I said.

"Tattletale," he said.

"Meanie."

"I don't want to walk with you."

"Fine. I don't want to walk with *you*."

"I'm going ahead."

"No, *I'm* going ahead."

"Well, go right ahead then!"

And, in a lather of irritation, we were both home before we knew it.

Our family took a dim view of snitching and tattling. Why, I don't know. I walked through the front door, weighing the cost of telling versus not telling, when I was saved from making a decision by Mother calling me into the parlor.

"Calpurnia. Come in here and tell me what's wrong with Travis."

"Um, maybe you better ask Lamar," I said, as he tried to slink past me in the hallway.

"Lamar, come in here and explain," she said. Travis was sitting on the carpet at her feet, hugging his knees, his face flushed and swollen. He threw a furious look at Lamar.

"What happened at school today?" she said. She nodded at Travis. "He won't tell me anything."

Lamar looked surprised. He hadn't expected that.

"Lamar?" said Mother. He looked away and wouldn't answer.

"Calpurnia? What happened?" I looked at Travis for guidance, but his face was blank. "Calpurnia, I'm not asking you to tell me, I'm *ordering* you to tell me. Right this minute."

So I told, hoping that both brothers would understand that I was under orders and had no choice. Mother listened in silence to my whole story, starting with Lula. To my surprise, she looked more sad than angry. She doled out a light punishment of extra chores, and that, we hoped, was the end of that.

But boys being boys, and Lula being a beauty, it was not.

The next several days were a cauldron of anxiety for me, and for Travis too, no doubt. Lula came to pick a kitten at a time she and I had arranged together, making sure that none of my brothers was around. To my relief, she chose Belle Starr.

I was constantly on guard against Lamar and Sam Houston on the trips to and from school, and it started to wear on me. I got to the point where I couldn't stand it anymore, and after dinner one night, I called them together out on the porch and said, "Look, you can't keep herding me and Lula about like sheep. I'm tired out. You've got to leave us alone. You've got to leave each other alone. If you don't agree not to fight, I'll make sure that she never speaks to any of you ever again. As long as you all live."

I wasn't sure how I could manage that, but I was the resident Lula expert, their beloved's best friend, and I spoke with such conviction that they believed me.

"Here's what we're going to do," I said. "Each of you can walk with us one day a week. Travis, you get Monday, Lamar gets Wednesday, and Sam Houston gets Friday. That's that."

"What about Tuesday and Thursday? Who gets those?" said Sam Houston.

"Nobody does. You leave us alone. I'm not kidding. Any questions?"

To my great satisfaction there were none.

CHAPTER 11
KNITTING LESSONS

Natural selection will modify the structure of the young in relation to the parent, and of the parent in relation to the young.

THE LULA SYSTEM I'd devised ended up working well enough, at least for the next few weeks. I invited her over to play piano after school, and we learned a couple of popular duets at our mothers' request. We knew we wouldn't have to play them at the next recital. Or any recital, for that matter. Then I made the mistake of inviting her over to work on one of our Domestic Arts assignments together and Mother got a good look at her stitches. Lord have mercy, how could I have been so stupid?

"Calpurnia," said Mother a few days later, in a tone I dreaded, "I think it's time you graduated from knitting scarves to socks. There's nothing like good, thick woollen socks made by a pair of loving hands. If we start now, you'll have time to make a pair for all your brothers before Christmas, maybe even for Father and Grandfather, as well. Wouldn't that be nice? Bring your knitting bag, and we'll sit in the parlor."

The pressure was on.

I sighed and put down my magnifying glass. I was in the middle of preserving a particularly nice specimen of Viceroy butterfly in a framed glass to hang next to Granddaddy's specimens in the library, but it was raining outside and the delicate work was tough without direct sunlight.

Mother seemed pleased by the skeins of new wool that she pulled from her own bag, which bristled with needles of every size. The wool was a fine dark chocolate brown and bound in thick hanks. She sat with her hands out like paddles while I unwound the skeins and rewound them into a ball. Although I was not excited at the prospect of knitting socks, the rhythmic shuttling of the wool back and forth was hypnotic, and I grudgingly had to admit that there might be worse ways to spend a rainy day. *Might* be. Mother also seemed calmed and relaxed by this timeless domestic ritual; knitting always seemed to soothe her headaches, and she didn't need such frequent doses of Lydia Pinkham's.

The weather had cooled somewhat. Although it wasn't warranted, a small fire of pecan logs popped in the fireplace to foster the illusion that summer was well past us. Travis wandered in with Jesse James and Billy the Kid. He dangled some wool before them and soon had them springing back and forth and tumbling on the carpet. Lamar came in and at Mother's request put some Schubert songs on the gramophone.

"Let's start with socks for Jim Bowie, shall we?" said Mother. "Some small plain ones. We'll learn about patterns later. Cast on a row of, oh, let's say forty stitches, and we'll start at the calf." She handed me four tiny knitting needles.

"Four?" I frowned. "What do I do with four?"

"You knit in a perpetual circle instead of turning back at the end of a row."

Help! I was clumsy enough with two needles. This was going to be much worse than I thought. Mother made encouraging noises while I cast on the first row of my first sock. There were so many sharp needle points sticking out at unexpected angles that it was like juggling a porcupine.

"Look," she said, "if you wrap the wool around your fourth finger like this, it's easier to control the tension, and the stitches stay even." I tried to do as she showed me, and to be truthful, the next row did look better. The one after that looked better still. I noticed that once you got into a certain rhythm, the stitches flowed down the needle so that you picked up the next one before you knew it.

"Now we begin to cast off to make it narrower toward the ankle. Yes, that's right."

Slowly—exceedingly slowly—the mess of wool in my hands began to take shape. The afternoon passed, and although I wouldn't call it fun, it wasn't as terrible as I had feared. At the end I had in my hand one small, funny-looking knitted brown thing. I held it up for inspection and decided that it looked more socklike than not. Mother seemed pleased with it. She said, "It looks just like the first one I made at your age."

"Well, that's that," I said, packing up my knitting bag. "Done."

"What do you mean, done? Where are you going?"

I looked at her, not comprehending.

"Let's start on the next one," Mother said.

"The *next* one?" I yelped. Was she crazy? It had taken me hours to make this one.

"Of course the next one, and kindly don't raise your voice like that. What's Jim Bowie going to do with only one sock?"

"I don't know," I said. I wanted to add, *I don't care. Maybe he can make a puppet out of it.*

"And what about the other boys? And Father? And Grandfather?" she said.

I counted up. There were the six brothers plus Father and Granddaddy, and they had many feet amongst them. So that meant there was also tomorrow, and the day after that and the one after that. My mind reeled. There was my whole life for you, socks stretching all the way to the infinite horizon, a yawning valley of knitting tedium. I felt sick.

"Please, Mother," I said in pathetic tones, "let me do it tomorrow. I think my eyes are strained."

She looked so concerned at this that I realized I must have touched a nerve. Perhaps the addition of spectacles to her only daughter's not-so-promising features didn't bear thinking about. This was a small but handy nut of knowledge, and I stored it away for future use. Also, perhaps I could cultivate sick headaches.

"All right," she said, "that will do for today."

I grabbed my knitting bag and got out of there before she could think of some other homegrown skill for me to learn. I took my bag to my room and then dashed downstairs and out to the darkened laboratory, but Granddaddy wasn't there. He was probably out collecting plants. Rainy days were a good time to collect plant specimens, which was just as well, as it was impossible to find animal or insect life, all of which melted away in the rain and stayed away until the sun came out again. I lit one of the lamps and sat in his shabby sprung armchair, contemplating the rows of glinting bottles. The lulling rain pattered overhead.

I awoke to Granddaddy hanging his dripping oilskin on a nail.

"Good afternoon, Calpurnia. Are you keeping well?"

"Yes, sir, but I'm tired out from all the knitting I had to do today."

"And how do you like knitting?"

"It's not the worst thing in the world," I admitted, "but there's such a lot of it. I'm supposed to knit socks for everyone before Christmas, and that's a tremendous number of socks. I'm hoping you like yours plain because I haven't learned any patterns yet."

"I like my socks plain. I never learned any patterns either."

"You can knit?" I asked, amazed.

"Oh, yes, and darn too. Several of the men in my regiment were accomplished knitters."

He saw the look on my face and went on, "We had to be self-sufficient in the field. If you needed a new sock, you made it yourself. There were no wives or sisters—or granddaughters, for that matter—to look after us, and parcels from home seldom got through. I remember one sergeant writing home at Christmas, asking his wife to send him a new pair of rabbit gloves. They arrived in the middle of the following summer, and by then he'd lost two fingers to frostbite. But he kept his thumbs, so he was happy about that. There was, of course, the problem of the empty fingers in the gloves. They interfered with his rifle grip, but he lopped them off at the knuckle and sewed them flat. Made a neat job of it, if I remember."

"Self-sufficient." I thought about this for a while. If our soldier boys had learned to knit, if my grandfather had learned, maybe it wouldn't kill me to learn.

He looked at me. "I imagine that your mother is hoping you learn cookery, as well. We had to cook for ourselves, too."

"Granddaddy, are you trying to make me feel better?"

He smiled. "I suppose I am."

"Mother's threatening to make me learn a new dish every week. It might not be so bad, except that you spend hours making it and then it's all gone in fifteen minutes. Then you sweep up the kitchen and you scrub the counter and you have to start all over again without a single moment's rest. What do you have to show for it? How does Viola stand it?"

"It's all Viola knows," he said. "And when something is all you know, it's easy to stand it. There is one other thing she knows: Her life could be much harder. Viola is 'house' instead of 'field.' She has aunts and uncles in Bastrop chopping cotton with the short hoe and pulling the long sack."

"Father won't allow a short hoe on the place."

"Do you know why not?" said Granddaddy.

"No sir, I don't."

"It's because I provided him with the opportunity to spend a full day in the field with one when he was about your age. I hope he provides your brothers with the same experience."

"Do you think he'd let me try it?"

"I doubt he would want to see his daughter out there."

"Hmm. So what did you find today?"

He pulled his spectacles from his pocket and lifted his satchel onto the counter. "Here are some nice specimens of *sangre de drago,* or dragon's blood. The Indians used it to treat gum inflammation. I did see an *Oxalis violacea,* but I think we have enough of those. And, look here, it's a *Croton fruticulosus,* which I've never seen blooming this late before. You may have heard it called bush croton. Let's try and root this one."

The plants were nowhere near as interesting to me as the insects, and the insects were not as interesting as the animals, but Granddaddy had shown me how they were all dependent, one upon the other, and you had to study and appreciate all of the phyla in order to understand any one of them. So I peered at the wilted wisps he sorted with his finger and tried to learn something.

"Do you remember," he said, "the hairy vetch we found a while back? The possible mutant?"

It had been an extremely boring plant, but I did remember it.

"Can you find it for me?" he said. "I think it's still here somewhere. I haven't had time to press it."

I scuffled through the jars and envelopes and came up with it, an unprepossessing dried brown scrap.

"The mootant," I said. "Here it is."

"The correct pronunciation is 'mew-tant.'"

"How do you spell that? And *please* don't tell me to look it up."

"Just this once. It's *M-U-T-A-N-T*."

"I think my pronunciation is better," I said. "Mootant. What is it? What does it mean?"

"Mr. Darwin discusses it in some detail. Have you not reached that chapter yet?"

I felt comfortable enough with him to admit how difficult I found the reading. "I'm still studying the chapter on Artificial Selection. It's taking me longer than I thought. It's dense reading."

"For someone of your tender years, I suppose it is," he mused, while inspecting the jar. He opened it and tipped the sample out onto a fresh square of blotting paper. "Hand me the magnifying glass, will you?" he said.

He studied the mootant for a full minute and then said, "Humh." Now, this in itself was odd. My grandfather normally spoke in complete sentences.

"Humh?"

"Let's go outside and look at this." It was still overcast, but the light outside was better than the gloom of the laboratory. We went out and he looked at the plant through the magnifying glass for a long time. I waited until I couldn't stand it anymore.

"What *is* it, Granddaddy?"

Pensively he said, "I don't really know." This was even odder. He always knew everything. "There appears to be a small uncinate leaf dependent from the main node, but it's difficult to say, as it's so desiccated. I don't remember this in any of the descriptions. And I don't recall seeing it in any of the drawings, and we have some excellent ones in Dr. Mallon's atlas."

"So what does that mean?"

"It's so dried out it's hard to say. It may be an aberration, it may be nothing." He looked at me. "Or it may be that we have found an entirely new species."

"No, " I breathed.

"It's possible. Let's sit down and have a drink and think about this." We went back into the laboratory, and he put the weed in the middle of the counter, then sank into his armchair, the springs echoing in a way that normally would have made me giggle. He stared at the vetch.

"There is a bottle for special occasions on the top shelf in the corner," he said. "Reach it down for me, will you? There's a good girl."

The heavy green glass bottle was covered with the dust of ages. The brittle label read Kentucky's Finest Bourbon Whiskey and showed a picture of a curvetting thoroughbred.

Granddaddy poured himself a full measure and downed it in one gulp. He repeated the process, then poured a third time and handed the glass to me. I shuddered at the memory of my first glass of whiskey (*might cause some coffing*—indeed).

But he was so lost in thought that he didn't see me trying to wave it away. I took it from him and set it aside. I waited, breathless.

After a long time he whispered, "Well, well. I've been waiting for this day for a long time." He looked up. "And here we are."

"Are you sure?" I whispered back. "How do we really know for sure?"

"We must find a fresh specimen and root it right away. We must make a detailed drawing. We must mark the precise spot we found it on the map. We must photograph it to send to the Smithsonian, perhaps a cutting later on. And then we'll see." He took a deep breath. "Do you care for another drink?"

"No, thank you, Granddaddy, but you go right ahead," I said, handing him back his glass.

"I believe I will," he said. "Yes, I believe I will."

He had his drink, and we regarded each other. "Now to work," he said. "Let us gather a fresh one so we can complete our documentation. And we need several others like it so that we have a good sampling. Where did we find it?"

I picked up the jar and looked at the label. And there, under "mootant," where I always marked the location the way he'd taught me, was . . . nothing. The earth tilted under my feet. I stopped breathing. My vision grew dim. I looked away for a second to give my deceitful eyes a chance to stop their trickery, to see what *had to be there*. I blinked hard and looked again at the label. There was nothing.

With great effort of will, I gasped for breath and air rushed into my lungs.

"Calpurnia, are you all right?"

I puffed like a landed catfish, "Uh-noh, uh-noh, uh-noh."

He stood up. "I agree, it's an overwhelming moment. Perhaps you should sit down for a minute. Sit here," he said, and gave me his chair.

I couldn't bring myself to speak. I couldn't tell him.

"Shall I get your mother?" he said, with consternation.

I shook my head and got control of my breathing. "No, sir."

"Do you need some whiskey?" he said.

"No, sir!" I shouted, throttled with fear.

"Be calm," he said, "and tell me what's wrong."

"It's the vetch," I cried. "I didn't write it down. It's not there."

He picked up the jar and looked at it. "Oh, Calpurnia," he said, softly. "Oh, Calpurnia." Each mild word was like a blow across my face.

I put my head in my hands. "I'm so sorry," I sobbed. "I'll find it, I'll find it!"

"How did this happen?" he said.

"I know what you taught me," I wept, "I know. We were coming back from the river. I was thinking about Ajax's turtle. I was thinking about the survival of the fittest." I wrenched my handkerchief from my pocket. "Oh, I'll find it, I promise. Please don't be mad at me, I *will* find it."

"Yes. Of course you will," he said quietly.

"I'll go right now."

"Calpurnia, it's getting dark."

"If I hurry," I said, jumping up and grabbing the jar. "Where's a pencil, I need a pencil, I'm sure there's a pencil around here somewhere," I gabbled.

"Stop. It's too late tonight. We'll have to go tomorrow. Sit down and calm yourself. Think back. You said we were coming back from the river," he prompted.

I sat down again.

"Close your eyes," he said, "and see it in your mind."

I closed my eyes, but I was too overwhelmed to concentrate. I listened to his words and tried to slow my breathing. "We were using the microscope. At the inlet."

"I remember," said Granddaddy. "Breathe deeply. Be still and think. We were coming back from the inlet."

"We were coming back from the inlet," I echoed. "That's right, Ajax had caught a turtle, the only time he's ever done that. I remember taking it from him. You led him away so I could let it go. There's . . . there's something else about Ajax . . . but I don't remember what it is."

"I'm sure you will remember," he said. His voice calmed me.

Ajax and the mootant. The mootant and Ajax. I knew I was on the right track. One had something to do with the other, but what? I cast about through the trails of my memory like a hunting dog trying to pick up a lost scent. This way, that way, all blind leads. What had Ajax been doing? It seemed like some-thing annoying, but then he was always doing something annoying in his bumbling, good-natured way, so that was no help at all. Hadn't he been out wooing Matilda? But then what?

"Oh," I moaned, "I can't think of it. It's in here some-where"—I smacked myself on the forehead—"but I just can't find it."

"I think, Calpurnia, that it's something you're going to have to sleep on. We will find it. We *have* to find it. Even if we must examine every green growing thing on this section."

Somberly he regarded the mootant jar. Then he sighed once, and even though I saw no blame in his face, I thought my heart would shatter. I resolved then and there that I would crawl on my hands and knees across our six hundred acres with a magnifying glass if that's what it took, for as long as it took. We closed up the laboratory and walked back to the house in silence. Never had I felt so wretched.

Do you think there was any sleep for me that night? I lay flat in bed like a corpse, unable to generate the energy to toss and turn. Question for the Notebook: How could Calpurnia Virginia Tate be so stupid? An excellent question, that. My grandfather had taught me to note the location of every specimen, and I had done so, right up to the one moment—the *only* moment—when it truly mattered. Another Question for the Notebook: How could I expect him ever to forgive me? Again, an excellent question, Calpurnia. Perhaps he won't forgive you. Perhaps he won't be able to bear the sight of you. In which case, you're done for.

I got up in the morning with huge, dark half-moons under my eyes; Mother regarded me with some alarm. I was unable to look at Granddaddy at breakfast.

School was an agony of exhaustion and nervous tension. I came perilously close to snapping at Miss Harbottle and being sent to the Corner of Shame for the rest of my natural life when she made me go to the board and solve a long division problem. Which I got wrong.

At recess, Lula said, "Callie, what's wrong with you?"

"Nothing, Lula, I'm *fine*!" I shrieked. She backed away from me and went off to play with that simp, Dovie Medlin. "Hey, Lula, I'm sorry. Come back," I called out, but Miss Harbottle rang her bell.

I dragged myself home at the end of the day, lagging far behind my brothers, who had given up trying to cajole me out of my mood. I thought about Ajax as I trudged along. If only I weren't so exhausted, maybe I could get my brain to focus. The stupid dog was the key to it all. I'd taken his turtle away from him. We'd walked away from the river. I'd hauled on his collar. Because. Because. Because he'd stuck his nose in a big hole.

"Yes!" I screamed and my brothers turned around to look at me. I jumped up and down and screamed, "Yes! The badger, the badger! I know where it is! I know where the vetch is!" I ran up to Lamar and Sam Houston and shoved my schoolbooks into their hands. "Take my books home for me, I'm going to find the mootant!" And I ran into the brush, heading for one of the deer paths.

"What are you doing?" Lamar called out. "What's a mootant?"

But I was too busy crashing through the brush, my heart pumping *yes yes yes* as I ran. It had been the biggest badger hole I'd ever seen, so big I'd meant to come back and investigate it further. Granddaddy had found the vetch a few yards away, hadn't he? I could find it, I *would* find it. The world was mine. My grandfather would be mine again.

Three hours later, scratched, blistered, thirsty, I stepped in said badger hole in the gathering twilight and almost snapped my ankle in two. I also woke the badger. He responded with an irritable hissing and thumping from deep in his burrow, causing me to pull my leg out of there double-quick, despite the pain.

There wasn't much time left. Soon it would be too dark to see, and besides, the badger would be emerging soon to make his rounds, terrorizing the local moles and gophers. A grouchy badger was something to be avoided. I hobbled a few feet away and thought. We had been coming from the river. We had been heading toward the house. So that meant we were traversing . . . that way. I set off limping, eyes fixed on the ground. And there—right there—was a small green clump of possible vetch. I fell to my knees, praying *let this be it, this has to be it, please let this be it*. I scrabbled in the hard-packed dirt with my fingernails, loosening the soil to free up the roots as much as possible, cursing myself as an idiot for not bringing a trowel and a jar of water.

Panting with anxiety, I got it out of the earth after a good five minutes' work. Most of the root was intact. I sank back onto my heels, drained, ignoring the pain in my ankle. I would have rested longer except for the indescribably rank smell and loud snuffling coming from a few feet away. I turned and saw the badger trundling toward me.

I made good time for a crippled girl bearing a priceless treasure.

VIOLA RANG her bell on the back porch as I reached the driveway. There'd be trouble for arriving late to dinner, especially since I was so filthy. Arriving late for dinner was a serious offense in our house, but if I went in right away, there'd be explanations and delays and cleaning up to deal with, all postponing the critical moment of putting the vetch in water. I drew back under the trees and skirted around the house to the laboratory, adding to my tardiness and the repercussions I'd have to face at the table.

The laboratory was dark. There were several empty jars and a carafe of drinking water on the counter. I filled a jar with water and put the vetch into it, thinking, *Please let this be the right one. If it's not, I'll have to kill myself. Either that, or run away from home.* I walked to the back door, trying to remember how much money was in the tin box hidden under my bed. At last count, I'd saved twenty-seven cents for the Fentress Fair. I couldn't run very far on twenty-seven cents. *Best not to be pessimistic, Calpurnia. It has to be the one.*

I got through the back door just as Viola pulled the roast from the oven. SanJuanna stood ready to take it into the dining room.

"You late," Viola said. "Warsh up in here."

"Sorry," I said. "Is Mother mad?"

"Plenty."

I pumped water at the kitchen sink and attacked my hands with the nail brush.

"Sorry."

"You said that already."

I looked down at my torn, dirt-stained pinafore.

"Take that off," Viola said. "Nothing you can do. Go get in there."

I took it off and hung it on the hook by the sink and hobbled into the dining room hiding behind SanJuanna and the roast. I may have exaggerated my lameness a tad. Conversation stopped. I ducked my head and murmured "pardon me" as I took my place. My brothers looked expectantly back and forth between me and our mother.

"Calpurnia," said Mother, "you are late. And why are you walking like that?"

"I stepped in the world's biggest badger hole, and I think I hurt myself. I'm sorry I'm so late, Mother, I truly am. It took me ages to get back, what with being so injured and all."

"See me after dinner, please," said Mother.

The older boys went back to eating, disappointed by the lack of a public scourging, but the baby, Jim Bowie, said, "Hi, Callie. I missed you. Where have you been?"

"I've been collecting plants, J.B.," I said in a loud, exuberant voice. Both my mother and my grandfather looked up. "And then I stepped in the badger hole," I added. "Maybe my ankle's broken."

"Really?" said J.B. "Can I see? I never saw a broke ankle."

"Later," I muttered.

Mother turned her attention back to her plate, but Granddaddy continued staring at me. I was about to bust a gut.

I turned to Jim Bowie and said, "J.B., I might have found something special, a special plant. Yes, indeedy. I left it out in the laboratory. I'll show it to you later, if you want. Best not to play with your peas like that."

I peeked at Granddaddy. He was still staring at me with intense concentration. We started the meat course. The port bottle was still a good thirty minutes away, but then Granddaddy did something unprecedented in the entire History of Dinner: He left before the port. Rising from the table, he patted his beard with his napkin, bowed to my mother, and said, "Another fine dinner as usual, Margaret. Kindly excuse me." He walked out through the kitchen, leaving us all gaping in his wake. I heard the back door close behind him and his boots on the steps. None of us had ever seen anything like it. My mother collected her wits and glared at me.

"Do you have anything to do with this?" she said.

"Not I." I kept my eyes on my plate.

"Alfred," Mother said, turning to Father for information, "is Grandfather Walter feeling all right?"

"I believe so," Father said, looking perplexed.

Seeing an opportunity, Jim Bowie, still playing with his peas instead of facing up to the ordeal of eating them, said, "Please, Mother, may I be ex—"

"No, you may not. Don't be ridiculous."

"But Grandfather is ex—"

"Stop it right now, J.B."

The rest of dinner passed in silence. I was made to sit at the table for a whole hour after they left and SanJuanna cleared up, and I missed the firefly competition. Who cared about that? But not being out in the laboratory was killing me. I caught myself wringing my hands, something I'd only read about in over-wrought sentimental stories. I was out of my chair and limping through the kitchen before the clock stopped bonging. Viola was feeding Idabelle the Inside Cat while SanJuanna washed the dishes.

"Listen, you—" said Viola as I crashed out the back door and came to a screeching halt. There, sitting on the back steps in the dark, stroking one of the Outside Cats, sat Grand-daddy, smoking a cigar and staring at the sky. From the kitchen behind us came the homey noises of the crockery being put away. From the darkness came the chitter of some night-flying bird. I stood there a moment, my whole world hanging in the balance.

"Calpurnia," he said, "it's such a lovely evening. Won't you join me?"

CHAPTER 12

A SCIENTIFIC STUDY

There are not many men who will laboriously examine internal and important organs, and compare them
in many specimens of the same species.

THE FOLLOWING SATURDAY, Granddaddy and I left for Lockhart
in the gig. The excuse I gave my parents was that I wanted to
visit the library. Granddaddy didn't give any excuse; he asked
Alberto to hitch up a horse. Even though he had removed himself from domestic matters, everyone still paid him enormous
deference. Invoking his name was like turning a golden key to
open doors that might otherwise have remained closed to me.

I held the precious specimen in a cardboard box on my lap
while he drove. Even though the day was overcast, I had one of
Mother's old parasols shading both me and the Plant, which was
snugly ensconced in a small clay flowerpot. I had watched
Granddaddy poke a hole in the dirt with a pencil before tenderly
easing the fragile green stalk into its new home. We watered it
with fresh well water. I felt honored to be entrusted with it.

To my horror, the Plant began to look a tad wilted on our
journey.

"Granddaddy, the Plant looks a little . . . tired."

He glanced at it but didn't appear concerned. "That's not unusual, considering we ripped it out of the ground not so long ago. Give it some water from the canteen. Isn't it a grand day for a drive?"

I agreed that it was and relaxed a fraction. He whistled some Mozart for a while and then broke into song, something rude about a drunken sailor and what should be done about him. To pass the time, he taught me the words.

In Lockhart, we pulled the gig up in front of Hofacket's Portrait Parlor—Fine Photographs for Fine Occasions. Once inside, Granddaddy had trouble making Mr. Hofacket understand what we needed.

"You want me to take a picture of a plant?" he kept saying. He may have been able to work a camera, but he was slow to catch on to our request. Granddaddy explained again what he wanted. The reluctant Mr. Hofacket said, "Well, I'll have to charge you my usual rate. That's one dollar for each portrait."

"Done," said Granddaddy without hesitating. Mr. Hofacket looked chagrined, like maybe he was kicking himself for not charging a special plant premium.

"All right," he said. "Come on back into my studio. Little girl, you wait out here."

"No, sir," said Granddaddy. "She's part of this expedition." Mr. Hofacket looked at him and then led us through the curtains without saying another word.

In the back were various chairs and chaises and wicker

stands. Everything looked familiar, which was disconcerting until I realized I had seen all this stuff before in different family portraits scattered throughout the whole county, the same props used over and over again. Mr. Hofacket fumbled in a drawer and produced a sheet of plain white paper. Then he opened another drawer and found an empty photo album, undid the binding, and pulled out a sheet of rough black paper.

"Like this?" he said to Granddaddy. "You want a black one and a white one both?"

"That will be fine."

"Okay," said Mr. Hofacket, still having trouble with the concept. "It's your money."

"Yes, sir, and soon it will be yours," said Granddaddy expansively, in as good a mood as I'd ever seen him, especially considering he'd taken no whiskey that I knew of. He winked at me, and I tried to wink back, but I could only do it with both eyes at once, which made me look stupid. Another important skill I needed to work on.

Mr. Hofacket tacked the white piece of paper to the wall and then placed the Plant on a wooden box in front of it. Then he rolled his big bellows camera into place and started fiddling with it.

"Closer," said Granddaddy. "As close as you can get while still preserving the detail. We need to be able to make out that hooked leaf, that one hanging right there."

"That there?" said Mr. Hofacket, amazed. "That's what you want a picture of?"

"Yes, sir."

Mr. Hofacket frowned. "If I move in too close, it'll be a blur. Let me think about this for a minute." He examined the Plant from this angle and that. Then he said, "I think we need some extra light coming from this direction. That will throw this part here into relief, and the flash will show it better." He wheeled a cunning rolling rack of stacked lanterns up next to the Plant and lit them, nine lanterns in all. He turned the rack this way and that until he was satisfied with the angle of the bright light it cast.

Then he looked through his lens, and said, "Okay, this is the best I can do. But I got to warn you, you got to pay me even if you don't like the results."

"Yes, sir, I understand." That didn't seem fair to me, but Granddaddy was not troubled.

"Even if you can't see that . . . that thing hanging there."

"Sir, I accept your terms. Here," he said, reaching into his pocket, "let me pay you now."

"Naw, naw," said Mr. Hofacket. "I just wanted to make sure you understood." He filled his tray with flash powder and then ducked under his black cloth, and a second later we heard a soft *foop* as the room erupted with brilliant white light, stunning my vision for several long seconds.

"Don't move around until you can see good again," warned Mr. Hofacket as he emerged from his tent. "Once I had a lady trip and nearly break her darn foot." He pulled the plate out of his camera, turned and saw me, and said, "Oops, missy, I'm sorry about the language. Pretend you didn't hear that and please don't tell your mama. I'll be back in a few minutes." He took the plate and disappeared into a tiny closet. We could hear him clinking and sloshing around in there, and he emerged a few minutes later holding a floppy photograph with a pair of wooden tongs.

"I don't normally bring it out while it's still wet, but I thought you'd like to see it," he said. "Don't touch it."

We looked and there it was: the Plant and, clearly visible at the base of the stem, the Very Important Tiny Leaf.

Granddaddy grinned. "That's fine work, sir, most fine."

Mr. Hofacket flushed and ducked his head, and I swear he would have kicked a clod if there'd been one on his studio floor. He mumbled, "You like it?"

"It's perfect. I am most gratified."

"The shape of that there leaf is real clear."

"It's admirable, sir. Admirable. Let's do the other one." I think Mr. Hofacket would have stood there all day and drunk in the praise he'd earned during this strangest of undertakings. He set the Plant in front of the black paper this time and repeated the process all over. I closed my eyes before the magnesium flared, but I still saw dazzling fireworks, even through my eyelids. Mr. Hofacket hurried out with the next picture to more praise. Now that he was part of the project, he peppered Granddaddy with questions about new species, the Smithsonian, Washington, et cetera.

I was putting the Plant back in its cardboard box to head home when Granddaddy said, "Wait, Calpurnia. Mr. Hofacket, one more picture, I think." He put the Plant on a fancy wicker fern stand.

"Calpurnia, you stand on this side, and I will stand here." I smoothed my pinafore, and Granddaddy patted his beard. I stood tall and proud in my very best posture.

"Hold your breath," called Mr. Hofacket. "Don't breathe, now. Three, two, one."

This time, the flare in our faces could have stopped a rhinoceros in its tracks. The whole world went white. I wondered if this was what snow looked like. Mr. Hofacket yakked away as my vision gradually returned. He carried all three portraits to the front counter and was about to stamp his embossed gold HOFACKET'S FINE PORTRAITURE seal on the lower left corner of each one when Granddaddy stopped him.

"Sir," he said, "kindly put your seal on the back of the portraits as they are scientific exhibits, and the images themselves must remain plain." Mr. Hofacket's face fell until Granddaddy said, "With your seal on the back, the world will still know that you took these photographs. You may put your seal on the front of the one of me and my granddaughter to memorialize this day." He handed him three silver dollars.

The photographer wrapped the pictures in brown paper and tied them with twine. It was time for us to leave, but he was loath to let us go. He walked us out to the gig, still talking. He insisted on holding the Plant in its box while I climbed into the gig. Fascinated, he stared at it as if expecting it to address him. I opened the parasol and took the Plant on my lap, and Granddaddy clucked to the horse. Mr. Hofacket stood in the road and yelled, "Good-bye, come back soon. Good-bye, and be sure to tell me what happens. Be sure to let me know if they like my photographs!"

"When we get home," said Granddaddy, "I'm going to write a letter and send the photographs off right away. Then we have nothing to do but wait, which is sometimes the hardest part. Give our specimen some more water, won't you?"

On the long drive back to Fentress, my grandfather and I had energy to spare. We burned up some of it singing sea chanteys and pirate songs with naughty words, being careful to switch to hymns when other riders came into view. We made it home at dinnertime, dusty and worn out but still elated by our day. We put the Plant to bed in the laboratory and joined the others inside.

Dinner lasted an eternity.

"What news from Lockhart?" said Father.

"Cotton futures are up, I believe," said Granddaddy, "and Calpurnia and I had our photograph made."

"You did?" said Sul Ross. He looked at me accusingly. "How come you got a photograph?"

"To mark a red-letter day," said Granddaddy. He looked around the table. "Calpurnia and I may have discovered a new species of plant."

"That's nice," said Mother, looking distracted.

"What kind of plant?" said Harry.

"Please pass the potatoes," said Lamar.

"It may possibly be a new species of vetch," said Granddaddy.

"Oh," said Sam Houston. "Vetch."

Oh. Vetch. Bloody red murder raged in my bosom. I wanted to fly across the table at him, but instead I frothed in silence through the rest of that interminable meal. Never before had the obligatory dinner conversation sounded so inane. Never before had I seen my family as such half-wits, such hayseeds, such dolts. The only saving grace was that Father, as a cattle owner, appreciated the importance of a possible new strain of "oh, vetch" and asked if it could be used for feed, but I was in too much of a snit to pay attention.

Finally, *finally*, it was over, and Granddaddy and I retired to the library and closed the door. He took one of the tiny keys off his waistcoat chain, opened the locked drawer to his desk, and pulled out some sheets of thick, cream-colored writing paper.

He said, "Light the lamp, Calpurnia. Let us cast some light in the shadowy corners of Terra Incognita. Let us hold high the lamp of knowledge and expunge another dragon from the map. We shall write to the Smithsonian Institution."

I set a match to the kindling in the fireplace and ran and got extra lamps and set them around the perimeter of his blotter like an intimate constellation. He dipped his pen, paused and stared into space, dipped his pen again, and then wrote in his old-fashioned hand,

August 8, 1899

Dear Sirs,

It has come to our attention during our daily rambles in this small corner of Caldwell County, located in the center of Texas, forty-five miles (approx.) due south of the State Capital of Austin, that there may be a new species of vetch, which we have the honor to present to you gentlemen. The plant is, on first inspection, a common member of the lowly pasture Vicia villosa, also known as hairy vetch. However, you will see, as described below and from the photographs . . .

It took him two full pages to describe the Plant and the Very Important Tiny Leaf. And at the end he signed it, as I looked over his shoulder,

Faithfully yours,
Walter Tate and Calpurnia Virginia Tate

He sat back in his chair. "There we are," he said. "We shall see. We shall have to wait and see."

I put my hand on his shoulder. He took a slow deep breath and said, "I thought the day would never come, my girl. I thought I might die before it happened."

And there we were. A new species. A photograph. And me, his girl.

CHAPTER 13

A SCIENTIFIC CORRESPONDENCE

When a race of plants is once pretty well established, the seed-raisers do not pick out the best plants, but merely go over their seed-beds, and pull up the "rogues," as they call the plants that deviate from the proper standard.

THE PLANT TOOK UP RESIDENCE in the southern windowsill of the laboratory and, after some anxiety on my part, grabbed a firm hold on life. We inspected it several times a day, vigilant for signs of under- or overwatering, too much or too little sun, spider mites, drafts, chlorosis, general malaise. Every time I found a ladybug, I rushed it to the Plant to stand guard for pests, but my tiny crimson sentries always wandered off. We made detailed daily notes in the log, a crisp new marbled-cover book reserved for the Plant. Terrified that somebody might toss the Plant out in some misplaced fit of tidying up, I tacked a small warning sign beneath the flowerpot:

EXPERIMENT IN PROGRESS. DO NOT MESS WITH THIS PLANT. I MEAN IT.
Calpurnia Virginia Tate (Callie Vee).

Twelve days later, we received our first correspondence about the Plant. From Mr. Hofacket. He wrote asking if we'd received word from the Smithsonian. He'd put copies of the photographs in his window between the stiff bride and the naked baby lolling on a white bearskin rug, and several new customers had come into the shop to inquire after the curious pictures of a nondescript weed.

"Calpurnia, you are part of this endeavor," Granddaddy said. "Would you please write to Mr. Hofacket and remind him again that it is far too soon to receive word about this? I told him repeatedly that it would be months. Nevertheless, we must cultivate enthusiasm in the layman whenever and wherever we find it."

Ah! An assignment to enter into a scientific correspondence—of sorts—with an adult. I wrote my draft in pencil, and when I was satisfied with my efforts, I sought out Granddaddy to show it to him. I knocked on the library door, and he called out, "Enter if you must." I found him poking through one of his lizard drawers, muttering something about a missing specimen.

"Calpurnia, have you seen my five-lined skink? It should be filed here between the four-lined and the many-lined, naturally, but I seem to have misplaced it."

"Uh, no, sir, I haven't, but I have written a letter back to Mr. Hofacket, and I need you to look at it."

"Mister who?" he said, rummaging.

"The photographer. You remember, in Lockhart."

"Ah, yes." He waved me away and said, "I trust you've

done a fine job. Yes, yes, go ahead and send it. Here are the newts," he murmured. "Here are the salamanders. Where are the rest of the skinks?"

I was thrilled to the marrow. I was about to run from the room when I remembered another problem.

"I have no stamp, Granddaddy," I said.

"Hmm? Oh, here we go," he said, digging in his pocket for a coin. He gave me a dime, and I took it and ran upstairs to my room. I pulled out a new nib and my box of good glossy foolscap paper reserved for special occasions. I arranged these items on my vanity and sat down. It wasn't a long letter, but it took me an hour to make the final copy.

August 20, 1899

Dear Sir:

Your letter of Wednesday instant at hand. My grandfather Captain Walter Tate requests that I inform you that we have, as yet, received No Word from The Smithsonian Institution. My grandfather, Captain Walter Tate, wishes you to know that he will send correspondints the moment he receives Word. My grandfather conveys his complimints and appreciates your interest in the Subject.

I remain, vy truly yrs,
Calpurnia Virginia Tate
(granddaughter of Captain Walter Tate)

I put it in a nice thick envelope and clattered down the stairs, determined to get it in the post that day.

Travis and Lamar were playing Cowboys and Indians on the front porch, firing popguns at each other. I ignored their cries of "Hey, Callie! Where you going?" and ran as fast as I could. I didn't feel like sharing, and I didn't feel like explaining. They had their own lives. *And now I have mine*, I thought, exulting as I ran.

I made it to the post office in record time, puffing and covered in fine road dust. Mr. Grassel, our postman, stood behind the counter. There was something wrong with Mr. Grassel, but I wasn't sure what. He always made a great show of waiting on the Tates; he kowtowed to my parents when they came in. He pretended to like children, most of all the Tate children, but I could tell he really didn't. He chatted with Lula Gates's mother and handed her a parcel. I waited like a polite child.

"Good afternoon, Callie," Mrs. Gates said, noticing me a minute later. "Is your family keeping well? Your mother is not too bothered by her headaches, I hope?"

"Hello, Mrs. Gates," I said. "We are all keeping well, thank you. And you?"

"We are all well, thank goodness."

After a few more pleasantries and her urging me to convey her respects to my mother, she left. I edged up to the counter and placed my envelope on it so that I wouldn't have to put it in Mr. Grassel's hand. His puffy palms were always sweaty. He made my skin crawl.

"So, Missy Tate," he said, picking it up and inspecting it, "you are writing to Lockhart, I see."

"I want a stamp," I said, teetering on the knife edge of rudeness.

He narrowed his eyes. Was I being impertinent or not?

"Please, sir," I added, a finely timed second later.

Mr. Grassel looked at the address on my envelope. "Going to get your pitchur made at Hofacket's?" He often asked who you were writing to and why. Mother said it was the height of rudeness for a public servant with privileged knowledge to pry, and for once I had to agree with her.

"Yes." A pause. "Sir." Then because I was filled with daring on this special day, I added in my sweetest little girl voice, "I'm going to get my *pic-ture* made."

His mouth tightened. Ha! I pushed my dime across the counter at him. He took a stamp, dampened it on a small sponge, stuck it on my envelope with a dramatic flourish and said, "Any kind of special occasion?"

"No. Sir."

He ostentatiously counted my eight cents change and held it out so that I was forced to hold up my hand to receive it.

"Whole family?" he said, pressing my fingers with his moist palm.

"What?" I said.

"Whole family going? Or just you, little lady? Why, you're a real pitchur unto yourself—oh, excuse me, make that *pic-ture*."

"Yessir!" I cried as I wheeled and ran out of there, hugging the private precious nugget of the Plant to myself. I would never share that knowledge with him. You might as well tell your news to the whole town.

And what if it turned out that Granddaddy was—God forbid—wrong? I could bear it if he was wrong, but I couldn't bear other people making fun of him. I had noticed in passing that he remained well-esteemed in the community due to his building of the gin and other business enterprises in decades long past, but there was sometimes a tinge of mockery of his present pursuits. I'd heard him called "the Perfessor" by various semiliterate wags about town in tones that might have been termed faintly derisive. My grandfather didn't care what others thought of him, but I did. I cared. My disloyal thoughts were followed by a stout, *And what if he's right?* Of course he was right; he had to be. In our time together, I'd never known him to be wrong about anything. He might misplace a five-lined skink from time to time (and who did not?), but he was never wrong about the facts.

I knew full well that the next few weeks were going to be an agony of waiting and that leaving myself unoccupied would make things much, much worse. I resolved to dive into a frenzy of specimen collecting, science, schoolwork—work of any kind—to make the time go faster.

What I did not foresee was that the work would be housework.

CHAPTER 14

THE SHORT HOE

Nature ... cares nothing for appearances, except in so far as they may be useful to any being.

I CONTINUED TO HOVER over the Plant with Granddaddy. To my great relief, it thrived under our tender care, first stretching for the light and then trailing along the windowsill. Granddaddy called it the Proband. He told me that's what you called the first of a kind. Every day I took it outside for a few minutes to expose it to the bees for pollination. I was vigilant in my duties and shooed away all grasshoppers and other plant eaters that dared to venture too close.

I turned my attention to other experiments of my own devising, anything to keep me away from Christmas socks. The cotton harvest was looming, so I considered the issue of the short hoe, which still raged through our part of the world. Granddaddy had taught me that the best way to learn about something was to undergo the experience or perform the experiment yourself, and he had given Father the opportunity to study the short hoe as a youngster, making him spend a day toiling with it. In my new campaign of activity to hasten time, I took one of the long hoes from the tool shed (we had no short ones on the property). I figured that if I held it halfway down, it would be the same thing as working with the short one. I walked out to our closest row of cotton, a good fifty yards from the back porch. Mother said that a proper lady always had a lawn and a garden; women who were not proper ladies had cotton planted right up to their windowsills.

The bolls were swelling on the plants, performing their miraculous transformation from hard green pods into fluffy white spheres. Cash money, coming right out of the ground.

I swung my hoe.

Oh, it was hard work, let me tell you. And the weather wasn't even that hot. And I didn't have to do it hour after hour for my daily bread. And I wasn't an old person with rheumatism like I'd seen some in the fields. All these things were going through my head when I heard a shriek like a screech owl coming from the house. I nearly jumped out of my skin.

"What are you doing?" Viola charged at me from the back porch. I had never in my life seen her so upset.

"I'm chopping cotton, what does it look like?"

"Lord a'mighty, you get inside! At once! Before anybody sees. Jesus help me." She grabbed the hoe from my hand and shoved me toward the house, hard. "What's the matter with you?" she hissed. "Have you completely lost your senses? Playing like you a Negro."

"I wanted to see what it's like, that's all. Granddaddy told me about—"

"I don't want to hear about that old man. That old man losing his mind, and now you losing yours." She muttered and prodded me all the way back to the house, "Little girl chopping cotton. *White* girl chopping cotton. *Tate* girl chopping cotton. Lord help me."

We made it to the safety of the kitchen with her looking around in alarm and griping at me the whole way.

"Gimme that pinafore," she said, snatching it off me. "You go get a new one right now. Your mama take a fit, she see you. Don't you tell anybody. I mean it."

"Why not? Why are you so mad? I was only trying it out."

"Jesus God, give me strength."

"Don't be so mad at me, Viola."

"I got to sit down for a minute."

"Here," I said, "I'll get you a glass of lemonade."

She sat at the kitchen table and fanned herself with a cardboard fan while I went to the pantry, where I spotted a stone crock of hard cider. I hesitated and then drew her some of that instead. She looked like she needed it.

"This will make you feel better," I said.

She drank it right down and stared off into space, fanning away. I brought her another glass, and she sighed. It seemed like lots of people I'd been around lately were either drinking or sighing.

"Callie," she said at last, "somebody coulda seen you, girl."

"So?"

"Your mama got *plans* for you, you know that? Just last

week she says she wants you to come out. And now this. No, sir. Can't have no debutante chopping cotton."

"Me, come out? What for?"

"'Cause you a *Tate* girl. Your daddy owns cotton. Your daddy owns the gin."

"Granddaddy still owns it, I think."

"You know what I mean, Miss Smarty," she said. "Don't you want to be a debutante?"

"I'm not sure what-all it means, but if it means being like that drip that Harry brought home that time, then no."

"That was a drippy lady, for sure. But that ain't what it means. It means lots of fancy parties and lots of the young gentlemen coming around. It means having lots of beaux."

"What do I want with lots of beaux?"

"You say that now. But later on."

"No, really, Viola, what's the point?"

"It would please your mama, that's the point."

"Oh."

"Miss Selfish," she said.

"I am *not* selfish," I retorted.

She went on, "Make you a young lady of *society*. Instead of a *scarecrow*."

I ignored this last ungracious remark and thought for a minute. "Did Mother come out?"

"They put her name down for it. But she never did."

"Why not?"

Viola looked at me. "You should ask her."

"The War?" I said, puzzled. Viola nodded.

"But it was over by then. Mother must have been . . ." I counted on my fingers.

"There was no money left, that's all," said Viola. "And then her daddy die of typhus, and that was the end of that."

"So I have to come out? Because she missed her turn?"

"I'm telling you, you got to ask her yourself. Go get cleaned up. You a mess. I got to rest my heart—it's beating like a kitten. Lord help me."

I left her fanning herself.

My mother had got one girl out of seven tries at it. I guess I wasn't exactly what she'd had in mind, a dainty daughter to help her bail against the rising tide of the rough-and-tumble boyish energy that always threatened to engulf the house. It hadn't occurred to me that she'd been hoping for an ally and then didn't get one. So I didn't like to talk patterns and recipes and pour tea in the parlor. Did that make me selfish? Did it make me odd? Worst of all, did it make me a *disappointment*? I could probably live with being thought selfish or odd. But a disappointment—that was another matter, a harder matter. I tried not to think about this, but it tailed me about the house all afternoon like a bothersome, bad-smelling dog demanding attention.

I sat in my room and looked out at the trees and paid the matter some mind, turning it this way and that. I hadn't intended to be this way. Could I be blamed for my nature? Could the leopard change her spots? And, if so, what were my spots? It all seemed so muddled. I came up with no conclusions, but I did get a middling headache. Maybe I needed some Lydia Pinkham's like Mother. Maybe I was more like her than I thought.

Would coming out as a debutante be so bad? Maybe I wouldn't mind it so much. Eventually. Meanwhile, I would have to find out more about it.

Granddaddy had taught me that the important questions could not be answered without the best scholarship you could lay your hands on, along with plenty of time to weigh and measure the alternatives. I had another six or seven years to think about it. That might be enough time. I didn't know anyone who could tell me about such things except Mother, but if I asked her, wouldn't that just get her hopes up, hopes that might have to be dashed later on? My head ached, and my neck started to itch.

Hives again.

THE NEXT MORNING, I found Mother outside examining the rows in the kitchen garden, a wide straw hat shading her face and a pair of white cotton gloves on her hands, following her own dictum that a lady always hid her hands and face from the sun. I approached her cautiously in case Viola had told her of my apparently shameful public experiment, but there was no special alarm in her eyes. No more than usual.

"Where's your bonnet?" Mother called out. "Go inside and get it."

I ran back inside for it. There was no point in starting this conversation off on the wrong foot. I grabbed it from the peg inside the back door and went out again.

"That's better," she said. "Are you coming to help me with the flowers?"

"I wanted to ask you something," I said. "Viola told me . . . Viola told me you were supposed to come out when you were a girl but that you didn't get to. Is that true?"

A shadow of something—surprise, annoyance, regret maybe—passed over her face. She stooped and clipped a Cherokee rose. "Yes. That's true."

"So what happened?"

"The War ruined us. It ruined many families. People were starving. Making one's debut would have been . . . unseemly."

"But you met Father anyway."

She smiled. "I did. I was one of the lucky ones. Your aunt Aggie wasn't so lucky."

My mother's sister Agatha lived unmarried and alone in Harwood in a house that smelled of cats and mildew.

"So you didn't need to be a debutante," I said, pulling a stray weed.

"No, I guess I didn't. But lots of girls still do." She looked at me.

I couldn't avoid the question any longer, so I squared up to it. "Do I have to come out?"

"You're the only daughter, Calpurnia."

I didn't want to be rude and point out that she hadn't answered the question. "Well, what does it mean? Exactly?"

Mother's eyes lit up. "It means that a girl from a good family has become a young lady and is ready to be introduced into Society. That she is ready to take her appointed place. That she can be introduced to young men from good families. It means cotillions and entertainments and a new gown for each one."

"How long does it last?" I said.

"A year."

"A whole year?" I didn't much care for the sound of that. "And then what happens?"

She looked confused. "What do you mean?"

"You said it lasts for a year, and then what?"

"Well, usually the young lady has found a husband by that time."

"So it's a lot of fancy parties to marry off girls."

Mother clucked. "Goodness, I wouldn't put it that way."

Why not? I thought. There was no disguising it.

"Mother?"

"Yes, dear?"

"So . . . *do* I have to come out?" Her face fell. I quickly added, "Do you *want* me to come out?"

She studied me. "Callie, I think there's lots of time to think about it. But yes, I would be glad if you had the opportunity I missed. Many young girls would be glad of the chance."

"What does Father think? It sounds expensive, a new gown and all every time."

She looked disapproving. "One doesn't speak of money

like that. It isn't done. Your father is an excellent provider. I am sure he would be proud to present you."

"Hmm." So there lay the matter. For now.

Later it occurred to me that I could ask Granddaddy his thoughts about it. But then I realized I didn't need to. I could just imagine his opinion on the matter.

CHAPTER 15

A SEA OF COTTON

Linnaeus has calculated that if an annual plant produced only two seeds . . . and their seedlings next year
produced two, and so on, then in twenty years there
would be a million plants.

A COUPLE OF WEEKS LATER, my father met with the other major
landholders at the Moose Lodge and declared the cotton harvest
date, by far the most important event in our entire county.

An army of colored workers from three counties around
descended on our acreage and picked from first light until complete dark, men and women and children, stopping only at midday for a meal and a short Bible reading by a preacher, one of
their number.

Viola recruited three of the women to help her cook in the
old stone kitchen in back of the house. Such a prodigious quantity of grits and fatback and beans and biscuits and syrup flowed
out of there, all loaded into the buckboard in giant hampers and
driven out to the fields, along with a barrel of fresh water and a
huge pail of coffee. Mother temporarily moved into the kitchen
to feed us. She also kept busy nursing the pickers' cuts and

blisters and other injuries deemed too small to be sent to Dr. Walker.

Harry drove the wagon back and forth to the store for cornmeal, sugar, flour, and other supplies. Sam Houston and Lamar scurried with messages from the scale house to the tally board and were sometimes rewarded with a penny, which translated into ten pieces of candy or a new pencil at the general store. Being a tally messenger was a highly coveted position.

Father labored late at the gin and came home long after we'd all gone to bed. The only one exempt from duty of any kind was Granddaddy. He had built up the ginning enterprise himself and overseen it through this seasonal spasm of mad activity for thirty years; he no longer had the slightest interest or obligation. He retired to his laboratory or else he headed off in the morning with his satchel over his shoulder.

The gin ran night and day. The blacksmith and the carpenter labored without sleep to keep the machines going and the cotton flowing, high-mounded wagons of it coming in and huge shedding bales of it going out, bound for Austin, Galveston, New Orleans. The bales were so heavy and piled so high that they were a real menace. Packing and balancing them was an art and, every year, scores of men across the South were crushed and killed by unstable loads.

In our house, we could hear the great leather belts of the machinery whirring and slapping rhythmically a quarter mile away. After the first couple of nights, you got used to it all over again, and although I'd never heard the waves of the ocean, the machinery noise in the distance made me feel I was falling asleep to the lapping of the surf, at least as I imagined it. But instead of water, prodigious waves of cotton lapped around our house.

Our school shut down for ten days. Many of my classmates came from families who couldn't afford to hire help, so everyone, children included, picked until they collapsed. I was conscripted into kitchen duty with Mother. One morning I sifted a whole sack of flour, and the next day my hands were too sore to grip my pencil and write in my Notebook. I made a point of complaining so bitterly about this that I was reassigned.

My next job was to keep an eye on the two dozen or so babies who played in the yard between the house and the outside kitchen while their mothers worked the fields, and to make sure they didn't get pecked by the busy, officious hens who were aggrieved by this invasion of their normal habitat. I was not happy with this unpaid duty, either, especially when I had to watch Sam Houston and Lamar prance off to the gin and come home with money. After a whole day of wrangling the babies and thinking disgruntled thoughts about those pennies, I launched a new campaign at dinner that night.

"Why do I have to mind the babies?" I asked Father.

"Because you're the girl," said Lamar offhandedly.

I ignored him. "Why do *I* have to mind the babies? Why can't *I* run messages? Why can't *I* earn money?"

"Because you're the *girl,*" said Lamar, alarmed, scenting possible danger.

"And what's *that* supposed to mean?"

"Girls don't get paid," scoffed Lamar. "Girls can't even vote. They don't get paid. Girls stay home."

"Maybe you better tell that to the Fentress Normal School," I said, proud of my retort. "They pay Miss Harbottle, don't they?" I said.

"That's different," huffed Lamar.

"*How* is it different?"

"It just is."

"Exactly *how*, Lamar?"

I harped on this so loud and long that my exhausted father, in desperate need of peace, said, "All right, Callie. I'll pay you a nickel."

I shut up in triumphant silence. Lamar looked relieved to keep his post as tally boy. Then my three younger brothers set up their own grizzling chorus about how unfair it was that they didn't get paid for anything. It took a sharp "Enough of this!" from Mother to make them quiet down. They glowered in sulky silence through the rest of dinner while I made light and pleasant chitchat as I'd been taught ladies do, discussing the weather and inquiring about everyone's day. Granddaddy looked amused; Mother looked as if she had a sick headache but gamely held up her end of the conversation.

The next day, I sat on the back steps and kept a close eye on my twenty-nine tiny charges. Now that I was being paid, now that I was a professional, I took my duties seriously. I counted heads over and over. The babies were mostly toddlers who played happily in the dust, but every now and then one would haul himself to his feet and stagger off in pursuit of a passing dog or cat, squealing with pleasure, and have to be dragged back, protesting. There was also the problem of them putting the odd item they found in the dust into their mouths; I saved the lives of a couple of beetles and a disoriented night crawler that way. I wanted to read a book, but I couldn't look away for a second. For such small, unsteady organisms, the babies sure could get away from you fast. And the hens were a bother, darting from the periphery into the thick of things, setting up a great hysterical hoo-hah. I chucked pebbles at them to drive them back.

Sul Ross came by as I was taking potshots at the hens. I guess he thought I was having fun. I was not. I was peeved and about to chase him off when I noticed he was looking on with interest, like maybe he wanted to join in. I looked at him from the corner of my eye and thought fast.

"This sure is a lot of fun," I said.

"Yeah," he said, "I'll bet it is. I always get yelled at when I do that."

"Too bad, because it's so much fun," I said. No mere Becky Thatcher I, but crafty old Tom himself.

A few minutes later, I ran across the meadow in the direction I had seen Granddaddy set off. "Wait, wait," I cried. He was disappearing into the shady pecan bottom when I caught up with him.

"I am delighted to have your company, but what are you

doing here?" he said. "I thought you were pressed into work with the others and hired yourself out."

"I traded with Sul Ross," I said.

"What did you trade?"

"Um, well, I didn't exactly trade, sir. I hired him. I told him if he looked after the babies that I would give him two pennies. Plus, I told him he was allowed to throw rocks at the hens to keep them away." I hastened to add, "But only small rocks—no bigger than my thumbnail, I made that *very* clear. He seemed pleased enough with the arrangement. This way, I make three cents. And I get to spend the day with you."

"Ah," said Granddaddy. "You may turn out to be a real young woman of commerce." And although he spoke genially enough, I sensed something—disappointment?—in his expression.

"No," I said after a moment's thought, "I don't think so." I put my hand in his. "Do you think we'll see something new today?" I said.

His expression changed to one of gladness. "I am certain of it," he said, and we set off for the riverbank.

CHAPTER 16

THE TELEPHONE COMES

Although some species may be now increasing, more
or less rapidly, in numbers, all cannot do so, for the
world would not hold them.

CHANGE WAS COMING, both on the small stage of my life and the
larger one of our town. The Bell Telephone Company had run a
line all the way from Austin to the county seat in Lockhart, and
one could now perform the astonishing feat of talking over a
thin strand of wire to a man thirty miles away. (Or, to be precise, shouting at him. The interaction was reputed to be noisy.)
Twenty years earlier, the journey to Austin had taken three
days by wagon; ten years earlier it was half a day by train; now
a message could be delivered in the time it took a man to
draw breath.

There was much debate about where the switching board
and the Telephone (there was only one) should go. Some
thought the gin since it was the center of commerce; others said
the post office; but our mayor, Mr. Axelrod, ruled that it should
go to the newspaper, the beating informational heart of our
community. The newspaper office was right across the street

from the gin, and so the apparatus could be used when needed to receive cotton orders and check market prices.

Granddaddy grew excited about the 'phone and had an extra spring in his step when we went out collecting specimens.

"By God," he said, "progress is a wonderful thing. That boy Alex has done it, by God."

"Alex?" I said. "You mean Mr. Bell?"

"I do mean him," he said. "The very one."

"Um," I said, "you know him?"

"A good boy. Known him for years through the Geographic. I'm surprised I haven't told you. I loaned him some money when he was starting out, and he gave me some stock in his company. Remind me to check the ticker next time I'm in Austin. Those shares might be worth something by now." And then he said, "By God, I can *telephone* the Exchange and get the quotes. No need to go to Austin. Ha!"

Our town talked of nothing else for a week. The Bell Company placed an advertisement in the *Fentress Indicator* announcing that it would hire a Telephone Operator and that this person had to be a dependable, sober, industrious young lady between the ages of seventeen and twenty-four. Apparently the Company had had plenty of bad experiences with its earliest operators, who had all been recruited from the ranks of telegraph men (a rough lot and prone to drunkenness, rudeness, and disconnecting patrons). The advertisement also stipulated that the young lady had to be tall, setting off all kinds of speculation, both polite and otherwise. It also offered room and board and the stunning sum of ten dollars a week on top of this. For a *girl*. Not a wagoneer, not a blacksmith, but a *girl*. And indoor work at that. This was unheard of. The money, the prestige, the independence! I burned for the position.

I asked my handiest brother, J.B., "Do you think I look seventeen?" He looked at me and spoke gravely through a thick mouthful of wet toffee, "You look real old, Callie." This pleased me, but then he was only five years old so it wasn't exactly reliable information. I went and found Harry in the barn, where he was mending a harness.

"Harry," I said, "do you think I could pass for seventeen?"

"Have you lost your mind?" he said, without looking up.

"No. Look, what if I do this?" I held my hair up in what I imagined were attractive bunches above my ears. "Don't I look seventeen?"

He glanced at me. "You look like a spaniel. The answer is no." Then he stopped his mending and squinted at me. "Why? What are you up to?"

"Oh, nothing. . . ." I had for a fleeting moment seen myself as Miss Tate, Girl Operator, dressed in a smart shirtwaist dress, perched on a rolling stool, connecting each call with great efficiency and presence of mind, and saying in a well-modulated voice, "Hello, Central. Number please. . . ."

I was even willing to lie about my age and "borrow" a dress and hat from Mother's dressing room in the face of such potential magnificence. I had it all worked out when suddenly the obvious flashed on me: Half the town knew me by name and the other half by sight. What kind of idiot was I? I thanked the Lord for showing me the stupidity of my ridiculous and dangerous proposition in time. But still . . .

On the big day, a dozen of our tall and not-so-tall young ladies presented themselves in their soberest hats, clutching letters of reference in their cleanest white gloves. They lined up along the raised wooden boardwalk in front of the newspaper office and stood for hours, some of them straining on tiptoe. When they went inside, they were made to stand with their backs to the wall and have the distance between their fingertips measured. It turned out that they needed someone with long arms who could plug in connections the length of the switching board. At the end of the day, they announced that Miss Honoria Goates from Staples would be our new Telephone Operator. There was considerable grumbling about this. She was tall, yes, and maybe she had long arms, but there were plenty of fine young ladies in Fentress, were there not? It was the *Fentress* Telephone Company, was it not? Why hire a foreigner from Staples, four miles away? Would she take the room and board or drive herself daily, and if so, how would she manage in bad weather? And on and on.

Honoria Goates and her tin trunk arrived two days later and were placed in a tiny room the size of a closet containing the switching board and a cot so that she could answer the phone at any hour of the day and night. Her meals were to be brought to her from Elsie Bell's Rooming House down the street. Such extravagance was unprecedented.

In any event, it turned out not to matter that Honoria was from Staples or that she had long arms. What the Company didn't know about her (but the rest of us did) was that her uncle, Homer Ray Goates, had been struck by lightning while plowing and had been found in the field, charred and smoking lightly, by Honoria herself. Mr. Goates lived, but lost most of his hearing and had to tote a huge ear trumpet about with him from then on. He also became prone to sudden fits of hilarious laughter over nothing, which, while disconcerting, nevertheless made him entertaining company.

Poor Honoria had lived in mortal fear of electricity ever since. And who in her shoes would not? So, when faced with having to plug her first line into the board, with the supervisor at her shoulder to teach her, she shrieked and fled the building, no doubt expecting to be fried like her uncle by some satanic spark leaping through the wires. She stumbled across the bridge, not even stopping for her things, and ran all the way home to Staples in teary disgrace. Her father sent for her trunk the following day.

Maggie Medlin, Backy Medlin's great-niece, was hired to take her place. Maggie was shorter than Honoria but sturdier of disposition. Her abhorrent younger sister, Dovie, basked in Maggie's reflected glory and took to beginning every sentence with, "Well, my-sister-the-Operator says. . . ."

We all hated her for it.

Finally, the Bell Company men made it out to Fentress, and the great day came for the opening of the telephone line. The company's representative arrived on the train from Austin. There wasn't room to hold the ceremony inside the newspaper office itself, so we gathered on the street outside. The Odd Fellows' Brass Band played a short selection, the Moose Band played at length, and the International Woodmen of the World, the band with the fewest members, went on forever. The mayor and the Company man made long, boring speeches about this great day. Mayor Axelrod cut a wide red ribbon with fake oversized cardboard scissors to officially open the Telephone Company in Fentress. Cheers went up, hands were shaken, and free lemonade and lager were passed around. Sam Houston tried to cadge a beer and was properly rebuffed.

And then, at noon on the dot, it happened. A shrill jangling noise rang out in the breathless expectant air. The crowd gasped and *oooh*ed. On the line was our state senator in Austin calling to congratulate our town as we hurtled toward the twentieth century. Maggie Medlin connected the line, and our mayor stepped into the closet and yelled at our senator, who yelled back at him from forty-five miles away, giving him that morning's price for cotton on the Austin Exchange.

Granddaddy murmured to me, "Do you realize what this means, Calpurnia? The days of whale oil and coal dust are over. The old century is dying, even as we watch. Remember this day."

Mr. Hofacket of Hofacket's Portrait Parlor ("Fine Photographs for Fine Occasions") was there with his big bellows camera to memorialize the day. He wanted to talk to Granddaddy about the Plant and was disappointed that we still hadn't heard back. He'd have gabbed about it all day except that Mayor Axelrod pulled him back to his duties as official photographer. We crowded around, spilling off the boardwalk and into the street. Mr. Hofacket set up his camera. Granddaddy gripped my hand. Then Mr. Hofacket ducked under his black veil and held up his magnesium flash powder.

"Don't move!" cried Mr. Hofacket. We all froze. Mr. Hofacket's powder lit us up like summer lightning and caught us for that one second in time. When we later saw a copy of the photograph, most of the faces were solemn and severe. I looked pensive. The only smiling face was that of Granddaddy, grinning away like the Cheshire Cat.

CHAPTER 17

HOME ECONOMIES

As more individuals are produced than can possibly survive, there must in every case be a struggle for existence, either one individual with another of the same species, or with the individuals of distinct species, or with the physical conditions of life.

AGAINST MY WILL, I had arrived at that age when a young girl began to acquire those skills she would need to manage her own household after marriage. And of course, all the girls I knew expected to get married. Everybody did, unless you were so rich that you didn't have to, or so hard on the eyes that no man would have you. A few girls went off to be teachers or nurses for a while before they got married, and I considered them lucky. And now we had the example of Maggie Medlin, Telephone Operator, an independent woman with her own money who answered to no man other than Mr. Bell. Since there was still only the one telephone in town, her duties were not onerous. She sat before her board, receiver around her neck, eating apples and reading the newspaper until the board buzzed with a call to be relayed. She then plugged in a cord and said in the same crisp voice every time, "Hello, Central, what number please?" She had to say this, despite the fact that there was only the one number. All the girls in school admired her. We played Operator with a scrap of cardboard and a length of twine for a switching station. This looked like the good life to me. But the telephone proved to be so popular that soon everyone had to have one. Maggie was not allowed to leave her station and became a veritable Company slave.

THE PLANT THRIVED. We heard no word from Washington. Granddaddy toiled on with me at his elbow whenever I could escape to the laboratory with him.

One Saturday morning, Mother looked up from her sewing as I was running out the front door, one of Granddaddy's butterfly nets and his old fishing creel slung over my shoulder. "Stop a minute," she said as my hand turned the doorknob. I didn't like the way she looked me over. "Where are you off to?" she said.

"Down to the river, ma'am, to collect specimens," I said, edging crabwise out the door.

"Come back here. Specimens are all very well," said Mother, "but I'm worried that you are lagging behind. When I was your age, I could smock and darn and had the essentials of good plain cookery."

"I know how to cook," I said stoutly.

"What can you cook?" she said.

"I can make a cheese sandwich. I can make a soft-boiled

egg." I thought about it some more, and then said triumphantly, "I can make a hard-boiled egg."

My mother said, "Lord above, it's worse than I thought."

"What is?" I said.

"Your ignorance of cookery."

"But why do I have to cook? Viola cooks for us," I said.

"Yes, but what about later? When you grow up and have a family of your own? How will you feed them?"

Viola had been with us always, since before I was born, since before even Harry was born. It had never occurred to me that she wouldn't always be there. My world wobbled on its axis. "Viola can cook for my family," I said.

There was silence. Then Mother said, "All right, you can go. But we will talk about this again soon."

I ran out of there and did my best to forget the conversation, but it nagged at me all the way to the river like a tooth beginning to go bad. All joy had fled the morning. Mother was awakening to the sorry facts: My biscuits were like stones, my samplers askew, my seams like rickrack. I considered my mother's life: the mending basket that never emptied, the sheets and collars and cuffs to be turned, the twenty loaves of bread to be punched down each and every week. It's true that she didn't have to do all the heavy cleaning herself—she had SanJuanna for that. And a washerwoman came on Monday and spent the whole day boiling the clothes in the dripping laundry shed out back. Viola killed and plucked and cooked the chickens. Alberto dispatched and butchered the hogs. But my mother's life was a never-ending round of maintenance. Not one single thing did she ever achieve but that it had to be done all over again, one day or one week or one season later. Oh, the monotony.

The day didn't begin to look up until I caught a spotted fritillary butterfly. They were swift and elusive and difficult to net. I knew Granddaddy would be well pleased, plus it helped keep my mind off cooking and mending. When I got home, it took me a whole hour just to set the delicate body in preparation for mounting, and by then I had forgotten what an ignorant girl I was. Just as well, as the campaign to bring me up to domestic scratch was, without my knowledge or cooperation, ginning up in earnest.

The campaign gained momentum when Miss Harbottle decided that all the girls in my class would enter their handiwork in the Fentress Fair. This was distressing news. I found sewing a waste of time, and I had been easing along doing the minimum. My work could charitably be described as sloppy, like Petey's cocoon. Stitches dropped themselves and later reappeared at random so that the long striped scarf I was knitting bulged in the middle like a python after dining on a rabbit. I fancied that a malevolent Rumpelstiltskin crept into my room at night and undid my best work, turning the gold of my efforts into pathetic dross on a wheel perversely spinning backward.

Although she'd been watching my knitting to some degree, it had been a while since Mother had inspected my fine sewing. One day she asked to check my work. I reluctantly took her my sewing bag, and she poked through it for a minute. "You did this?"

"Yes, Mother."

"Are you proud of it?"

Was I *proud* of it? I pondered this. Was it a trick question or not? I couldn't tell; I didn't know which way to flop. "Uh..."

"I'm asking you, Calpurnia."

"No, ma'am, I guess I'm not too proud of it."

"Then why don't you do work you can be proud of?"

I thought again. I had no snappy answer, so I had to fall back on honesty. "Because it's boring, ma'am?" A truthful answer, but one I knew to be foolish, even as it exited my mouth.

"Ah," said Mother. "Boring."

A bad sign when she repeated your own words back to you like a parrot. Now, parrots. Those were some interesting birds, living to such a great age that they were passed down in the family will. Why, Granddaddy had told me about a parrot who had lived past his century and learned over four hundred conversational phrases, as acute a mimic as any human being...

"Calpurnia, I don't believe you're..."

Although I doubted I'd be allowed a parrot (Granddaddy had also told me they were very expensive), this didn't necessarily exclude the possibility of something smaller, a cockatiel, say, or maybe a budgie. . . . Mother's lips were moving. . . . Something about practicing?

"Have to do better . . ."

A budgie would do as the bird of last resort. They could be taught to speak, couldn't they?

"When I was your age . . ."

And if I had a budgie, would I be allowed to let it fly loose in the house? Probably not. It would drop white dollops like antimacassars on the good furniture, and that would be the end of that. And you couldn't forget Idabelle the Inside Cat in her basket by the stove. Maybe I could let it fly in my bedroom. It could perch on my headboard and chirrup in my ear, a pleasant sound—

"Calpurnia!"

I jumped. "Yes, Mother?"

"You're not listening to me!"

I stared at her. How could she tell?

"You'd better listen to me. This situation is intolerable. Your work is unacceptable. I expect better from you, and you will do better, do you understand me? I'm surprised Miss Harbottle hasn't sent me a note about this."

She had. Two, in fact.

"You will show me your work every night until the fair."

This meant that I'd have to pay more attention for a few weeks. Gloom tolled its heavy bell in my ear. I was a marked girl.

IT WAS GETTING on in the day. I'd had an inordinate and unfair amount of homework, and there were a couple of hours of decent working light left. I headed for the door at top speed. Mother sat in the parlor reviewing her housekeeping accounts. "Calpurnia," she called, "the river again?"

Too late. "Yes, Mother," I said, in my best cheerful-obedient-good-girl voice.

"Bring me your sewing first."

"What?"

"Don't say *what* like that, my girl. Bring me your sewing before there's any talk about going to the river. And where's your bonnet? You'll freckle."

How could I freckle? It was practically dark out. I tromped back up the stairs, feeling as if I were carrying the weight of the world on my shoulders.

"And stop stamping about like that," Mother called. "You're not carrying the weight of the world, you know."

Her comment startled me into proper behavior. It was scary how she could read my mind. I crept the rest of my way up to my room and closed the door. I pulled my sampler from my sewing bag and looked at it. It had started out life as a perfect square but had evolved into a skewed rhomboid, with all the letters leaning sharply to the right. How were you supposed to make the stitches the same size? How were you supposed to keep the tension even? And, most of all, who cared about this stuff?

Well, I could answer the last one. My mother cared, and the rest of the world apparently did too, for no good reason that I could figure out. And I, who did not care, was going to be forced into caring. It was ridiculous. I threw the embroidery hoop across the room.

Two hours later, I took my work downstairs. The assignment was to embroider "Welcome to Our Home" in flowery script. I had made it as far as "Welco," but it was all wobbly, so I had picked it out and reworked the entire *W* to show Mother.

"Is this all you have done?" she said.

"It's a big letter! It's a capital!"

"All right, all right. Lower your voice. You have done better, which shows me, Calpurnia, that you can do this if you would only apply yourself."

Oh, how my brothers and I hated that word *apply*.

"Can I go?"

"Yes, you *may* go. Don't be late for dinner."

As Mother lit the parlor lamps, I shoved my handiwork away and dashed out the front door. There wasn't much light left. Too late to collect diurnal samples. Great. I could see the newspaper: Girl Scientist Thwarted for All Time by Stupid

Sewing Projects. Loss to Society Immeasurable. Entire Scientific Community in Mourning.

I seethed my way to the river and got there at darkfall. And then Viola's bell clanged in the distance.

I clomped through the kitchen on the way to washing up and said to Viola, "How come I have to learn how to sew and cook? Why? Can you tell me that? Can you?"

I'll admit it was a bad time to ask her—she was beating the last lumps out of the gravy—but she paused long enough to look at me with puzzlement, as if I were speaking ancient Greek. "What kind of question is that?" she said, and went back to whisking the gravy in the fragrant, smoking pan.

My Lord, what a dismal response. Was the answer such an ingrained, obvious part of the way we lived that no one stopped to ponder the question itself? If no one around me even understood the question, then it couldn't be answered. And if it couldn't be answered, I was doomed to the distaff life of only womanly things. I was depressed right into the ground.

After dinner I went to my room, put on my nightie, and read. I was munching my way, so to speak, through Granddaddy's volumes of Dickens with great satisfaction and had made it all the way to *Oliver Twist*. Please, sir, could I have some more? The poor wretch's circumstances were grim enough to make me reconsider my own situation.

I went downstairs for a glass of water. Mother and Father were sitting in the parlor with the door open.

"What will we do with her?" said Mother, and I froze on the landing. There was only one *her* they ever talked about, and it was me. "The boys will make their way in the world, but what about her? Your father feeds her a steady diet of Dickens and Darwin. Access to too many books like those can build disaffection in one's life. Especially a young life. Most especially a young girl's life."

I wanted to yell, *We're doing important work! There's the Plant!* But then I'd really catch it for eavesdropping.

"I don't see the harm in it," said Father.

"She runs wild all day with a butterfly net. She doesn't know how to sew or keep house," said Mother.

"Well, plenty of girls her age don't know yet," said Father. "Don't they?"

"She can't cook a dry bean. And her biscuits are like . . . like . . . I don't know what."

Rocks, I thought. Isn't that the word you're looking for?

"I'm sure she'll pick these things up," said Father.

"Alfred, she keeps frogs in her room."

"She does?"

I wanted to call out, *That's a lousy lie—they're only tadpoles.*

But then it happened. My father fell silent. And it was his silence, his long pause while he digested this information, that filled the hallway and my heart and soul with such a great whooshing pressure that I couldn't breathe. I had never classified myself with other girls. I was not of their species; I was different.

I had never thought my future would be like theirs. But now I knew this was untrue, and that I was *exactly* like other girls. I was expected to hand over my life to a house, a husband, children. It was intended that I give up my nature studies, my Notebook, my beloved river. There *was* a wicked point to all the sewing and cooking that they were trying to impress upon me, the tedious lessons I had been spurning and ducking. I went hot and cold all over. My life did not lie with the Plant after all. My life was forfeit. Why hadn't I seen it? I was trapped. A coyote with her paw in the trap.

After an eternity, Father sighed, "I see. Well, Margaret, what shall we do about it?"

"She needs to spend less time with your father and more time with me and Viola. I've already told her I'm going to supervise her cookery and her stitchery. We'll have to have lessons. A new dish every week, I think."

"Will we have to eat it?" said Father. "Heh, heh."

"Now, Alfred."

Tears sprang to my eyes. That my own father could joke about his only daughter being pressed into domestic slavery.

"I trust these things to you, Margaret," he said. "I always feel such matters are safest in your hands, despite the burden it places on you. How are your headaches these days, my dear?"

"Not so bad, Alfred, not so bad."

My father crossed the room, and I saw him stoop and drop a

kiss on my mother's forehead. "I am glad to hear it. Can I bring you your tonic?"

"No, thank you, I'm fine."

My father returned to his seat, rustled his newspaper, and that was that. My life sentence delivered.

I leaned against the wall and stood there, empty, for a long time. Empty of everything. I was only a practical vessel of helpful service, waiting to be filled up with recipes and knitting patterns.

Jim Bowie came padding down the stairs. Without speaking, he wrapped himself around me and gave me one of his long, sweet hugs.

"Thanks, J.B.," I whispered, and we walked upstairs together hand-in-hand.

"Are you sick, Callie Vee?" he said.

"I reckon I am, J.B."

"I can tell," he said.

"It's true. You can always tell."

"Don't feel bad. You're my best sister, Callie." We climbed onto my bed, and he curled up next to me.

He said, "You said you were going to play with me more."

I said, "I'm sorry, J.B. I've been spending time with Grand-daddy." *But it's all coming to an end soon enough,* I thought.

"Does he know about Big Foot Wallace?"

"He does."

"Do you think he'd tell me about Big Foot Wallace?"

"You should ask him. He might, but he's kind of busy."
Busy without me, I moped.

"Maybe I'll ask him," said J.B. "But he scares me. I got to
go. Good night, Callie. Don't be sick."

He gently closed the door. My last thought, before I fell into
a restless sleep, was of the coyote. If only I could figure out how
to gnaw my own leg off.

CHAPTER 18

COOKING LESSONS

Battle within battle must ever be recurring with varying success....

MY TIME WITH GRANDDADDY slipped away as the domestic mill
wheel gathered momentum, grinding its principal raw material—
namely, me—into smaller and smaller scraps.

"Calpurnia," Mother called up the stairs in that particular
tone of voice I'd come to dread, "we're waiting for you in the
kitchen."

I was in my room reading Granddaddy's copy of *A Tale of
Two Cities*. I put it down and didn't answer.

"I know you're up there," said Mother, "and I know you
can hear me. Come down here." I sighed, slipped an old hair
ribbon into the book to mark my place, and trudged downstairs.
I was the condemned young aristocrat holding my head high in
the tumbrel. It was a far, far better thing—

"There's no need to look like that," said Mother as I walked
into the kitchen, where she and Viola sat waiting for me at the
scrubbed pine table. "It's only a cooking lesson."

On the table was the marble slab, the sugar tin, a rolling pin, a large bowl of green apples, and one bright yellow lemon. And a book. I perked up until I got a closer look at it.

"Look here," said Mother. "It's my Fannie Farmer cookbook. You can borrow it until you get your own copy. It has everything in it that you need."

I doubted that. She presented it to me in the same way that my grandfather had handed me his book—the other book—a few short months before. Mother smiled; Viola looked determinedly blank.

"We're going to start with apple pie," Mother said. "The secret is to add a splash of lemon juice and a handful of lemon zest to give it that nice tart flavor." She smiled and nodded and spoke in that coaxing voice mothers use on reluctant children.

I tried my best to smile back. Lord knows what I looked like because Mother looked alarmed, and Viola cut her eyes to the corner.

"Won't that be fun?" said Mother, wavering.

"I guess so."

"Viola's going to show you how to make the crust. It's her specialty."

"Get two scoops of flour out of that bin, Miz Callie," Viola said. I blinked. She had never called me Miss before. "Dump 'em in this bowl. Okay."

Mother thumbed through her cookbook and planned our Sunday dinner while Viola tried to lead me down the tricky path of pastry-dough making. I must have seen her make a million pies as I wandered through the kitchen, and it had always looked so easy. She never measured anything, instead cooking by eye, by instinct, and by touch, throwing in handfuls of flour and thumb-sized chunks of lard and drizzling in more or less cold water, depending. There was nothing to it. Any idiot could learn it in two minutes flat.

An hour later, I stood panting and thrashing around with my third bowl of dough, with Mother and Viola growing more incredulous by the minute. The first batch had been watery and lumpy; the second so dense I couldn't roll it out with the pin; the last had turned out as sticky as wallpaper paste and with the same unappealing consistency. It was all over my hands and pinafore, smeared across the counter and the pump handle, and there were streaks of it stuck in my hair. I think there was even a glob on the fly paper hanging from the ceiling several feet above my head, but how it got there, I had no idea.

"Next time a kerchief, I think, Viola," Mother said.

"Mm-hmm."

"I tell you what," said Mother. "Maybe we'll let Viola finish the dough. You go ahead and peel and core the apples. Hold the apple like this, and draw the knife toward you. Be careful. It's sharp."

I held the knife and apple in imitation and, with the first paring motion, sliced my thumb open. Fortunately, I only bled on a couple of the apples. Viola plunged them in water, but they were still tinged pink. We all pretended not to notice. Mother went off to get me a sticking plaster. Viola and I sat at the table and looked at each other. We didn't speak a word. I sighed and put my chin in my hand. I wanted to put my head down on the table, but that would have meant more dough in my hair. Idabelle, as if sensing my despair, climbed from her basket and came over to butt her wide forehead against my shins. I couldn't even stroke her, I was so covered in goo. Viola got up and threw flour and water and lard together with seeming thoughtlessness and rolled out a nonsticky, nonrunny, perfect crust in no time. Then she skinned the lemon for me, whether to spare my wound its acid or to stop me from bleeding on any more fruit, I wasn't sure.

After Mother returned and patched my cut, Viola said, "Miz Callie, you got to check the temperature of the stove."

"How do I do that?"

"You stick your hand in there. If it's too hot to hold it in there for more than a blink, you got a medium oven."

"You're joshing me." I looked at her. "That's what you do?"

"That's what you do."

"How do you tell when it's a hot oven?" I said.

"Why, you can't get your hand in that far. It's too hot."

"Isn't there a thermometer or something?" I asked. They both laughed like this was the funniest thing they'd heard all week. Oh, funny, all right. I opened the stove and was met by a blast of hot air as if from a dragon's cave.

"Go on, girl," said Viola. "Go on."

It hadn't killed her yet, so I guessed it was safe. I took a deep breath and plunged my arm deep into the heat and pulled it out a split second later.

"Yep," I said, fanning my hand in the air, "medium oven for sure. Maybe even hot."

"Put those pieces of apple in the dishes. Get some sugar, like this much here," she said, showing me sugar cupped in her palm, "and put it over the apple, you don't need to stir it up. That's right. Now we got to put the top crust on."

She handed me a spatula to lift the tops from the rolling board onto the pies, which was easier said than done. The uncooperative dough flopped in all directions. When I touched it, it stuck to me; when I manhandled it, it turned leathery. It took me a good ten minutes to finish putting three pies together. I looked at them. They were a sorry-looking exhibit.

"They don't look so good," I said.

"You got to crimp the edges with your thumb, like this. That makes 'em look nice. You go ahead and do it."

I pinched my way around the pies with my good thumb, and they did look better, although no one would be fooled into thinking they were Viola's handiwork.

"Okay," said Viola, "you only got to do one more thing."

"What?" I croaked, exhausted.

"You got to put the letter *C*, for Callie, on top. Make a letter *C* out of dough and put it right there on top. Put it in the middle, show everybody you made it. Then you brush it with the egg yolk. Makes it all shiny."

I rolled out three worms of dough and curled one on top of each pie as instructed. I brushed the yolk on top, and we all stood back and looked.

"There you go," said Viola.

"Well," said Mother. "Very nice."

"Whew," I said.

That night, when SanJuanna had cleared the main course and brought dessert in, my mother called for quiet and said, "Boys, I have an announcement to make. Your sister made the apple pies tonight. I'm sure we will all enjoy them very much."

"Can I learn how, ma'am?" said Jim Bowie.

"No, J.B. Boys don't bake pies," Mother said.

"Why not?" he said.

"They have wives who make pies for them."

"But I don't have a wife."

"Darling, I'm sure you will have a very nice one someday when you're older, and she'll make you many pies. Calpurnia, would you care to serve?"

Was there any way I could have a wife, too? I wondered as I cut through the browned *C* and promptly shattered the entire crust. I tried to cut slices but mangled the job and ended up spooning out pie that looked more like cobbler. Father smiled at his dessert, smiled at Mother, smiled at me. My brothers made exclamations of appreciation and fell on their portions like hungry dogs. My cooking lesson had taken all afternoon; the results were downed in four minutes flat. None of them could flatter me enough to make up for the fact that I had lost hours with my Notebook, my river, my specimens, and my grandfather. Granddaddy chewed his pie, deep in thought.

CHAPTER 19

A DISTILLERY SUCCESS, OF SORTS

We have seen that man by selection can certainly produce great results, and can adapt organic beings to his own uses. . . .

"CALPURNIA," GRANDDADDY CALLED up the stairs, "will you come out to the laboratory with me? I require your assistance if you're not otherwise engaged."

Since I'd heard my domestic life sentence delivered, I had sunk into the deepest quagmire of ill temper and low spirits, keeping apart from the others as much as possible, so much so that there had been the occasional talk of cod-liver oil. It held no healing powers for the mangled paw caught in the cruel trap.

When Granddaddy called, I was sulking in my room and knitting yet another sock in the endless series of Christmas socks. But I did not consider myself otherwise engaged *at all*, and here he was, offering me temporary respite from the tyranny of the house. I dropped the needles, ran from my room, and slid down the banister.

Granddaddy smiled. "An efficacious method of transportation. Remind me to talk with you some other time about

Newton's laws of physics and how they apply to banister travel."

"What are you—what are *we*—working on today?"

"Do you remember the whiskey sample we put in oak in July? I think it's time to see how it's coming along."

We headed through the kitchen for the back door. Viola sat sifting soft hillocks of white flour with Idabelle for company. She gave us the walleye and said, "Dinner in an hour."

The laboratory shelves were crammed with scores of bottles, the inspiring—or depressing—results of years of work, depending on your point of view. The Plant had gone to seed, and we had swept every tiny fleck into a labeled envelope, which had then been placed in a labeled jar, which had then been locked in the library cabinet. The room smelled of pecans, must, and mouse. I would have to appoint one of the Outside Cats to clear the mice out. Granddaddy opened his log book and riffled through it in the gloom, his thick yellow fingernail running down the columns.

"Here it is, the one with your notation. Number 437, on the twenty-first of July. I wonder where we put it?" You'd think it would be difficult to lose an oak barrel, even a small one, in the laboratory, but the space had become so crowded with failed samples and the detritus of various old and new experiments that it took a few minutes of pawing through it all before we located it buried deep under one of the counters.

"Ah," said Granddaddy. "Careful, we don't want to disturb any sediment. Let's see how it looks first."

I lit all the hanging lamps while Granddaddy cleared a spot on the counter and gently placed the barrel on it. He tapped the barrel and turned the wooden spigot, spilling a couple of inches of warm golden-brown liquid into a clean glass. He raised the glass and held it up before the brightest lamp, handling it as if it were nitroglycerin. He inspected it, both with his spectacles and then without. The glass glowed. But I knew that no matter how good the stuff might be, no matter how successful the run, it was death to practically-twelve-year-olds.

"No real sediment to speak of," he said.

"Is that good?"

"I believe it to be a good sign. I don't remember ever drinking a glass of good bourbon with any particulate matter floating in it, do you? What do you think of this color?"

"It's nice. It's the same color as Mother's amber beads. Is it supposed to look like that?"

"It's hard to say," he said. "We are crossing the bar of distillery without a pilot." He looked at me, and I could see the explorer's excitement stirring beneath his calm expression.

"Let's see how it smells," he said, lifting the glass to his nose. He took a tentative sniff, as if it might be noxious smelling salts. Then he inhaled deeply. He looked gratified and held it out to me. I shied like a nervous pony. He'd nearly killed me before, and he'd forgotten about it. My feelings were hurt.

"Um," I said, "you're not going to make me drink any of it, are you? You do remember what happened last time, don't you?"

He saw the look on my face and said, "Ah, no, you're

232

absolutely right. Dreadful. We mustn't let that happen again. You don't need to drink it. Just tell me if you like the way it smells."

I took the glass from him and stuck my nose into it. A powerful pecan essence wafted into my face, not at all unpleasant, considering how sick I was of pecans. "It smells like Viola's pie," I said.

"Ah," he said, "here comes the real test." He saluted me with the glass and said, "To your good health, Calpurnia, my companion in sailing uncharted waters." He took a good mouthful.

I still remember the look on his face as if it were yesterday. The spasm of surprise. Followed by a long, contemplative gaze fixed somewhere in the middle distance. Then, a slow smile.

"Well," he said at last. "I have done an amazing thing."

"What, Granddaddy, what?" I breathed.

"I doubt that any other man alive can make this claim."

"Oh, *what*?" I wailed.

Calmly, Granddaddy said, "I have managed to take perfectly good pecans and ferment them into something approximating cat piss."

My mouth flopped open.

"And what is the lesson we can take from this?" he went on.

I sat there and gawped at him.

He said, "The lesson for today is this: It is better to travel with hope in one's heart than to arrive in safety. Do you understand?"

"No sir."

"It means that we should celebrate today's failure because it is a clear sign that our voyage of discovery is not yet over. The day the experiment succeeds is the day the experiment ends. And I inevitably find that the sadness of ending outweighs the celebration of success."

"Should I write it in the log?" I said. "Cat piss, I mean."

He chortled. "A good idea. We must be honest in our observations. Take up the pen and kindly do the honors, my girl."

It was a red-letter day, after all, so I put aside the black ink and held up the bottle of red. He nodded his approval. I dipped the pen in the blood-red liquid and made a slow, careful notation. I showed it to Granddaddy.

"Excellent," he said, "but I believe there are two *s*'s in the word *piss*."

CHAPTER 20

THE BIG BIRTHDAY

We have many slight differences which may be called individual differences, such as are known frequently to appear in the offspring from the same parents. . . . No one supposes that all the individuals of the same species are cast in the very same mould. . . .

THE YEAR GROUND ON, and there was still no word about the Plant. My days consisted of a cycle of schoolwork, piano practice, and cooking lessons with Viola. I learned, against my will, how to make Beef Wellington and Lamb Parsifal. I learned how to fry chicken, catfish, and okra. I made white bread, brown bread, corn bread, and spoon bread.

None of this seemed to wear well on Viola. It didn't wear all that well on me, either. In the shrinking scraps of free time I had left, I traipsed after Granddaddy as often as I could.

We made it to October. Ah, October. That time of ecstasy for me and three of my brothers, each of us with a birthday that month, *plus* Halloween to look forward to. It was almost too much excitement to bear. And that year it did in fact prove to be too much, at least for Mother, who called me, Lamar, Sul Ross, and Sam Houston in for a talk.

"Children," she said, "this year we are going to have a birthday party for all of you to share. One big group birthday, instead of four ordinary ones. Won't that be nice? We'll invite all your friends and have a real celebration."

"What?"

"Hey, that's not fair!"

"Wait a minute."

"Motherrrrr."

Did she expect general joy about this arrangement? There was none. The chorus of grizzling was so loud and long that I was surprised she didn't relent and go back on her plan. But she stuck it out.

"Enough!" she commanded. "It's all too much. For me and for Viola, both. If she has to make four birthday feasts in one month again, she'll quit us, I swear she will. And I'll not have you complaining to her about it, either. It wasn't she who suggested it."

"Callie Vee could help her cook," Lamar said loftily. "She's learning how. Let her help. I want my own birthday party."

I threw him such a venomous look that he took a step back.

Mother prevailed, and so began an entire week of preparations, during which she and Viola and SanJuanna went full-steam ahead (since it was my birthday too, I was excused from cooking, despite my rotten brother's comment). We four children stayed out of their way and continued to vent our group spleen amongst ourselves, muttering about the unfairness of it all. Then the first Saturday of October came, and we were herded together for our communal birthday, in a peculiar mood both celebratory and sullen.

Viola's job was to cook the mountains of food; SanJuanna's was to keep it coming. Alberto's job was to erect the pavilion tent in case of rain and lead Sunshine, a bitter, elderly Shetland pony, around on a tight rein, making sure she didn't perform her favorite trick of whipping around like a snake and taking a chunk out of her rider's leg.

Our initial collective pique melted away as the party began, and why not? It was the biggest party Fentress had ever seen. All of the children in town were invited, and many of their parents came too. There were pony rides, sparklers, bottle rockets, croquet, horseshoes, taffy pulls, and apple bobbing. There were favors and crepe-paper hats and streamers.

There were mounds of dainty sandwiches and sausage rolls; there were cool aspics and hot ham served with apricot preserves; cold roast beef sliced thin and served with fiery horseradish, which the children assiduously avoided; all the jelly roll and ice cream you could possibly eat; pecan pies and lemon meringue pies; there was a towering four-layer dark chocolate cake with the name of each birthday child written in fancy white icing on the sides, with candles on the top for all of us, a total of forty-nine, covering the top layer. (Twelve for me, fourteen for Lamar, fifteen for Sam Houston, and eight for Sul Ross. It was a veritable sheet of flame, and I could see that if we kept up the communal birthday, we'd soon have to convert to some other candle system, or else get a much larger cake.)

Things started out decorously enough but deteriorated into unprecedented pandemonium. Ajax swiped a sausage roll and managed to gulp down his prize while running at top speed, a mob of gleeful children pounding in pursuit.

My one responsibility for the day was to chaperone Sul Ross and make sure he didn't stuff himself on birthday cake to the point of getting sick. A futile undertaking. Sul Ross *always* got sick on cake, whether watched by me or not.

Father and Mother played the gracious host and hostess. Granddaddy stood with the adults and had a convivial glass of beer. He announced that there was a birthday present for all of us coming from Austin but that it had been unexpectedly delayed and would arrive later in the week. This caused all sorts of speculation, but he wouldn't tell us any details. Then he retreated to the library to take a refreshing nap.

Travis and Lamar and Sam Houston circulated in Lula Gates's vicinity like planets around the sun, pestering her with constant questions: "More ice cream, Lula?" "Can I get you more cake, Lula?" "Are you having a good time, Lula?"

Nobody asked me if I wanted anything. But then, I was perfectly capable of getting my own cake. I surely was. A good, sturdy girl like me.

Lula stood talking with her mother, the tiniest beads of sweat on her nose, her loose hair a silver-and-gold cataract in the sun.

Mrs. Gates smiled at Travis and then Lamar. *So, I thought, she is hoping to land a Tate boy for Lula, and it doesn't look like she cares which one, either.*

"Callie," said Mrs. Gates, "we were talking about the fair. How is your handiwork coming along? If I may be permitted to toot my own daughter's horn, I must say that Lula is surprising me with her skill these days."

"Ah," I said.

"We're hoping she takes a ribbon in cutwork, although her lace making is progressing as well."

"Well," I said, and then realized I could think of not one single word about the subject. The gap in the conversation yawned wider until Travis chimed in.

"Callie Vee is making me some socks for Christmas, Mrs. Gates. Aren't you, Callie?"

"Yes. That's right. Socks."

Travis said, "It will be nice to have wool socks when it's cold, don't you think? I hope they'll be done in time."

"Oh, Travis," said Mrs. Gates, smiling, "I'm sure they'll be done in time for Christmas, won't they, Callie? Why, socks don't take any time at all."

I felt like saying, Don't bet on it.

"Lula can make a pair of socks in an afternoon," Mrs. Gates went on.

"Really?" said Travis, digesting this information and then looking at me with puzzlement.

I didn't like the way this conversation was going. "Lula," I interrupted, "do you want a ride on Sunshine? It's okay, Alberto's got her, she won't bite. But if you're worried, I'll go first if you want."

"Okay, Callie, that would be nice," Lula said, and we excused ourselves.

Travis, again showing admirable social skills for his age, followed Lula with his eyes but cannily stayed behind to woo Mrs. Gates with his attentions. That boy was growing up fast.

As we passed the groaning trestle tables of food, I saw Sul Ross head for the trees with two mounded plates of cake. I had forgotten that I was supposed to shield him from his own excesses. I felt guilty, but in truth an eight-year-old should know better, shouldn't he? Besides, it was my birthday party too.

We passed the horseshoe game, which Harry was supervising. He kept one eye on Sam Houston, who was known for his wild pitches, and the other on Lula's older cousin, Fern Spitty, who swanned about nearby, twirling her white lace-trimmed parasol.

"Callie," Lula said tentatively, "it seems like you've been in such a bad mood. Are you sick?"

I was torn about explaining it to her. Could she, the budding princess of bobbins and lace, understand what I was going through? We'd been friends for years, yet lately it seemed that we didn't speak the same language. But the thought of not being able to tell my best friend that my paw was caught in the trap was too sad. So I screwed up my courage and said, faltering, "I . . . I don't like all that sewing and knitting stuff, not like you, and besides, I'm not any good at it. I want to do something else with my life."

"Like what?"

"I'm not sure."

"You mean you want to be a schoolteacher? Like Miss Harbottle? But then you wouldn't get to have a family of your own. Don't you want a family of your own?"

"I'm not sure," I said.

She looked confused. "Everybody has a family. Don't they?" She thought for a moment and said, "Oh, you mean you want to be like the Telephone Operator, like Maggie Medlin. She doesn't have a family." Lula thought some more and said, "She does get paid real money of her own. That would be nice, real money of your own. . . ."

"I don't know what I want to do, Lula." And then it came to me, like the first shocking glimpse of the sun's disk rising over the horizon, what it was I *did* want to do. It was so obvious that I wondered why I hadn't seen it before. I only had to say it aloud. Did I have the courage to do that? To reveal it in the open air? Maybe I should try it out in front of Lula to see how it sounded.

"I think," I said, then stopped. "I think maybe I want to go to the university."

"Really?" Lula was either impressed or appalled, I wasn't sure which. She said, "I don't know anyone who has gone to the university. Wait, did Miss Harbottle go?"

"No, she went to the Normal School. She's only got a certificate."

"What do you do at the university?" said Lula.

"You study things."

"What kinds of things?"

"All kinds of things," I said, a trifle pompously. I had no real idea what you did at the university—I was making it up as I went along—but I didn't want her to know that. "Science and things," I said. "They give you a special diploma that shows you've been there." I was afraid she would ask me what you did with your special diploma once you got it, and the truth was I had absolutely no idea. The sudden, ridiculous superstition seized me that if she asked the question and I couldn't answer it, I would never get to go. "Come on, Lula," I said, grabbing her hand, "let's go for a ride!"

She smiled with pleasure and swiped at the sweat beads scattered on her nose like freckles, and we ran off to find the cranky pony. As we passed the horseshoe pit, I saw Harry talking to Fern Spitty, and there was something about his attentive attitude that made me think we were in for the mating dance again.

After riding Sunshine, a group of us played at Civil War games, enacting the battles of Fredericksburg and Chancellorsville, skirmishing with wooden swords and firing log cannons. All my brothers except for Sam Houston lamented that they had missed the heroics and the romantic glory. (Sam Houston was the one who had seen Mathew Brady's gruesome photographs in the library and hadn't found them any too glorious.) We had to maintain a strict rota to determine whose turn it was to play the Federals, as no one wanted to enact their part.

We tried playing a few times without the North, but this turned out to be so boring that we abandoned the game altogether.

Then we had a watermelon-seed-spitting contest, which Lamar won, naturally, as the biggest gas-bag in attendance. Next we opened gifts, and I received a tiny brown bag of licorice from the three youngest boys, who had pooled their resources to buy it. Sam Houston gave me a buttonhook, and Lamar gave me a pincushion shaped like a fat red tomato. Harry gave me a book of music for the piano, *Jolly Songs for Family Fun*. From my parents, I got a dress of the finest white lace-trimmed lawn and a new pair of winter slippers made of rabbit fur to replace the ones I'd outgrown. I gave each of my brothers a bookmark of a waving Texas flag that I'd inked and colored myself.

By the time the fireworks were set off, all of us were worn out. There was much laughter. There were tears and snits and several small bruises and scrapes, all the hallmarks of a grand party. Dovie got a black eye from running smack into another child's fist. (It could easily have been my fist but it wasn't, I swear.) Since she was generally esteemed an unbearable Miss Priss, this did her a world of good and earned her much approval.

That evening Mother took to her room with a large bottle of her tonic. Viola went to lie down with a cold cloth and a headache powder and was given an unprecedented two whole days off to recover. SanJuanna and Alberto shouldered the thankless burden of cleaning up. Alberto reported that when he led Sunshine back to her stall at the end of the day, she was too exhausted to try and bite him even once.

And Granddaddy's gift did arrive at the end of the week, although we all came to wish soon enough that it had not. It came in a large crate with ventilation holes, always a promising sign in a gift. We assembled on the front porch and watched as Harry pried it open. It contained a scrolled wire cage, in which sat a gorgeous parrot. How on earth had Granddaddy known?

And it wasn't just any parrot. It was an enormous, full-grown Amazon, three feet (excuse me—*one meter*) long from crest to tail feathers, with a brilliant golden breast, azure back, and wings of shocking crimson. We all stared at it in awe. Granddaddy had read about it in the Austin papers and had bought it from an estate sale, the bird having outlived its previous owner. It was the most beautiful thing we'd ever seen. And it looked like it could take your eye out without the slightest effort.

As we gaped at it, it reached through the bars with its great scaling beak and delicately opened the latch, then swung itself onto the top of the cage in a practiced move, despite the impediment of a thin silver chain that ran from one ankle to its gnawed perch. It preened a long iridescent feather, shook its head, raised and lowered its crest in a gesture that was somehow threatening, and turned to gaze at us with a perfectly round, yellow eye.

We were stupefied. None of us had ever seen anything like it. Mother looked at the creature with some alarm, but then, as if realizing its future was at stake, the bird broke into an amazing whistling rendition of "When You and I Were Young, Maggie," complete with trills and cadenzas. Was this pure chance? Or had the bird somehow divined that my mother's name was Margaret and that this was her favorite song? There was some cruel intelligence in its jaundiced eye that made me ponder this and made me grateful for the chain. His name was Polly, of course, and he was our birthday gift. What could my mother do?

So he stayed, at least for a while. He turned out to be as tetchy and irritable as he looked. With his huge beak and tremendous black claws, no one dared think of unchaining him from his perch. He intimidated all of us: parents, children, dogs, cats. Everyone gave his corner a wide berth except to feed and water him and change his paper. He had his own cuttlebone that he rubbed the sides of his beak against like a knife grinder honing his blade. I wanted to examine it up close but didn't have the nerve. Polly didn't seem to care that he was a friendless bird. He spent his days muttering dyspeptically to himself and singing naughty sea chanteys, with the occasional random earsplitting screech thrown in just to make you jump.

We took to covering his cage more and more often so that we could have some peace. I suspect everyone wanted to get rid of him, but no one had the nerve to come out and say it; we were waiting for some decent excuse to present itself because he was, after all, the Birthday Bird.

The decent excuse came during one of Mother's afternoon teas when he cheerily greeted her guest, Mrs. Purtle, with the suggestion to "bugger off." I didn't know what that meant, but it appeared that both Mother and Mrs. Purtle did. Within the hour, Polly was carried by Alberto down to the gin and given to Mr. O'Flanagan.

Mr. O'Flanagan was the assistant manager of the gin and a former merchant sailor, and he loved having a bird around. He had once kept an ancient raven, which he'd dubbed Edgar Allan Crow, and he'd labored for years to get the bird to speak the word *nevermore*. It remained mute until the day it squawked once and then fell off its perch from old age. Mr. O'Flanagan, on hearing that we had a real parrot that talked, was thrilled to take possession of Polly. Being an old salt himself, he took no offense in rough company. It turned out that he and the bird knew many of the same indecent songs, and they would pass the time when he wasn't busy with customers by singing together, with the door shut, of course.

Polly was missed by no one in our house, including, I suspect, Granddaddy.

CHAPTER 21

THE REPRODUCTIVE IMPERATIVE

Selection may be applied to the family, as well as to the individual, and may thus gain the desired end.

SURE ENOUGH, HARRY was soon asked to have dinner with Fern Spitty, although the invitation was not so blatant. He was invited to the Gateses' house, but Cousin Fern just happened to be visiting for a fortnight. It was a few short months after the Minerva Goodacre debacle, but Harry looked as if his broken heart had mended. Fern had just come out in Lockhart, and it was time to buckle down to the business of meeting bachelors. Lockhart was nowhere near the size of Austin, of course, but that year for the first time there were five prosperous-enough merchants who felt compelled (by their wives, no doubt) to certify their daughters as marriageable. In other words, up for bid on the block. Mother read about this in the *Lockhart Post*, and a gleam came into her eye, a gleam I didn't like, a gleam that I knew had something to do with her only daughter.

Harry resumed anointing and pomading himself. He polished his riding boots so that you could see yourself reflected in them, brushed his suit, and went off to dinner. I figured he was irresistible, he looked that dashing.

The next day Lula reported to me that, after dinner, Harry and Fern sat outside in the darkness on the porch swing for a good half hour with no chaperones except the mosquitoes.

"Did they spoon?" I asked. I wasn't one hundred percent sure what that involved, but I hoped Lula would know.

"What?" she said. "What?"

"Did he whisper sweet nothings in her ear?"

"Huh?" Lula said. "What's a sweet nothing? How can you whisper nothing?"

"Never mind. Did he hold her hand?" I said.

"I couldn't see."

I went way out on a limb. "Did he kiss her?"

"*What?*" Lula cried, "Oh, Callie, they barely know each other!"

"Well, I understand that, Lula, but people do kiss, you know. I wondered if you saw it, that's all."

She blushed, and the pinpoint dots of sweat across the bridge of her nose beaded up. (Question for the Notebook: Why does Lula's nose sweat like that? Nobody else's does.) She yanked her hankie out of her pocket and dabbed at herself over and over and said, "How can you ask me about things like that?"

"Because he's my brother, and I'm trying to figure out if he's going to run off and marry Fern. She's your cousin, so that would make us related, wouldn't it? I think it would, but I'm not sure how."

I knew better than to interfere with Harry's courting. I had learned my lesson hard. But, maybe, if someone else gathered intelligence and it happened to fall in my lap . . .

"Lula," I said, "do you ever think about getting married?"

"I guess I do. Doesn't everybody?"

"You have to let your husband kiss you once you're married. And you have to kiss him back."

"No," she said.

"Yes." I nodded, as if I knew everything there was to know about husbands and wives kissing. "That's what they do together."

"Do you *have* to?"

"Oh, absolutely. It's the law."

"I never heard of that law," she said dubiously.

"It's true, it's Texas law," I said. "And while we're on the subject, you do know that a whole bunch of my brothers are sweet on you, don't you?"

Even as this interesting information fell from my mouth, I remembered the promise I had made to all three. "Drat! I wasn't supposed to tell you that."

Lula looked shocked by my profanity. "Callie! You shouldn't swear."

"Sorry," I said. "It's supposed to be a secret. Forget I said anything."

She hesitated and then said, "So who is it?"

"Who is what?"

"You know . . . sweet on me."

"Take a guess," I said. "I shouldn't tell you." But I was sick of the burden of carrying their secrets. And why shouldn't Lula know? "Oh, all right, it's Lamar and Sam Houston and Travis."

"My goodness," she said, turning bright pink.

"You can have your pick. Which one do you like best?"

"I—I don't know."

"Well, d'you want any of 'em? I'm not sure I would, if I were you. Which one is the handsomest, do you think? Harry is, of course, but he's not in the running."

She flushed and said, "They're all nice-looking boys."

"Yeah, Lula, but do you *like* any of them?"

"They're all nice boys."

"Yeah, yeah, but do you *like* any of them?" But she wouldn't answer me, just dabbed at her beads of sweat and looked flustered.

I went on, "If I were you, I'd pick Travis. He's the nicest one. Maybe kissing him wouldn't be so bad. There must be something to it—otherwise, they wouldn't want to do it, don't you think?"

Lula looked thoughtful. "I don't know if my mother and father enjoy it. I mean, I can't remember seeing them kiss."

I had seen my parents kiss each other on Christmas Eve, and once I had seen my father put his arm around my mother's waist and pull her to him at the dark end of the hall as they went into their bedroom. And when you lived on a farm with chickens and pigs and cows and cats, there were always litters being born; so, naturally at a certain age, it occurred to you to wonder how all this teeming life came about. I had seen the dogs mating, and one night I had stumbled on two cats in the dark, something you never saw. The cats and I were equally shocked.

Lula said something to me that I didn't catch.

"What?" I said.

She looked away. "So . . . Travis is . . . sweet on me?"

"Yep. Snag him, Lula. He's the pick of the litter."

"But he's so young. After all, I'm twelve and he's only eleven. Isn't he?"

"Um. Right." He was actually ten, but I was not going to stomp all over his tender campaign of first love. "Remember, Lula, that I wasn't supposed to tell you. You won't let on, will you?"

She swore the deepest double-Injun-blood-brothers oath for me. I was willing to seal it with spit, but that was too much for her.

That evening I cornered Harry as he wrote a letter.

"Hello, my own pet," he said absently.

"Harry," I said, "have you ever kissed a girl?"

He looked startled. "Why do you ask?"

"I wondered what it's like, that's all."

"I did kiss a girl once," he said, smiling, "and it's very nice."

"Why is it so nice?"

"It just is. You'll have to wait and see."

"Who did you kiss?" I asked.

"Callie, I cannot tell you. A gentleman would never tell."

"Why not? You can tell me. I can keep a secret." Well, I thought, maybe not. "Did you kiss that Minerva Goodacre?"

"No. It was not she. But she did let me hold her hand once."

"Was that nice too?"

"Very nice. Terrifically nice. Go away."

"Why was it nice?"

"You're being my own pest. Leave me alone," he said, but he smiled at some pleasant memory.

"Do you pine for her, Harry? Do you sigh?" As long as the wretched Goodacre was well out of our lives, some degree of pining and sighing might be indulged in strictly as a romantic exercise.

"I guess I did for a while."

"But you don't anymore?"

"No, not anymore. Would you please go away?" I turned to go when he called out, "Wait. What's all this interest about?" He looked sly. "Do you have a boy you're not telling us about? Your first beau?"

"No, no, no." I gargled out a strangled laugh. "No."

"Why not? One day I'll lose you to some charming prince offering you a glass slipper, Cal."

"Don't say that," I said, rushing at him and throwing my arms about him. I felt like crying for no good reason. "Why do you have to get married? Why do I have to get married? Why can't we all stay here in our house?"

"It's okay, pet. One day you'll want a family of your own."

I mumbled into his vest, "People are always saying 'one day' to me, and I'm sick of it."

He said, "They said that to me, too."

"They said it to you?"

"It's infuriating, isn't it? They say it to everybody, and here I am saying it to you. Here, let's fix your hair. You're all mussed up."

"Harry," I said, choosing my words carefully while he fiddled with my ribbon, "do you think . . . do you think I could be a schoolteacher?"

"A schoolteacher? Is that what you want to do?" he said, retying my bow.

It wasn't, but I couldn't yet tell him what I really wanted.

"Do you think I could do that, Harry?"

"Yes. I think you could do that. Have you talked with Mother and Father about this?"

I ignored this and said, "Do you think I could be . . . oh, I don't know, maybe a Telephone Operator?"

"I'm sure you'd be good at that, too, if your arms grow long enough. Hold on, let me fix your ribbon. There we go."

"Harry. Do you think I could be"—I stopped, then spoke again, my voice studiedly casual—"a scientist?"

"A scientist?" He stepped back. "That's kind of far-fetched, don't you think?"

I fixed him with my gaze. My question, and his answer, were too important to look away.

"Ohhh," he said, "I see. It's coming from Grandfather,

isn't it? He's egging you on, isn't he? Maybe you shouldn't spend so much time with him. Really, Callie, it's so far-fetched."

"Why?" I said, flatly. "Why is it so far-fetched?"

"Because I don't know of any lady scientists, do you? How would you live? Where would you work? Look, one day you'll get married, you'll have lots of children, and you'll forget all about this. Don't you want to have a house of your own?"

"I already have a house of my own."

"You know what I mean," he said.

I took a step back from him and said, "Harry. If I did want to be a scientist, would you help me?"

He looked skeptical. "Help you how?"

"I'm not sure," I said, since I had no plan. "Just help me. If I need it."

"I don't know what to say, pet." Seeing the look on my face, he said, "I'm not saying no. I just don't understand what you're getting at."

"If it was important to me . . ."

"I'll always try to do what I can for you, Callie, you know that. Although it's more than you deserve after telling Mother about Miss Goodacre. Now, go away. I've got to finish this letter."

I jumped on this change of subject with relief.

"Is it a love letter?"

"None of your business."

"Is it to Fern Spitty?"

"Go away."

I had extracted no promise of help from him, but he hadn't refused me, either. I counted the conversation a wash. Now I knew that, finally, the time had come to go to Granddaddy. Lula and Harry had been mere dress rehearsals. I had been putting it off, but it was time.

I kissed Harry's bent head and went out to the porch, where the others were assembling to watch for the first firefly. The weather was cooling. The insects were diminishing in number, and soon their season would be over, which was just as well, as the Fentress Firefly Prize ribbon was grubby and limp.

Granddaddy sat in a wicker rocker at the far end of the porch. I was glad to see that he was off some distance by himself. I took my Notebook and pencil and sat in the chair next to his. The end of his cigar glowed brighter when he inhaled, like some fat red firefly. I half expected to see the few remaining insects circling him and semaphoring their romantic intentions. (Question for the Notebook: Has a firefly ever mistaken a cigar for another of its species? A painful—possibly lethal—mistake.) We sat in silence until he said, "Calpurnia, do you intend to inflict a mortal wound on that chair?"

I looked down and realized that I had been jabbing a hole in the wicker arm with my pencil.

"I haven't seen much of you lately," he said.

"It's because I'm in training to be a cook. Or a wife, I guess."

"Ah. And we have all enjoyed the fruits of your labor."

"You don't have to say that," I said unhappily.

We sat in silence, and I felt an unseen mosquito feasting on my ankles, adding to my general misery. I couldn't see it until it had bitten me several times, and in its own gluttony, had transformed itself into a visible flying droplet of my own blood. It settled on the porch near my feet, and I stamped at it. It tried to fly, too engorged to escape. I caught it with the edge of my shoe and a tiny fountain of my blood spurted against the gray paint of the porch. I thought about this. Apparently too much of a good thing could kill you, like the old song said. Look at the smeared evidence. The mosquito was a clear success in terms of getting plenty of food, but a failure in terms of living to a good old age and expiring peacefully in her sleep, surrounded by her many keening grandchildren. So was she fit or unfit? Although it might not matter, depending on what Granddaddy had to say next. Would he commute my life sentence of domestic drudgery?

Travis spotted the first firefly and claimed the ribbon at the other end of the porch. I cleared my throat. "Grandfather. . . ." And then I faltered.

"Yes, Calpurnia?"

"Girls . . . girls can be scientists, too." We both pretended not to hear the quiver in my voice. "Can't they?"

He took a long puff on his cigar and then tapped the ash clean.

He said, "Have you asked your mother this? Or your father?"

"What?" I said. "No, of course not. Why would I do that?"

"Because they may have something to say about the matter. Has that occurred to you?"

"Oh," I said bitterly, "I *know* what they have to say about the matter. Why do you think I never get out of the kitchen anymore? That's why I'm asking *you*."

"I see," he said. "Do you remember when we sat by the river some months ago and talked about Copernicus and Newton?"

"I remember." How could I ever forget?

"Did we not talk about Mrs. Curie's element? Mrs. Maxwell's screech owl? Miss Anning's pterodactyl? Her ichthyosaur?"

"No."

"Miss Kovalevsky's equations? Miss Bird's travels to the Sandwich Islands?"

"No."

"Such ignorance," he muttered, and quick tears pricked my eyes. Was I such an ignorant girl? He went on. "Please forgive my ignorance, Calpurnia. You have made me well enough acquainted with the primitive state of your public education, and I should have known you would be left in the dark about certain matters of Science. Let me tell you about these women."

I soaked up what he told me like a living sponge. It was galvanizing information. But was there something in his voice, some hesitation, some reservation I hadn't heard before? We were interrupted by Mother herding the children inside for bed. Lately, it seemed that all my talks with Granddaddy were interrupted. Lately, it seemed that there wasn't any time.

By unanimous vote, my brothers and I retired the Fentress Firefly Prize at bedtime, declaring the season of 1899 officially over.

Travis's firefly was, in fact, the only one spotted that night. Although I knew the fireflies would return in a year, it felt like the extinction of a species. How sad to be the last of your kind, flashing your signal in the dark, alone, to nothingness. But I was not alone, was I? I had learned that there were others of my kind out there.

CHAPTER 22

THANKSGIVING

One of the most remarkable features in our domesticated races is that we see in them adaptation, not indeed to the animal's or plant's own good, but to man's use or fancy.

I WOKE EARLIER than usual the next morning and knew, before I was completely awake, that something was different. I came fully awake and realized that I was cold. I was *cold*! The temperature had dropped a good forty degrees in the night in one of those unpredictable fronts that swept down from the Amarillo plains. I reached out a goose-fleshed arm to pull up a quilt, but of course there wasn't one. Our household had been caught unprepared, so long had the heat hung over us like a suffocating shroud. I flung back my thin cotton sheet and stretched my arms to the ceiling and luxuriated in the chill air. I wondered, If I lay there long enough, would I start to shiver? But there wasn't time for this kind of experiment. A lovely day waited to unroll before me.

I came downstairs dressed in my summer clothes because I had nothing else in my press to wear. Viola was singing "The Willow Bends Her Boughs for Me" as she stoked the kitchen stove. Idabelle was tucked tightly in her basket. Mother came down in her dressing gown, over which she'd thrown her prize cashmere shawl, which reeked of camphor. Father had bought it for her on their honeymoon in Galveston, a city into which an unimaginable profusion of fabulous goods flowed every day.

"Soft as a baby's bottom," Father always said about the shawl when she wore it, twinkling at Mother, who would flush. She fought a running battle against mouse and moth for possession of her shawl, and kept ahead by such heavy and diligent applications of mothballs that the smell wafted about in her wake like some vile perfume. By spring the smell would fade, but by then she'd have to pack it away again.

Viola made pecan sticky buns served with hot syrup, and we fell on them like ravenous beasts. Granddaddy celebrated the day by briefly giving up his shabby frock coat to SanJuanna to allow her another futile stab at making it presentable; the benzene had little effect except to make him smell like a walking laboratory.

On the back porch, the Outside Cats were curled into themselves. Ajax and the other dogs snuffled and pranced in the grass. Everyone had a brighter eye. Tempers were soothed, gladness filled our souls. We could go on.

That day on the way to school, my brothers and I raced each other for the first time in months. Miss Harbottle was in such a good mood that no one got the switch, and no one had to stand in the Corner of Shame. Lula Gates and I celebrated by jumping rope all the way home. It had been too hot for months to even think about it. When I tripped myself up, I realized that I had grown taller over the summer.

I stopped in at the gin on the way home, and since Father was engaged in a meeting with some other planters, I went to Mr. O'Flanagan's office and asked him to cut me a longer length of jump rope.

"Certainly, certainly. Come in and say hello to Polly," he said, getting up from his desk. Polly looked happy and healthy enough standing on his cage, but he still gave me the evil eye.

"Old Polly's a good bird, aren't you?" Mr. O'Flanagan said, and affectionately ruffled the feathers on his back the wrong way. I watched in alarm, but instead of ripping Mr. O'Flanagan's scalp off with his talons, Polly winked slowly in obvious pleasure and leaned into his hand.

"Polly's a good boy," said the bird in its disquieting nasal counterfeit of a human voice.

"Yes, he is," cooed Mr. O'Flanagan, "yes, he is. Here, Calpurnia, you can pet him while I get some rope."

Not likely. I stood well across the room. Polly and I looked at each other. He raised and lowered his crest and then I swear he hissed at me like a feral cat. I was backing out of the room when Mr. O'Flanagan returned with a length, saying, "Let's see, how long should we cut this?"

I was glad to see him back. I was glad that Polly had found his proper place in the world but gladder still that it was not with us.

When I got home, I joined my brothers and SanJuanna and

Alberto in carrying quilts and winter clothing outside for airing. The lighter patchwork quilts were hung over the clothesline, and we set to beating them with all our might. It was one of those rare times that we were actually encouraged to be boisterous, and it was grand. The heavier feather quilts were spread out on clean sheets in the sun, and we took turns shooing the inquisitive dogs and cats and chickens away from them. Mother put a dilute solution of vinegar in a Flit gun and misted everything. She believed firmly in the disinfectant qualities of vinegar and sunshine, and who's to say she was wrong? It's practically all we had. Diphtheria, polio, typhus lurked everywhere, and we had no weapons against them, although living in the country instead of Austin gave us some protection.

With the change in the weather came the realization that Thanksgiving was sneaking up on us. We'd all been too hot for too long to give it much thought. It was unfortunate that this year the task of feeding our small flock of turkeys (numbering exactly three) fell to Travis. One turkey was destined for our table, one was for the hired help, and one was for the poor at the other end of town. This was traditional in our house. What was not traditional was that this year the softest-hearted child had been assigned to look after them.

Travis had promptly christened his charges Reggie, Tom Turkey, and Lavinia. He spent hours communing with them, preening their feathers with a stick while sitting in the dust and gobbling softly at them. They, in turn, seemed attached to him and followed him about within the confines of their pen.

Helen Keller could have seen what was coming, so why couldn't my parents?

I don't think it sank in for Travis until early November, when I went out to the pen with Viola so that she could inspect our prospective dinner. Travis sat on a stump holding Reggie on his lap, talking to him and feeding him corn from his lips. Oh, dear. He looked up and paled when he saw Viola.

"What are you doing here?" he said.

"Honey, you got to face facts," she said. "Get the others out here and line 'em up so I can see 'em."

"You go away," he said. His voice was thin and tight. I'd never heard him talk like that before. "Go away right now."

Viola went straight to Mother and said, "You better think about that boy. Those turkeys is his pets."

Mother went to Father and said, "Shouldn't you turn the turkeys over to Alberto?"

Father summoned Travis and said, "You can't let yourself get too attached, little man. This is a working farm, and you have to be big about such matters."

Travis came to me and said, "They're my friends, Callie. Why would anybody want to eat them?"

"Travis," I said, "we always have a bird at Thanksgiving. That's what they're for. You know that."

I thought he was going to cry. "We can't eat my friends. What am I gonna tell Reggie?"

"I don't think you should discuss it with him," I said. "It's better that way, don't you think?"

"I guess," he said sadly, and shuffled off.

The next day I sat in the kitchen with Viola and watched her punching down the bread dough, the cords working in her forearms. She was a marvel of efficiency.

"What's on your mind?" she asked.

"Why do you think there's something on my mind?"

"You got that look about you. You wearing it right now."

This was news to me, that I was so transparent to the world. I said, "Viola, what about Thanksgiving? What about Travis? Can't you do something? It's going to kill him."

"I talked to your mama," she said, sprinkling flour on the board, "and she talked to your daddy. I done my part. If you can think of something else, you go right ahead."

"Why did *he* have to get the birds this year? That was dumb."

She shot me a look. "*I'd* never say."

"Is it really his turn?" I counted my brothers on my fingers. "Let's see, last year it was Sam Houston, and the year before that, it was Lamar, I think, so that means that this year it's supposed to be . . . oh."

"That's right, baby girl."

I pondered this and concluded that they shouldn't have skipped over me. I would have made a better choice than Travis, now that I had been annealed in the furnace of the Scientific Method. Creatures sometimes had to die to advance knowledge; they also had to die to advance Thanksgiving. I knew this. I could have done it.

Probably.

The next day, I collared Travis after he fed his birds.

"Look," I said, "think of them as chickens. We eat the chickens all the time, so try and think about the turkeys like that instead. You don't care about the chickens like that, right?"

"But they're *not* chickens, Callie. They know their names. They wait for me to come every morning."

"I *know* they're not chickens, Travis, but I'm saying if you practice thinking about them *like* they're chickens, it's going to be easier on you."

He looked at me doubtfully.

"Or," I said, "think of them like Polly. You didn't get attached to Polly." (And neither did anybody else.)

"Polly is a scary bird," he said. "My turkeys aren't scary—they're tame."

"Travis," I said, "you've got to try. And you've got to stop spending all your time with them. I'm not kidding."

Two days later, Reggie went missing, apparently having wormed his bulky body through a tiny rent in the corner of the pen.

Oh, there was pure heck to pay, no doubt about it, but Travis stuck fast and stoutly denied that he'd engineered the escape. Unfortunately for my brother and Reggie both, the bird showed up at first light the following morning and waited outside the pen for his breakfast and morning grooming from his best friend. I didn't see it, but Lamar reported that Travis burst into tears when he saw the bird and tried to shoo him into the brush, but Reggie was determined to return to the soft life. Alberto was assigned to reinforce the pen, which was then personally inspected by Father, followed by yet another talk with Travis behind closed doors.

As the holiday grew closer, Travis grew paler and quieter.

In desperation, I went to Harry, who disappointed me by saying only, "Look, we've all had to go through it."

"Yes," I said, "but none of you made pets out of your birds. It's different for him, don't you see?"

"It's supposed to be your turn, you know."

"I know."

"But I talked Father out of it," said Harry.

"*You* did? Why?"

"Because we both figured it would be too hard on you."

"Well, that sure makes me laugh. Poor old Travis is about to fall apart, in case nobody's noticed."

"Okay." Harry sighed. "What do you suggest?"

"I don't have anything *to* suggest. That's why I'm asking you to help."

"Have you talked to Granddaddy about it?" he asked.

"I'm afraid to," I said. "He believes in survival of the fittest. And it looks to me like those turkeys are only fit for Thanksgiving dinner."

Despite admonishments from nearly every family member, Travis spent more time with the turkeys instead of less.

I went to the parlor one afternoon, where Mother was

sewing, and I said, "I have a terrific idea. Why don't we have a ham this year for Thanksgiving?"

"We have a ham at Christmas," she responded, inspecting a frayed cuff.

"Yes, but we could have ham twice, couldn't we? It wouldn't kill us," I said. Travis liked the shoats too, but fortunately, that year none of our present piglets had evidenced a singular enough personality to earn a name.

"We're not going to spoil Thanksgiving dinner because Travis has become overly fond of a bird." Mother was the court of last resort on household matters; there was no appeal, but I laid out my next suggestion anyway, feeble as it was.

"What about this?" I said to her. "We can trade our three turkeys for someone else's. That way, at least he won't have to eat his own bird."

Mother sighed and looked at me. "He's causing such a lot of trouble. All right, but they would have to be birds of the same size, not a pound less. Bring him to me, and I'll tell him."

I found Travis in the pen, sitting in the dust with Reggie and Lavinia and Tom Turkey.

"You need to come in," I told him. "Mother wants to talk to you."

"Is it about my birds?" he said, excited. "It's about my birds, isn't it? Is she going to let me keep them? She's going to let me keep them, right?" He followed me to the house, chattering all the way.

Mother said to him, "Travis, we can't not have Thanksgiving. But Callie has an idea, and I am willing to go along with it. We can trade your birds for someone else's—that's if we can find someone who'll do it. But they have to be just as big as ours."

"Trade? What do you mean?"

"Well, we would give someone our turkeys, and they would give us theirs."

"But I would get to go visit them. Wouldn't I?"

"No, dear, you wouldn't," she said.

"Then why would we do that?" he asked.

"It's so that we could have someone else's bird for Thanksgiving, not one of yours. So you don't have to watch us eating Ronald."

"Reggie," he said, sniffling.

"Reggie, yes. And this way, you could have some turkey for Thanksgiving too. Wouldn't that be nice?"

"No," he cried.

"That's enough. Please wipe your nose and try to collect yourself."

I wondered why he wasn't relieved of turkey duty and given something else to do instead. I guess it's because once you were assigned a chore you did it. We lived daily with the birth and death of every kind of animal, and we were expected to get used to it, or at least the boys were. Tender sensibilities didn't enter into it; life was hard, but life for animals on a working farm was harder. And a whole lot shorter.

I enlisted my brothers, and we started looking for replacement birds. Nearly everyone in town raised a few chickens, but turkeys were less common, being bigger and having a more pronounced tendency toward meanness, except of course for Travis's birds. We checked with our classmates, with the mayor, with Alberto, who came from a huge family of brothers and sisters and cousins at the other end of town. We put up a small handwritten notice at the newspaper office and made sure that old Backy Medlin, the gin's most maundering gossip, knew what we were looking for. I even bribed Lamar to go to the post office and tell Postmaster Grassel so that I wouldn't have to see the man.

It was a great plan, or at least a decent one. And absolutely nothing happened. As the day approached and Travis became more and more distressed, I went to Granddaddy in the library and explained the problem.

"Which one is Travis again?" he said.

"He's the ten-year-old. The one who's been crying all the time lately."

"Ah. So that's what's wrong with him. I thought perhaps he had worms."

"Not that I know of. Mother's always giving us purgatives. We've got to help him, Granddaddy."

"Calpurnia, our whole existence on this earth is a cycle of life and death. That is a fact. There is no stopping it."

"You're not going to help," I said and turned to go. "And you with your bat. If we were going to eat your bat for Thanksgiving, instead of turkey, you'd do something about it."

"Calpurnia," he said, "is it so important to you?"

"Not to me, it isn't," I said. "But it is important to Travis. So I guess that makes it important to me."

"Well, then."

THE FATEFUL DAY drew close, and I went to my brother. "Travis," I said, "I have found you three substitute turkeys. I've found a man who'll trade. But you can't watch. You have to say good-bye to them tonight. It's better this way, do you understand?"

"No," he said miserably. "I don't understand any of it. It's no good."

"We have to do it this way," I said. "You have to trust me."

Travis sat in the pen that afternoon until dusk. I could see him from the window upstairs in the back hall. Finally, he gave each of the birds a hug, pressing his face deep into their feathers, then tore himself away and ran into the house. Sobbing, he ran past me and slammed the door to his room.

Next morning, looking down at the pen, you could see there were three new turkeys. They were a different color from ours, and they had fewer tail feathers, as if they'd been fighting, but Mother was happy enough to see that they looked about the same size and weight as our old ones. Alberto went out early and chopped off their heads on the chopping block, and San-Juanna plucked and singed them clean. I noticed them conferring over the dead, naked turkeys on the back porch, speaking low in Spanish.

By noon, Viola had her choice of bird to put in the oven.

SanJuanna and I sat in the pantry and polished the good silver. Then we pulled the pink floral china that Mother had inherited from her mother out of its straw-filled crate and wiped it all down. Viola clanged about in the kitchen nonstop for hours with a plug of snuff in her lip, bringing forth our massive dinner out of clouds of steam. Travis stayed in his room the whole day, and no one had the courage to drag him out.

Finally, by six o'clock, the house redolent of enticing smells, Viola rang her bell at the back door and pounded the gong. Travis came out of his room and trooped silently in to dinner with the rest of us. Nobody looked at him.

Father said a grace of thanks that felt like it went on forever and then he carved the enormous bird. I studied the pattern of pink roses on my plate. Travis kept his head down. He didn't speak a word; he didn't cry. We passed the platter of turkey self-consciously and did our best to pretend he wasn't casting a wet tarpaulin over our entire feast. Mother excused him from holding up his conversational end. He never noticed that I bore some substantial scratches on my arms and that Granddaddy's nails were rimmed with crescents of dark paint.

We slowly plowed our way through the turkey, the giblet-and-smoked-oyster stuffing, the braised sweetbreads, peppery venison sausage, sweet glazed yams, crusty roasted potatoes in their jackets, buttered limas and wax beans, velvety corn pudding, tart stewed tomatoes with okra, cabbage with chunks of sugar-cured pork, puckery pickled beets, creamed spinach-and-onion compote. For dessert we had a pecan pie, a lemon pie, a mincemeat pie, and a tart apple pie (my only contribution, made by me two days prior to keep me out of Viola's way on the big day itself), all grandly displayed on the sideboard. Despite the pall hanging over us, small pockets of spontaneous merriment broke out here and there.

Harry got the wishbone, and while we waited for SanJuanna to cut the pies, he got up and walked around the table to share it with Travis. I didn't think Travis would pull it but he did, and he got the long end. When we urged him to tell us his wish, he stared into space and said quietly, "I wish I had a donkey. Just a little one. And maybe a little cart for him to pull. I would name him Dinkey the Donkey. That's what I would call him."

"Why do you want a donkey?" said Harry.

"Because I don't think people eat donkeys. Do they?"

Mother looked drawn. "No, dear, not as far as I know."

"Then Dinkey would be safe, and that would be all right. And that's my wish."

The table was silent except for Jim Bowie, who looked alarmed and said, "Are we eating a donkey? I don't want to eat a donkey. They have pretty eyes."

"No, J.B., we aren't eating a donkey," said Mother. "It's turkey. Please finish your plate or there'll be no dessert."

"Are we eating Travis's turkey?" said J.B.

"No, it's someone else's turkey," I said quickly. "We traded, remember?"

"Oh. Okay. Can I look after the turkeys next time?" J.B. said in his innocence. None of us knew what to say to him.

"No, you can't," said Mother. "It's Sul Ross's turn."

"No," I said. "It's my turn, remember?" Wondering, even as I opened my mouth, how much I was going to regret this. I meant only to sound determined, but apparently there was a measure of grimness in my voice because the conversation momentarily stopped, and everyone, including Travis, looked at me. But it was part of the hard bargain I'd made with Granddaddy, who only regarded me from his end of the table and nodded in approval.

CHAPTER 23

THE FENTRESS FAIR

How fleeting are the wishes and efforts of man! how
short his time! and consequently how poor will his prod-
ucts be, compared with those accumulated by nature. . . .

I HAD NO CHOICE. Miss Harbottle had proposed the motion on
the floor that all the girls in school enter handiwork in the fair,
and Mother had seconded it. So Mother and Viola came to my
room and inspected the various projects that I had laid out on
my bed. There were three pairs of brown woollen socks for my
brothers, a crocheted baby's jacket to give to the poor, and an
asymmetrical tatted lace collar, rather awkward on the side
where I'd begun it and somewhat tidier where I'd finished up. I
also had a piece of pathetic quilting so primitive that it looked
like it had been done by Toddy Gates, Lula's addle-brained
brother. Mother shuddered and turned away, and she and Viola
conferred and clucked over the remaining pieces. With much
sighing, they chose the tatted collar.

Mother mused absently as she wrapped it in tissue paper, "I
wonder if the family name has to go on it." She looked up and saw
our shocked expressions and said hastily, "Of course it does."

On reflection, anonymity sounded like a fine idea to me, and I said, "Do you think I *could* enter anonymously? That would be all right with me."

Mother flushed and said, "Don't be silly. You should have thought of that while you were making it, young lady. Of course your name—our name—will be on it." Still, she looked thoughtful. But whether she did or did not ask Miss Harbottle if this was possible, it didn't matter. My name was going to be stuck on my work. I knew it served me right.

None of the boys had been forced to enter anything, but Travis voluntarily entered his Angora rabbit, Bunny. Bunny was an enormous, docile, fluffy white creature that Travis combed regularly for his silky hair, which he then gave to a local spinner, who in turn re-presented it to Mother in the form of the world's softest wool. Travis had briefly considered entering a calf in the yearling division, but fortunately Harry had had the presence of mind to point out to him what inevitably happened to the winning specimens in the cattle divisions. Following this, Travis had driven us, and the fair organizers, mad with his obsessive checking and rechecking that Bunny was entered in the rabbit/fur competition and not the rabbit/meat competition.

Sam Houston had carved a recognizable profile of President McKinley out of pecan wood, a difficult wood to work, and entered it in the juvenile whittling division.

Except for my pathetic entry, it was bound to be a stupendous day, especially since we all had some money in our pockets saved up from working at the gin; I still had fifteen cents left over from babysitting during the harvest, despite subcontracting to Sul Ross. I considered spending some of it on a brand-new drink we'd all heard about, Coca-Cola.

The day dawned clear, and although we had to travel only a mile to the other end of town, the whole family, including Granddaddy, piled into the long-bed wagon. Travis held Bunny on his lap in a chicken-wire cage that was too small for him. The rabbit's fur pressed through the wire, and white wisps of it floated away in the sunlight like tiny clouds. We parked among a motley collection of farm wagons and gigs and dogcarts pulled up higgledy-piggledy on the grassy field adjoining the many tents.

Mother gave us our final instructions before we scattered. Travis took Bunny off to the Small Livestock tent, and I headed for Domestic Arts with my entry safely shrouded in brown paper so that no one could see it.

I went by the cakewalk in a marquee festooned with many curls of flypaper. Along with the cakes, various young ladies of the county had prepared picnic lunches, and whoever bid highest on the lunch got to sit with the young lady to enjoy her company and share the delectables from her hamper. All the money raised went to the Volunteer Fire Department. I guess this was the rusticated equivalent of coming out.

I hurriedly dropped off my entry and went wandering around. The Odd Fellows' band wheezed away, pumping out a steady supply of festive waltzes and marches that could be heard all over the grounds. I saw my brothers here and there in the crowd, and some of my friends from school. I watched Sam Houston win a tin whistle at the ring toss, and later I saw one exactly like it in Lula's hand, although she seemed to be holding it limply and not paying it much attention.

I passed a pavilion with a sign out front—HOFACKET'S FINE PHOTOGRAPHS FOR FINE OCCASIONS—and there was the photographer himself, having set up a temporary shop to catch business from fair-goers dressed in their good clothes with money jingling in their pockets. He was too busy posing a young couple to notice me, which was lucky. I'd received another letter from him inquiring after word about the Plant, and then yet another before I'd had a chance to answer the previous one, and it was all getting annoying. How quickly the bloom had gone off the whole idea of scientific correspondence.

Then I made my way to the Domestic Arts tent, which smelled of enticing baked goods. Mayor Axelrod got up with a megaphone on the platform at the front and started calling out the winners, starting with the novice classes. We ran through breads, breads/fancy, pies/fruit, and pies/otherwise, and then he began on the handiworks.

He consulted his list and called out, "In third place, Novice Tatting, Miss Calpurnia Virginia Tate!"

What? *What?*

"Calpurnia Tate, where are you? Come on up here!" he shouted.

In shock, I threaded my way through the onlookers and

climbed up on the platform. There was some light applause from the crowd and a conspicuous lusty cheer from the back of the tent that could only have come from a clump of my brothers. Mr. Axelrod pinned the white ribbon to my dress. Mother was nowhere to be seen.

"In second place, Miss Dovie Medlin!"

Dovie simpered her way up and stood next to me while the mayor pinned on her red ribbon. She sniggered and admired it. I was mightily relieved that she hadn't won; she was bordering on unbearable as it was. I almost expected her to turn and stick her tongue out at me. She was just that type.

"Ladies and gentlemen, boys and girls, the first place ribbon in the novice tatting category goes to . . . Miss Lula Gates! Let's have a big cheer for Miss Lula Gates!"

Lula came up. I wanted her to stand next to me, but she had to stand next to Dovie while they pinned her blue ribbon on her. I was still in shock and looked down at the upturned faces in the tent, trying to find my family. How had I won a ribbon? My tatting was nothing to write home about. After a final round of applause, I stumbled back down off the stage to pats on the back and words of congratulations.

"Well done, Lula," I said, always the good sport, especially in a contest where there was absolutely no chance of my winning. "You deserve to win. Your tatting's the best."

"How would *you* know?" said Dovie, flouncing by. I would have punched her except that there were too many witnesses.

Lula graciously said, "Thank you, Callie. I'm sure you deserve a ribbon too."

"The trouble is that I don't," I said. And I didn't, although Mother would probably faint with happiness when she heard. Mrs. Gates came up to us, flushed with pleasure.

"Well, girls," she said, "this is certainly a fine occasion."

"Hello, Mrs. Gates," I said. "Lula did a good job. She deserved to win."

"Thank you, Calpurnia. I'm sure you deserve a prize as well," said Mrs. Gates.

"Hmm," I said, doubtfully. "Have you seen my entry, ma'am? Do you want to go look at the other work?"

"We'd like to, but we can't. Lula is also entered in knitting and embroidery."

I wished them luck and headed off to the exhibition tables and pushed through the crush to the tatting table. Each entry had been pinned to a square of black velvet, the better to display its intricacy. The adults' entries were delicate works of art, collars and antimacassars as detailed and fine as a spider's web. Next to them were the few—very few—novice pieces. I pushed forward and saw my own lopsided collar on display, the black background nicely pointing up every dropped stitch of white thread. And my name, my *full* name, prettily lettered on a card to tell the whole world who had created this mess.

I surveyed the entries suspiciously. Yep, there were three. Even though I knew full well that I wasn't any good at tatting, having this fact confirmed by strangers was not pleasant. So much for my future in lace making, I thought sourly. Of course, I had absolutely no interest in going down that particular path, but now that others had said I couldn't, I felt oddly unhappy. And if there was to be no Science for me, and no Domestic Arts either, what was left? Where was my place in the world? This was too big and too frightening to ponder. I consoled myself with Granddaddy's words on the fossil record and the Book of Genesis: It was more important to understand something than to like it. Liking wasn't necessary for understanding. Liking didn't enter into it.

I headed out of the tent wearing my fancy rosette. Should I take it off? If I wasn't going to care about the work, then I shouldn't care about the prize, either. My hand moved to the ribbon but then froze. My brain clearly said "take it off," and my hand distinctly replied "no." I walked that way, my hand on the ribbon, mired in my ambivalence, to the refreshment tent. I would treat myself to a glass of Coca-Cola while thinking what to do with my prize. I was ready for "the Delicious and Refreshing Drink." Ethical questions were always so tiring.

A long line of folks waited to sample the new invention. My spirits sank when Mr. Grassel lined up right behind me.

"Hello, Callie," he said jovially. "I see you got a ribbon there. Let me see." He made as if to finger my ribbon, and I shrank away from him.

"It's for tatting," I said flatly. "Sir."

"Your family keeping well?" he said.

"All well."

Travis wandered up, sporting a big blue ribbon, happier than I'd seen him in a long time. He came over to show it to me, and I grabbed his arm and pulled him into line with me.

"Say, let me see your ribbon, boy," Mr. Grassel said. "What's it for? 'Best Angora Rabbit.' There's considerable money in Angora, son. Off to an early start there, aren't you?"

"Thank you, sir," said Travis, looking surprised, "but Bunny's my pet. I can't sell him. He's the biggest, furriest rabbit I've ever had."

"No need to sell him," said Mr. Grassel. "You can put him at stud and charge breeding fees."

Travis looked intrigued by this. He dealt mainly in cats, and no one had ever suggested money could be made by breeding Jesse James or Bat Masterson.

"So you don't have to sell your rabbit?" he said.

"No, Travis," Mr. Grassel said. "It's when someone rents Bunny for an hour to put with their lady rabbit to get babies."

"And then I get him back?"

"Sure, then you get him back," Mr. Grassel said.

"And you get money for this?"

"Cash money. On the nose," he said.

"Gosh, I never thought of that. And you think Bunny wouldn't mind?"

"Oh," said Mr. Grassel, winking with a sly smile, "I'd wager Bunny would like it a lot. He'd hop to work with a spring in his step." He tittered.

Travis looked thoughtful, and I could tell that whole new

worlds were opening up to him as we slowly inched toward the counter.

I turned my back on Mr. Grassel and pretended to study the red-and-white advertising bunting overhead. Mr. Grassel finally struck up a conversation with the folks behind him and left us alone. Then it was our turn, and we each paid our nickel for a Coca-Cola. We carefully carried our fizzing drinks outside. Travis lifted his to drink and exclaimed, "Oh! It tickles!" I held mine up and felt the bubbles dancing against my lips, then sipped it, feeling it burn in my throat, raw and sweet and unlike anything I'd had before. How could you ever drink milk or water again after this? We both downed the stuff greedily and straightaway ran back into the tent to stand in line again. This time we bought two cups apiece, spending the last of our money. We drank them more slowly, looking at the rising bubbles and making them last. We both felt extraordinarily peppy and, I would say, extremely refreshed. Travis let loose a rip-roaring belch that had us both giggling uncontrollably.

"Don't let Mother hear you doing that!" I said.

"No, no!" *Uuurp*. "Not me!" *Uuuuuurp*.

Lula and Mrs. Gates went by, Lula covered with so many rosettes that she looked like a walking Christmas tree. She and Travis waved at each other, and he ran off after her. I no longer cared that I was third out of three novice lace makers. Who cared? I wondered where Granddaddy was while I staked out my dubious claim to lace-making fame. Lamar came by, looking for Lula. "Lamar," I said, "have you seen Granddaddy?"

"Last time I saw him he was over in the machinery tent. I think he's been there all day. It's over past the livestock. Say, Callie, can you lend me a nickel?"

"I don't have a cent."

Lamar looked at me suspiciously. "What about your prize money?"

I laughed. "*Prize* money! That's a good one! They gave me this ribbon, that's all."

"What good is a ribbon? Why are you laughing like that? Why don't they give you some money instead? I need some money for the shooting gallery. I never have any money."

"You made lots of money at the gin. What happened to it?"

"Nothing," he said sullenly.

"You spent it at the store, didn't you? All that penny candy." He had no answer to that. I left him grousing about the state of his finances and headed off to the machinery tent. Of course that's where Granddaddy would be. I should have thought of it earlier. Cattle and cotton no longer held any allure for him. As I got closer, the smell of tobacco in the air grew denser. Actual clouds of smoke were rolling out of the tent flap and seeping through the seams. There were so many men smoking inside the tent that it appeared to be on fire.

Coughing, I made my way inside, pushing through the throngs of men and boys, all clustered excitedly around the latest in threshers and plows. But the biggest clutch of admiring onlookers milled around something at the far end of the tent. I shoved my way down there, mouthing a token *pardon me* in the

noisy crush, and ran into Harry escorting Fern Spitty and trying to clear a path for her through the near riot.

"Harry!" I shouted. "Have you seen Granddaddy?"

"He's over there right next to it. He hasn't moved all day."

"What is it?" I screamed.

"An auto-mobile!"

"Oh!" Fern and I mouthed and mimed hellos and good-
byes to each other, and he led her away. I noticed that she had
her arm tucked through his.

The place was absolutely packed. It took me another five
minutes to get through there, and I thought I'd suffocate with
all the cigars and pipes, but at least I was near the ground where
the air was slightly fresher. You couldn't see the top of the tent
at all—it was completely obscured by rolling clouds of smoke.
Finally, just when I thought I would pass out, I shoved my way
through the last ring of spectators and there it was, in all its
dazzling glory, something never seen before: a carriage without
a horse.

How to describe it? It looked like speed incarnate, its every
line carved by the wind. There were the shining brass appoint-
ments, the gracefully curved mudflap, the tufted black leather
seat. And there was my own grandfather sitting on that seat,
peering intently at the steering wheel as if mesmerized. A tall
man sat in the machine next to him, shouting in his ear and ges-
turing at the controls. He turned out to be the owner, and
Granddaddy was offering him cash on the spot for the machine—
twice what he'd paid, then three times, then five times—but the

tall man would not sell at any price. I wormed my way up to the auto-mobile and tugged on Granddaddy's coat as the owner shouted "Sorry! She's not for sale!" and climbed out of the machine.

Granddaddy saw me and then spoke again with the owner and pointed at me. I couldn't hear what they were saying, but Granddaddy was claiming me as his own, and so a second later the tall man lifted me up and placed me on the seat next to my grandfather. The crowd evidently liked this from the buzzing cheer it sent up, increasing the din to an unbelievable level. The noise momentarily stunned me, and all I could think about was that the backs of my legs were sticking to the leather and I needed to pull my dress down over my knees. But a second later someone whisked me out of the car and set me back on the ground. Granddaddy climbed out the other side, and the tall man nodded at two more bystanders, who scrambled to take our places. There was no question of driving the thing; it was an overwhelming experience to merely sit in it, to see it and touch it, to be in its presence, even at rest.

Granddaddy took me by the hand, and we began our struggle back to the entrance. The noise and the smoke and the press of people made me lightheaded and limpsy. I thought, *Right, I'm going to see what it feels like to faint after all, but if I faint in here I'll have to do it standing up because there's nowhere to fall. That might be a first.* At the moment when I thought I couldn't stand it anymore, we pushed outside and stood panting in the fresh air.

I puffed, "You tried to buy the machine, didn't you?"

"He would not sell at any price, and I don't blame him," he said. "We have to hurry home. I must write—no, telephone—the Duryea factory in Massachusetts and place an order at once. The internal combustion engine. Think of it! The power of four horses!"

"I don't feel so well," I said. "I think I'll rest awhile. You go on ahead."

Granddaddy peered at me, saying, "You look flushed. Are you sure you're all right?"

"It's the smoke. I'm fine," I said feebly as the world went black and I pitched over backward.

Now, FAINTING. There's a subject I'd always wondered about. The heroines in books seemed to faint a lot, swaying genteelly onto a handy padded couch or into the convenient arms of some concerned suitor. These heroines were always willowy and managed to land in graceful postures of repose, and were revived with the merest passing of a decorated flagon of smelling salts under their noses.

I, on the other hand, apparently went over like a felled ox and was lucky to land on the grass and avoid cracking my head open. What brought me to was not the whiff of smelling salts but a half bucket of cold water thrown in my face. I opened my eyes and looked up at the sky. A ring of faces peered down at me. *How blue the sky is,* I thought. *And look, there goes a cirrus cloud, it looks like Bunny's fur, and why are all my family staring at me like that, and which one of my stupid brothers is throwing water on me?*

"Pet, pet, can you hear me?" Harry's voice came from a long way off.

I located his face, which for some odd reason was undulating, and croaked, "Sure I can, Harry."

Next to Harry I saw Fern Spitty. She was vibrating strangely, her enormous hat blocking out a good part of the horizon. And even though I had seen her half a dozen times before, I said dreamily, "Hello. I'm pleased to make your acquaintance." For this I got another half bucket of water in the face.

All right, enough of that. I pushed myself up and shook water from my face like a wet dog and glared at the circle around me. Granddaddy took my wrist and felt my pulse. "Calpurnia," he said, "what is the order of the spider commonly known as daddy longlegs?"

"Opiliones," I said tartly.

"Very good," he said. "I believe she is coming around."

"Stop that water," I said to the circle at large.

Next to Granddaddy were Travis and Sam Houston. I couldn't see a bucket anywhere. No doubt one of them was holding it behind his back. Then of course there followed a big foofaraw about getting me to my feet and slapping the grass off me and getting me a lemonade and putting me into a borrowed gig to get me home. It wasn't far, but no one would let me walk.

Mother and Father weren't to be found, so Harry drove, and Fern came along for the ride.

The fresh air blowing across my face as we trotted smartly home made me feel worlds better. The attention was welcome at first but then quickly became oppressive as I perked up.

Viola met us at the door, took one look at me, and said, "Lord, what now, Mister Harry?"

I didn't think there was any need for her to take that tone, especially in front of a visitor.

"It's nothing, Viola," I said with great dignity. "I fainted, that's all. You need not concern yourself with me."

"She's fine, Viola," said Harry. "It was smoky and hot in the tent. Let us sit down. Miss Spitty, do you care for a cup of tea? Perhaps a glass of cold lemonade?"

Well, Miss Spitty thought a cup of tea would be delightful, and Viola went off to make it. We sat in the parlor and looked at each other. I searched her face closely and found her expression entirely lacking in the grasping quality that Minerva Goodacre had displayed. Miss Spitty had strawberry blond hair, which was definitely unfashionable, but I found it a beautiful color. Her complexion was a faint pink, and her eyes were a light blue, and although she gave an overall impression of paleness and delicacy, her alert expression and mobile features saved her from looking insipid. Compared with the odious Miss Goodacre, she stood up well. Perhaps I would have to bestow my approval on her after all. Everyone would be greatly relieved.

She smiled at me. I smiled at her. The clock ticked on the mantel.

Viola came back in with a tray of the best china and set it down. She looked at me. "Miz Calpurnia," she said.

"What?"

"I think it's time for you to go rest. After you fainting and all."

"I feel all right."

"I *think*," said Viola, "it's time for you to go rest."

"I'd like some tea," I said.

"I *think*," she said, "it's *time. Right. Now.*"

"Oh."

"I'll get you tea in your room," she said.

"Okay." Unwanted again. Still, the idea of curling up with *Treasure Island* and a cold cloth wasn't such a bad one. I left the parlor to the accompaniment of the inviting clash of crockery and the light tinkle of teaspoons, and went upstairs. SanJuanna brought me a pitcher of cool water and a fresh towel. Viola came up later carrying a tray set with the second-best china as a peace offering for my banishment.

She said, "You be careful with this tray. If you break one thing—"

"You don't have to tell me that."

She put the tray down and inspected my ribbon, which I'd put on my dresser.

"You got you a prize," she said. "How did that happen?"

"How do you think it happened?" I said grumpily.

"The judges was all blind peoples?"

"Ha ha."

"I got it," she said. "There was only three entries."

"Yep."

"Hmm. Still, you don't need to be telling folks that part. Now, don't chip nothing."

She closed the door as she left. I admired the graceful gold-and-pink rose pattern on the translucent bone china and figured that some of the trappings of civilization weren't so bad after all. I sipped my tea and turned back to my afternoon companions of pirates, parrots, and the sea.

CHAPTER 24

HARRY WOOS AGAIN

Feeble man can do much by his powers of artificial selection. . . .

COD-LIVER OIL. The grim specter of the teaspoon laden with the reeking oil suddenly leaped into my brain when I heard the wagon coming up the drive a couple of hours later, with Mother and Father and the three younger boys. If Mother thought I'd fainted due to sickness, I'd be in for it. Harry told me later that he and Fern had gone back to the fair and found our parents and told them the story. Harry stressed the smokiness of the tent in an effort to avert the deadly dosing, and this apparently did the trick. That and the fact that I ran out and met them all on the front porch looking as cheerful and lively as I could, wearing my prize ribbon, practically capering with girlish good health.

"Look, look what I won. Isn't it exciting?" I called out, gleefully pointing at my ribbon. I wasn't above being a big, fat imposter if it diverted attention away from a potential drenching with the world's foulest substance.

"My goodness! A prize!" There were many exclamations of approval. Mother looked startled and pleased. She didn't mention cod-liver oil, but she did say, "Do you feel all right, Callie? Your color's high. Alfred, do you think we should send for Dr. Walker?"

Father said, "She looks fine to me, my dear, but if you're worried—"

"I don't feel sick, ma'am," I said. "I'm excited because I won a ribbon, that's all."

Jim Bowie said, "How come you got a white ribbon and Travis got a blue one?"

"It's because I'm so special, J.B."

"Really? Gosh, Callie."

"No, not really. I'm fooling you. A blue ribbon is lots better than a white one. Travis and Bunny won the best prize there is." As I said this, I wondered if Mother would make me come clean about my entry, but she kept twinkling at my ribbon. Strange. Then I realized that she didn't know. Perhaps she hadn't noticed, or maybe she hadn't gone by the display, or maybe Lula and Dovie had taken their pieces down before she got there. Mother looked so gratified. Did I have to be the one to tell her?

"Uh, J.B.," I said in a loud voice, "tatting wasn't a strong field this year."

"Huh?"

I glanced at Mother, who was chatting with Travis.

I raised my voice. "The entrants. In the tatting class. Not so strong."

"Wha—?"

"Anyone could have won a ribbon, J.B., is what I'm saying."

"Why are you talking so loud? Can I have your ribbon? I never win the Firefly Prize. I'd like to have a ribbon."

Mother didn't look as if she'd heard me. My courage, watery and irresolute to begin with, ebbed away. I took off my so-called prize and pinned it on J.B., and he dashed away to admire himself in the hall-tree mirror. Mother started up the stairs to take off her hat.

"Ma'am, where's Harry?" I called.

She stopped on the landing, one hand on the rail, the other reaching for her hatpin. "He's walking Fern Spitty home," she said. Her expression was shuttered.

"And . . . ?"

"What do you mean, and? And nothing."

"I wondered if . . ." I wondered if this was good news or bad, that was all. But I had no intention of meddling.

"Please don't wonder, Calpurnia. I find it's dangerous when you wonder." Mother started up the stairs again. "And kindly don't meddle."

There she went, reading my mind again. It was scary. And me, *dangerous*? That was a laugh. At least I had the answer though: Fern was good news. But if Mother thought Harry courting Fern was a good idea, what did this mean about her ambitions for him to go to the university? I couldn't figure it out.

A FEW DAYS LATER, Harry went to dinner at the Spittys' home on the San Marcos Road. He came home long after we were all asleep. I noticed that nobody quizzed him the next morning at the breakfast table. I opened my mouth once or twice but thought better of it. Then Fern and her parents came to Sunday afternoon tea at our house. This was in truth the slimmest of formalities, as our families had been acquainted for years. I wondered why they were coming to tea instead of dinner. Did it have anything to do with the fact that the children were banished from these genteel afternoon entertainments? Or that Granddaddy wouldn't have stuck around for tea at gunpoint?

I got to see Fern arrive before we were all ordered outside to play (meaning, disappear). Her dress was rose-colored silk. Her hat was an enchanting confection of plumes and gossamer silk, dyed to match her dress. She made an appealing picture, unlike the loathsome Goodacre.

I went out through the kitchen. Viola was bent over an elaborate cake, holding her breath and applying the final decorations of nonpareils, those tiny edible metallic nuggets that crunched thrillingly between the teeth. SanJuanna was arranging crustless finger sandwiches and candied flowers on an enormous silver tray. Neither one of them looked up. The atmosphere was tense. They were both dressed in their good dark clothes and wearing spotless starched white aprons, ruffles standing out at their shoulders like wings. I walked out the back door to the laboratory. Why waste time "playing," as I'd been ordered, when I could spend some valuable time with Granddaddy? He didn't find me dangerous when I wondered about something. In fact, he encouraged it.

"Good afternoon, Calpurnia," he said. "Are you not having afternoon tea today?"

"Mother said we had to go outside while the Spittys are here. She's probably worried I'll frighten them off."

"That may be," said Granddaddy, "although why Margaret finds you a frightening child, I don't understand."

"Thank you, sir. Neither do I."

"Good, we're in agreement. Kindly set this beaker up for another run, will you?"

We busied ourselves in the shabby laboratory while the mating dance went on in the parlor.

"It's funny," I said, "that girls have to be pretty. It's the boys that have to be pretty in Nature. Look at the cardinal. Look at the peacock. Why is it so different with us?"

"Because in Nature it is generally the female who chooses," he said, "so the male must clothe himself in his finest feathers to attract her attention. Whereas your brother gets to choose from the young ladies, so they have to do their best to catch his eye."

"It's much too much work," I said. "All the clothes, the hats. And the hair dressing. When Mother dressed my hair for the piano recital, why, it took ages. And the corsets! Mrs. Parsons faints all the time in the summer from her corset. I don't know how they stand it."

"Neither do I. It's a silly idea. Your grandmother wasn't one for such nonsense."

"Granddaddy."

"Hmm?"

"Tell me about her. Grandmother, I mean."

"What do you want to know about her?"

"Everything. I've never heard any stories about her. She died before I was born."

"She did? Yes, I suppose she did. She was a woman who grew hard later in life."

"Was she interested in science?"

"Not particularly. And you must remember, we were struggling to recover from the War. The economy was in shambles. I was trying to build up a business and had no time left over for studying the natural world or anything else for that matter. Hand me that other beaker, will you? She was an excellent needlewoman. And she did enjoy reading novels in the spare time that she had."

"I got a prize at the fair for tatting." I grimaced.

"Did you? I didn't know you were interested in that sort of thing."

"I'm not. I hate it, and I'm no good at it. I haven't told Mother that it was third place out of three."

"Never mind. Tatting was never my strong suit, either."

I thought he was joking but you could never be sure. We worked side by side for a few peaceful hours until Viola rang the bell. I was grateful for those hours. I had been missing him.

CHAPTER 25

CHRISTMAS EVE

I would almost as soon believe with the old and ignorant cosmogonists, that fossil shells had never lived,
but had been created in stone so as to mock the shells
now living on the sea-shore.

I CHERISHED THE INFREQUENT hours I had with Granddaddy. As
Christmas loomed on the horizon, our paltry time together
shrank even further. I worked in the kitchen at Viola's elbow,
which I think she found more aggravating than usual, as she had
to cook and teach me at the same time.

J.B. quizzed me. "Callie, how long until Christmas?"

"Look, J.B." I held up my hand. "See my fingers?"

"Yes."

"Well, this finger is for today, and this one is for tomorrow,
and this one is for the day after that, which is Christmas.
You see?"

"Yes."

"Do you understand now?"

"Yes."

"Good."

"But, Callie, how long until Christmas?"

Question for the Notebook: When does the young human organism get a grasp of time? The five-o'clock possum living in the wall understands time, so why doesn't J.B.? He's driving me batty.

I looked at this last sentence. Granddaddy had taught me that a scientific log was a citadel of the facts and that opinion didn't enter into it. I erased my comment, relieved that I'd only written it in pencil.

Father and Alberto came through the door with a stunted pine they had found in the oak scrub (evergreens did not do well in our part of the world). J.B. went into a positive frenzy. "Look, look, Callie, it's our Christmas treeeeeee! It must be Christmas!"

We spent the afternoon making decorations from colored paper and clamping tiny candles in tiny holders to the branches. Harry made a star out of shiny silver cardboard and placed it on top of the tree with no need of a ladder, it was that puny. As a finishing touch, we arranged cotton bolls on the boughs to look like snow, something we had all heard about but never seen.

The world of Methodist Fentress was divided into those families who opened their presents on Christmas Eve and those who opened them on Christmas Day. Fortunately we were Christmas Eve-ers. According to our minister, Mr. Cornelius Barker, presents were a pointless, expensive, pagan diversion. Yes, well, good luck explaining that to seven children. My mother had no success with it, and neither did the Reverend Barker, although to give him credit, he didn't try all that hard. He came to dinner once a month, and as far as I could tell, he was the one guest Granddaddy looked forward to. They addressed each other as Walter and Cornelius, which scandalized Mother, and they baited each other in genial discussions of Genesis versus the Fossil Record. Mother scored the coup of having the Reverend come to our house for supper following the Christmas Eve services.

We spent a large part of Christmas Eve day making sure that everyone was well scrubbed—no small undertaking, as it meant heating a huge amount of water. Then we assembled in the front hall for inspection. For once, no one was sent back to the washroom for more work on his neck or her nails.

The night was clear and cold, and we bundled up in our thickest coats and scarves. Harry penned up the dogs so that they wouldn't troop along after us, and then we set off, all except for Granddaddy, who stayed behind to tend the fire in the parlor and enjoy some peace and quiet. Alberto and San-Juanna took the wagon to Our Virgin of Guadalupe in Martin-dale. Viola went off to her own service at All God's Children. I would have liked to have gone with her, but that would never have been allowed. I had walked past her church before and heard music spilling from the falling-down clapboard building; the spirited singing and proclamations of joy emerging from it beat the other churches all hollow, to my mind.

We set off with lanterns and sang carols on the way. I held J.B.'s hand and pointed out various constellations to him.

"Look, J.B., there's Canis Major and Canis Minor. That means the big dog and the little dog."

J.B. looked concerned. "There's no dogs in the sky, Callie."

"They aren't dogs, they're stars. Some people a long time ago thought they looked like dogs."

"They don't look like Ajax. They don't look like Matilda. I think you're fibbing. Mama says you're not supposed to fib."

I myself had trouble making a dog or a bull or a lion out of the distant pinpoints of light. How had the ancients come up with such cockeyed fancies?

We rounded the corner, and there was the Methodist church, lit with a thousand lamps. We filed into our pew, all except for Harry, who went up to assist Miss Brown at the organ. She played vigorously, pulling out the stops with a flourish and treading away like mad on the bellows pedal while Harry turned the pages. We sang "Hark, the Herald Angels Sing," and the music made my feelings about Miss Brown thaw. A little.

When it was over, Mr. Barker walked home with us. Sam Houston pinched me, daring me to cry out as we walked behind the grown-ups. In retaliation, I shouldered him into a puddle. Wet shoes would teach him.

We smelled the fragrant smoke from our own chimney as we rounded the bend. Viola was back from her service, and she and Granddaddy stood at the front door. As we entered the parlor, she lit the dozens of tiny candles on the Christmas tree, and they flickered like fairy lights. The fire roared high. On the sideboard, a cut-glass punch bowl glinted, filled with mulled red wine redolent of cloves. There was a silver pitcher of hot cider for the children (sweet cider, of course, not hard). I noticed the quiet passing of another milestone: For the first time, Harry got a cup of Christmas wine.

My parents were about to exchange their brief Christmas kiss, the only time they bussed in front of us, when Mother remembered the presence of the minister and ducked her head in embarrassment. Father took her hand and kissed it instead, murmuring, "Margaret."

The minister inquired whether Granddaddy had yet received any word about the Plant. I could tell that his interest, like that of the irrepressible Mr. Hofacket, was genuine.

"No, Cornelius, no word as yet." Granddaddy lit a cigar and politely blew the smoke toward the ceiling. "You can't rush science. These things take time."

After a ham supper, during which we children grew increasingly restless, my parents took pity on us and distributed the presents. Despite his philosophy of presents, Mr. Barker stayed on and exclaimed over the fineness of our spoils.

For the family at large there was a new stereoscope, which all the children were to share equally (fat chance of that happening). There were viewing cards of the Great Sphinx of Egypt, the Fabulous White City of Chicago, the Fascinating

Lives of the Esquimaux. Everybody got a big bright orange, a rare and expensive present during the winter. I saved mine for later.

There was a handsome new rocking horse for J.B., who had worn the rockers of his old one down to nubbins. It was covered in cowhide and had a real horsehair tail. For Sul Ross there were several wooden pull toys and a spinning top. Travis received a book on raising rabbits for fun and profit and a new curry comb. I knew he'd been hoping for a donkey, but he seemed happy enough. Lamar got a leather case containing a steel protractor, a ruler, and a compass. Sam Houston got *The Adventures of Sherlock Holmes*. Harry got a new suit of the finest dark navy wool, perfect for the young man about to make his mark in the world. And of course they all got brown woollen socks knitted by yours truly, displaying various degrees of competence. J.B.'s socks, the first ones, were lumpy and deformed, but by the time I got up to the older boys, they looked passable; I had even managed to knit a modest cable pattern into Father's and Granddaddy's. Much was made over this later handiwork, which, while not too embarrassing, did not warrant the fervent praise it received. (I suspected a put-up job.)

I gave Mother a selection of pressed flowers. She received a pair of garnet and jet earrings from Father and in turn gave him a dashing green-checked vest to wear on his business trips to Austin.

Viola was working in the kitchen but had received her gifts

of snuff and a thick red flannel petticoat from Mother earlier in the day.

Granddaddy got a handsome box of cigars all the way from a place called Cuba. On the label was a colorful picture of a woman dancing in a long flounced skirt; the box was attractive and the perfect size in which to keep one's treasures. I could tell that Lamar coveted it but was too afraid to ask Granddaddy for it.

"Go on," I whispered. "Ask him if you can have it. He won't bite."

"He won't bite *you*, you mean. He *might* bite *me*."

"Don't be a sissy, Lamar"—I used the magic word on him. Worked every time.

He wheeled and marched up to Granddaddy. "Sir, can I have that box? When you're through with it?"

Surprised, Granddaddy looked at him. "Of course you can . . . um, Travis."

Lamar blinked. "Thank you, sir," and scuttled back to his place.

"See?" I whispered. "He's actually nice once you get to know him."

"He called me Travis," he hissed.

I giggled, and he glared at me. I said, "At least you got first dibs on the box."

"How come you don't want it?"

"I already have two—no, wait, three—of them."

"Well, bully for you."

Lamar could be such a pill sometimes.

And I, what did I receive? Well, the little boys gave me a crumpled bag of sweets, and the older boys gave me new hair ribbons. My parents gave me a beautiful silver locket engraved with my initials. And then there was one more present for me. I could tell it was a book, even wrapped up as it was in brown paper. Ah, a book. How satisfying to have another one to add to the small library accumulating on the shelf above my bed. The book was so thick and hefty that I knew it was a reference book of some kind, a text, maybe even an encyclopedia. I peeled back the stiff paper to reveal the word *Science* printed in curlicues.

"Oh," I exclaimed. Such magnificence! But even better than the solid reality of the book in my hand was the gladsome fact that my mother and father at last understood the kind of nourishment I needed to survive. I beamed at my parents with excitement. They smiled and nodded. I ripped the paper off to reveal the whole title: *The Science of Housewifery*.

"Oh!" I stared in befuddlement. It made no sense to me. What could it mean? Was the writing even English? *The Science of Housewifery*, by Mrs. Josiah Jarvis. This couldn't be right. My hands turned to wood. I fumbled the book open to the Table of Contents and read: "Cooking for the Invalid." "Favorite Pickles and Relishes." "Removing Difficult Stains." I stared at these grim subjects.

Conversation trailed off, and the room became silent except for the monotonous thwacking of J.B. riding his rocking horse in the corner. All eyes were on me. I looked at Granddaddy, whose brow puckered in concern. I looked at Mother, who paled and then flushed. I was committing the sin of embarrassing her in front of a guest. Her face turned grim.

She said, "What do you say, Calpurnia?"

What does Calpurnia say? What *could* I say? That I wanted to throw the book—no better than kindling—into the fireplace? That I wanted to scream at the unfairness of it all? That at that moment I could have done violence, that I could have punched them all in the face? Even Granddaddy. Yes, even him. Encouraging me the way he had, knowing that there was no new century for me, no new life for this girl. My life sentence had been delivered by my parents. There was no pardon or parole. No aid from any corner. Not from Granddaddy, not from anybody. The stinging whip of hives lashed my neck.

"Calpurnia?"

Great fatigue washed over me like a tidal wave, drowning my anger. I was too tired to fight anymore. I did the hardest thing I'd ever done in my life. I reached down into the depths of my being, and I dredged up the beginnings of a watery smile.

I whispered, "Thank you." Just two words. Just two artificial words, coming from my own hypocritical mouth. Tears came to my eyes. I felt like I was disintegrating.

At that moment J.B. fell off his rocking horse and set up a tremendous squalling. In the general confusion, I gathered up my presents and slipped upstairs to my room. I stared out my window into the blackness. A few minutes later, I saw the receding glow of the minister's lantern like a distant firefly in the black night. Sul Ross and J.B. thumped and laughed on the stairs. I changed into my nightgown and climbed into bed. I looked at the ribbons, the locket, and the book, all laid out on my dresser next to the hummingbird's nest in its glass box. I closed my eyes, too exhausted to cry myself to sleep.

CHAPTER 26

WORD COMES

Although the beaks and feet of birds are generally quite clean, I can show that earth sometimes adheres to them: in one instance I removed twenty-two grains of dry argillaceous earth from one foot of a partridge, and in this earth there was a pebble quite as large as the seed of a vetch.

FOR MONOTONOUS MONTHS I had circled the mail on the hall table like a buzzard, poking through endless boring letters and bills before turning away each day in blank disappointment. Word did come, two days after Christmas, but not in the letter we had been expecting.

It came in the form of a personal telegram, a frightening event. Businesses used telegrams to buy and sell, but an individual got a telegram only for a death in the family. It came with Mr. Fleming, the telegraphist, who bicycled over to our house with it in his pouch. He had been a private in the War, and although he hadn't served under Granddaddy, he admired him and was determined to be of service to him when he could. I met Mr. Fleming at the end of the driveway, where I was dolefully flailing about in the drainage ditch looking for water striders. There were none, and there was no point to it, but it was either this or sit in my room and read my Christmas present.

"Callie Vee," he said, dismounting his bike, "I got a telegram here for Mr. Tate." I assumed he meant my father, and I scoured my brain to think of who might have died. It had to be his aunt in Wichita, an old lady I'd never met.

"Is it from Wichita, sir?" I asked.

"Naw. I ain't supposed to say. Oh, all right, you forced it outta me—it's from Washington."

"What?"

"It's from someplace in Washington."

"My father knows someone in Washington?" It had to be something to do with the cotton trade, although it was odd that it wasn't addressed to the gin.

"It's not for your father. It's for Captain Tate."

"Pardon me?"

"It's not for your father. It's for your grandfather."

"My . . ."

"I figured he'd want it right away," he said.

I found my voice. "Give me that!"

He shied away and looked at me as if I were crazy. "What are you talking about? I can't give it to you."

"*Give me that telegram!*"

"Little girl, you are being extremely rude. What's got into you? I can't give it to you. I got to deliver it to an adult over the age of eighteen. Company regulations dictate that I got to give it to an adult—"

"Sorry sorry—"

"—and I take the responsibilities of my office real serious."

My heart was thumping so hard I thought it would vault through my ribs. "Come *on*, Mr. Fleming." I took his arm and tried to drag him up the drive, but he was a man in a huff with a bicycle, and he wasn't very draggable. Those fifty anguished yards to the house took a lifetime. I felt like I was trapped in one of those nightmares where you're churning in quicksand. "Hurry!"

We made it to the porch, where Mr. Fleming paused to shake me off and square his cap. I burst through the door shouting, "Granddaddy! Granddaddy, where are you?"

Mother called in a cool voice from the front parlor, "Calpurnia, dear, there's no need to shout. Mrs. Purtle is visiting. Come in and say hello, darling."

Normally I'd have quick-marched into the parlor in response to her tone, but there was the library door, tantalizingly close. What to do? I spun in the hallway like a bobber in the river. Mother caught sight of Mr. Fleming behind me in the hall and frowned. She knew what telegrams were about.

He tipped his cap. "Good afternoon there, Mrs. Tate. Sorry to interrupt you, ma'am, but I got a telegram for Captain Tate. It's from Washington."

"Washington?"

"My goodness," twittered Mrs. Purtle, "how exciting."

"Come in, Mr. Fleming. The captain is out collecting his specimens at the river," Mother said, "but I have no idea how to find him."

"I do, I do!" I shouted and ran out the front. The screen door slammed on my mother's words, "You must forgive my daughter. . . ."

I flew to the end of the drive and veered off into the dense brush on the deer path that led to the river across the crescent parcel. I bounded like a deer and swerved like a fox; never had I felt so strong or run so fast.

"It's come!" I cried. "It's here! Word has come! Granddaddy!"

He wasn't at the inlet where I expected to find him. I turned south and ran along the river, calling out his name. I got to the small cliff above the island, the next likely place, but he wasn't there, either. I headed for the dam at the gin, a good five minutes away. I wanted to yell in frustration. I had always known where to find him. And now this.

A startled red-tailed hawk screamed at me from an oak tree. Winded, I kept running but no longer had breath to call out. My brain took up the chant to the pounding rhythm of my feet: Granddaddy Granddaddy Granddaddy. On I ran, right through a family of feral black pigs foraging for pecans, scattering them indignantly in my wake.

At the gin, I came upon Mr. O'Flanagan, who had moved

Polly's stand outside so that they could both take some air. He stood on the steep bank above the water turbines, contentedly puffing on a cigar, looking over his portly belly at the river below. Polly flared his crest and stared at me with a baleful jaundiced eye as I puffed up.

"Have you seen my grandfather, sir?" I cried. I could tell by Mr. O'Flanagan's face that he had not.

"Is something wrong?" he called out in alarm. "What's the matter?"

I dashed across the street to the newspaper, threw open the door, and rushed into the telephone office, where a startled Maggie Medlin was eating a sandwich at the switchboard.

"Have you seen my grandfather?" I croaked.

It took her a moment to swallow her mouthful and say, "No, not today. Is everything all right?"

I turned to go and ran smack into the belly of Mr. O'Flanagan, who'd followed me from the gin. Maggie called out from her room, "Do I need to call the doctor?"

"Calpurnia, is someone hurt?" Mr. O'Flanagan said. He was in my way. I ducked right and dodged left, but he ducked and dodged with me. He moved admirably fast for such a fat man. He grabbed me by the shoulders and shook me and made me look at him.

"Calpurnia, tell me. Are you hurt? Is someone hurt?"

I stood there trying to catch my breath. And suddenly I felt exhausted and overwhelmed. I felt . . . abandoned. What had happened to our time together? How had I let it get away? Why hadn't I *fought* for it? And where was he, on this, the day of all days? I had always been able to find him when I needed him. And now he'd gone off collecting somewhere other than our regular haunts, somewhere I didn't know about and where I couldn't find him. Somewhere secret. Somewhere private. Collecting without me.

Question for the Notebook: Why would he do that? Answer: He'd do that if he was tired of Calpurnia and wanted to be alone. If he was tired of her and her childish company. Right, Calpurnia? Right? Was that it?

"No one's hurt, sir," I managed to get out when I could finally speak, but all I could think was, Had there been the fleeting ghost of irritation on Granddaddy's face when I had interrupted his reading in the library a few days before? Had Mother and Father spoken to him? Told him he was an unhealthy influence on me and advised him to cultivate one of my brothers instead? And then there was the pall of the lost vetch. Oh, I'd found it again, but had he truly forgiven me for being so stupid about losing it in the first place? He had encouraged me to learn how to cook and to knit months earlier when Mother had thrust those chores upon me. He had not comforted me when I held *The Science of Housewifery* in my hands. He must have known all along that the scientific life was not for me, that the jaws of the domestic trap were well and truly sprung. I burst into tears.

"My goodness, girl, what's the matter?" Mr. O'Flanagan

patted me awkwardly. "There there. Let me take you home to your ma."

"No, thank you, Mr. O'Flanagan. I'm all right," I sobbed.

"You sure? You don't look all right." His expression darkened, and he said, "Has someone . . . been . . . after you?"

"No, no, I just need my grandfather," I blubbed, but he didn't look convinced. I pulled my hankie out of my pinafore and soaked it in seconds. I couldn't stop wailing.

"Here you go," he said, handing me his handkerchief. "You look like you need this more than I do. You keep it. Let's go home to your ma."

I could see that Mr. O'Flanagan wasn't going to leave me alone until I calmed down. I blew my nose and with a great effort got a tenuous grip on myself.

"I'm okay," I sniffled. "I'll go home. I'm all right. Thank you. Good-bye." Reluctantly he let me go. I trudged into the street and turned toward home.

My grandfather had given me Mr. Darwin's book to read. He had given me the possibility of a different kind of life. But none of it mattered. Instead, there was *The Science of House-wifery* for me. I was blind; I was pathetic. The century was about to change, but my own little life would not change with it. My own, little, life. One I had better get used to. I erupted in tears again like a fountain, a running tide of tears and snot soaking Mr. O'Flanagan's hankie. There was only one last Question left for the Notebook before closing it and putting it away forever, and that was the telegram: Yes? Or No? My grandfather would have to tell me that. I would make him tell me. He owed me that much.

I scrubbed my face with the last dry piece of Mr. O'Flanagan's hankie and glanced back. There he was, fifty yards behind me, seeing me safely home, trying to look like he wasn't following me. At least *somebody* cared about me.

He saw me to the end of the drive before turning around. I collected myself as best I could in an attempt to avoid further interrogation.

My mother was still in the parlor with Mrs. Purtle, pouring tea. Viola came in wearing a clean white apron and bearing a lemon pound cake on a silver tray. Mr. Fleming sat on a spindly chair with one of the good teacups perched on his knee, his delivery pouch at his feet. He looked like he was dug in for the duration and wasn't going to leave until he knew what was in the only telegram he'd ever delivered from Washington.

My mother looked up. "Calpurnia, whatever's the matter? Did you find your grandfather?"

"Nothing's the matter," I said, my voice flat. "And no, I didn't find him."

"Excuse me, ma'am," said Viola, "I believe Captain Tate is working in the shed out back." Viola refused to call it either the laboratory or the former slave quarters.

In the shed out back? The laboratory?

Mother frowned. "I could have sworn he went to the river. Calpurnia, go and fetch him, please. We can't keep Mr. Fleming waiting all day."

"Oh, that's all right, ma'am," he said and nudged his cup an inch or two in the general direction of the teapot, "quite all right."

Not at the river?

"Will you have more tea, Mr. Fleming?"

"Why, thank you kindly, ma'am. I believe I will."

He was not at the river collecting without me. He was in the laboratory working without me.

"Calpurnia? Did you hear me? Go and fetch him. Mrs. Purtle, do try some of this excellent cake. It's Viola's special recipe."

Numbly, I nodded. "I guess I'll go and get him."

I went through the kitchen, where Viola was starting on dinner. She looked up. "What you up to? You look funny."

"I'm not up to anything." I pumped cold water over Mr. O'Flanagan's hankie and pressed it to my face. "And I *am* funny," I muttered through the cloth. "That's the reason I *look* funny, okay?"

"What?" she said over the noise of the whistling kettle.

I dried myself with a scrap of towel and looked in the cracked mirror at the back door. I was still flushed and swollen, but at least I no longer looked completely crazed. I scrutinized myself. Was this the face of a child who bored an old man or an idiot who jumped to conclusions?

"Viola. Do you think I'm boring? Do you think I'm an idiot?"

"Huh. You may be many things, girl, but idiot? Bore? Not those."

"Are you sure?"

"Where do you come up with this stuff?"

"Viola, it's important."

"Not those," she said, and turned back to her cooking. I looked at her narrow shoulders and wiry arms working over our dinner, and I realized that I had always counted on her for other things besides food. Viola had never lied to me. She would not lie to me now. I went over to her and put my arms around her waist and hugged her. I was freshly amazed at the lightness of her person, her tiny bird bones. It was interesting that such a slight frame could contain so large a person.

"Go 'way," she said. "I'm busy."

"Yes, ma'am." And grumpy, as usual, which was reassuring.

"I told you not to give me no ma'am stuff. I ain't no ma'am in this house, girly," she called after me as I closed the door behind me. I threaded my way through the Outside Cats milling on the back porch and headed for the laboratory. My feet were leaden ingots. The short walk took a lifetime.

I pushed back the gunny sack hanging in the doorway and there he sat in the sprung armchair, staring at a flask of something on the counter. He looked up at me, his expression inscrutable.

"It's come, Granddaddy," I said.

"It's come?"

"The word about the Plant has come."

He was silent.

"A telegram from Washington," I said.

"Ah." He tilted his gaze to the ceiling and said quietly, "What does it say?"

I was stupefied. "I don't know," I stammered. "I didn't open it. I'd never open it. It's for you."

"Heavens, Calpurnia, I thought you might have opened it because we're partners in this endeavor, are we not? Are you all right?"

I nodded, not trusting myself to speak.

"Well, then. We must look our best when we get a telegram from Washington."

He stood up and straightened his disintegrating coat and then reached for me, smoothing my hair with his big hands and adjusting my bow. "Are you ready?"

I nodded again. He held out his hand. "Shall we?"

I took his hand, and we walked together to the house, not saying a word. We were about to go up the back steps when I said, "Wait." We stopped and he looked at me. "Yes, Calpurnia?"

"I think," I quavered, "that we should go through the front door today. Don't you?"

"Absolutely right," he said, and we promenaded slowly around the house on the walk, passing the parlor window where three curious heads swiveled after us. All my senses sharpened as we headed for the porch. The lilies had died back to the ground; the bark of the crepe myrtles had all peeled away; there was a mackerel sky. I could feel the press of something important in the atmosphere, the pressure of chill air against me. Hand in hand, we walked up the wide front steps, and my grandfather opened the door for me, bowing me through. My heart raced like a rabbit's.

"Captain Tate." Mr. Fleming snapped to attention in the parlor. "I am glad to find you, sir. I have a telegram here for you all the way from Washington. That's District of Columbia, sir. Not state of."

"Thank you, Mr. Fleming. I am most grateful."

"I figured it was important, so I rushed it right on over."

"Thank you, Mr. Fleming. Most grateful."

"I couldn't trust it to one of the boys."

"Thank you, Mr. Fleming. Grateful."

"Oh—don't get me wrong. They're good boys, or I wouldn't have 'em working for me. But sometimes they get sidetracked, and I figured—"

Mother broke in with, "Mr. Fleming, perhaps you'd care to give the captain his telegram? Now?"

"Oh, yes, yes, ma'am." He dove into his pouch and pulled it out. "Here it is. All the way from Washington. Yessir. All the way."

Mrs. Purtle squeaked and patted her bosom. We all stared at the envelope as if mesmerized.

Granddaddy stepped forward, and Mr. Fleming laid it in his palm. My grandfather's hand slowly closed around it. "I thank you for your trouble, Mr. Fleming," he said, reaching into his vest pocket for a coin.

The telegraphist was having none of it. "No, no, Captain Tate. I'll take no gratuity from you, sir. My pleasure, sir." He saluted smartly and clicked his heels together.

"You are too kind." Then, seeing that Mr. Fleming would not relax, Granddaddy said, "Please be at ease."

Mr. Fleming's posture relaxed a fraction. We all stood there, staring at my grandfather, who in turn contemplated the telegram.

"Ah," he said, looking up. "Thank you again for your trouble, Mr. Fleming." He bowed to my mother and Mrs. Purtle. "Ladies." He pressed the telegram between his hands and turned and walked out. Our collective mouths flopped open, we were that shocked. The unfairness of it, depriving us of this once-in-a-lifetime moment. Who could bear it? How could he do this to us? How could he do this to me?

"Calpurnia," he called from the hallway, "are you not coming?" For a second, I was paralyzed and then I found my powers of locomotion and ran from the room—parlor manners be damned—to join him. I skidded into him at the library door. He opened the door in silence and we went in. The room was chilly with no fire in the grate. The green velvet curtain was drawn back to let the thin winter sunshine wash in.

He sat down at his desk. "Bring a lamp, won't you?" His face was alight with a curious balance of eagerness and gravity.

Trembling, I lit the lamp. What if the answer was no? What would that make us? Nothing more than a deluded old man and a silly little girl. But what if it was yes? Would we not be acclaimed, exalted, famous? Would we not join the immortals? Was it better to know, or not? Either way, he had to still love me. Didn't he?

I sat down on the camel saddle, wishing I could stop time.

Granddaddy looked at the envelope's plain white aspect. Then he took his ivory paper knife and carefully slit it open. The telegram was a single sheet of paper folded once upon itself. He held it out to me.

"Read it to me, dear child."

My hands shook as I reached for the paper. I unfolded it, bent toward the lamp, and read, stumbling over the longer words:

Dear Mr. Tate and Miss Tate:

We, the members of the Plant Taxonomy Committee of the Smithsonian Institution, are pleased to inform you that, after much research and study, we have concluded that you have identified a new species of hairy vetch heretofore unknown. The class is Dicotyledon; the order is Fabales; the family is Fabaceae; the genus is Vicia. It is customary for the first identifier to have the species named after him, or any name he chooses, so long as it is not already in use. May we suggest to you that the plant be known as Vicia tateii? Such would be in keeping with the

regular customs of taxonomy. You may, however, elect
to name the plant otherwise. The choice is yours. The
Institution congratulates you on your perspicacious find.
We remain, yours in Science, et cetera,

Henry C. Larivee, President
Taxonomy Committee, Plants

I carefully refolded the paper in my lap and then looked at him. Motionless, he stared off into space for a long time. I felt an urgent need to say something, but I didn't know what. I couldn't sort anything out. The room was completely still. Far off in the distance, a dog howled. It was Matilda, sounding her unique yodeling call. Odd that she would register with me at that moment. Closer at hand, a pan clattered in the kitchen. The wooden screen door banged shut, and a couple of my brothers scuffled past in the hall. We heard the piano start up in the par-lor, a limpid, haunting melody; Harry had been pressed into playing for our visitors. The music drew my grandfather back from wherever it was he'd gone. His face was wistful, contem-plative, sad.

"Yes," he said at last.

"Yes?" I didn't know what else to say.

A minute later, he said, "It's Chopin. I have always liked that piece. Do you know, Calpurnia . . ." He trailed off.

"Yes, Granddaddy?"

"Do you know . . ."

"Yes, Granddaddy?"

"That I have always liked it best. Of all his work."

"No. I didn't know."

"It's commonly called 'The Raindrop.'"

"I didn't know that."

I could hear Viola ringing the dinner bell on the back porch. Soon she would sound the gong at the foot of the stairs.

He ignored the bell. "The only question, really, is how are we to spend the brief time that is allotted us?"

I wondered if we were going to talk about the telegram. I didn't want the gong to sound. Dinner was only dinner; dinner could wait. By rights we should be free to sit there forever. I looked around the room. I looked at the books, the armadillo, the bottled beast.

"Granddaddy?"

"Yes?"

"What about the telegram?"

"What about it?"

"Well . . ." Viola pounded on the gong. The sound was intrusive, hateful.

"Do you have any questions about it?" he asked.

"No," I said slowly, "I guess not."

"Were you ever in any doubt?"

"I suppose not, but—"

"There are so many things to learn, you see, and so little time is given us. I am old. I thought I would die before it happened."

I stood up and went to him. I tried to hand him the telegram, but he said, "You keep it. Press it in your Notebook."

I pocketed it and put my arms around him. He slipped his arm around me and kissed me, and we leaned together awhile until the inevitable knock came at the door.

I HAD EXPECTED a celebration. I had expected streamers and cake and confetti. I had expected our family to hoist us on their shoulders and carry us aloft in triumph. But Granddaddy never said a word all through dinner, and I spent the meal feeling lifeless. What was wrong with me? Why did I feel so flat on what should have been the happiest day of my life, and my grandfather's life?

Mother glanced at Granddaddy all through dinner and smiled and nodded encouragement at him whenever he looked up, giving him every opportunity to explain the once-in-a-lifetime communication, but instead he chose to apply himself to his plate. Generalized rustling and surreptitious glances from my brothers indicated that they knew something was afoot.

We ate our dinner. It wasn't until SanJuanna was clearing the dessert course that Granddaddy went to the sideboard and poured himself a generous measure of port. He held his glass aloft until the table quieted and all eyes were on him. The port caught the light from the chandelier and splashed a ruby wave across his beard.

He looked like he was about to address us, but then he

turned and pushed open the swinging door to the kitchen and called out for Viola to come into the dining room. She hurried in, wiping her hands on her apron, her brow furrowed in concern.

"Ladies"—he bowed—"gentlemen, I propose a toast. Something rather wonderful has happened. Today I received a telegram from Washington. It came from the Smithsonian Institution, informing me, and Calpurnia, that we have discovered a new species of vetch. A previously unknown specimen. It is henceforth to be called *Vicia tateii*."

Father said, "Well done!"

Mother studied Granddaddy with a puzzled expression, and then turned her gaze to me.

Harry said, "Grandfather, you've put our name down in history."

"Did you win a prize, Callie?" said Jim Bowie. "What did you win?"

"We won a place in the science books," I said.

"What books? What does that mean? Will we get to see them?"

"You will one day, J.B."

Father started clapping and the others followed with applause and hoorays. Here is what I had been waiting for, and it did make me feel more cheerful, although not as much as you'd think.

Father joined Granddaddy at the sideboard, poured himself a good dose of port, and said, "Margaret, will you join us?"

Mother scrutinized me.

"Margaret?"

"Oh," she said, and turned to Father. "Perhaps a small one, Alfred, seeing as it's a special occasion."

Granddaddy said, "Viola, won't you have a glass?"

Viola glanced at Mother and then said, "No, no, Mr. Tate, I couldn't—"

He ignored her and shoved a glass into her hands and then another into SanJuanna's hands—she looked like she would faint. They all stood and raised their glasses. We imitated them with glasses of milk.

Father spoke. "To our good health, to our continuing prosperity and, on this grand occasion, to Grandfather and his scientific endeavors. I must admit that there were times when I wondered about the way you spend your time, but you have proven it to be all worth the while. We are a proud family tonight!"

Harry started up a chorus of "For He's a Jolly Good Fellow" and then led them all in giving three cheers.

"Let's not forget Calpurnia," said Harry, "with her Notebook. I claim some credit for your accomplishments, pet, for having given it to you. Well done."

Another cheer, this time aimed at me. I had to smile at their bright, excited faces.

"It's true," said Granddaddy, raising his glass in my direction. "None of this would have happened without the help of my only grandchild, Calpurnia." He drank serenely.

His only grandchild! There was stunned silence from my brothers, followed by a rising swell of muttering and hissing.

"Pardon me," said Granddaddy, catching his mistake and bowing. "I meant, of course, my only granddaughter." He calmly drank and then sat down. My brothers were in a snit, but I didn't care. My heart pumped gladness through my veins. I was all to him, wasn't I? And he was all to me.

CHAPTER 27

NEW YEAR'S EVE

Man can hardly select, or only with much difficulty, any deviation of structure excepting such as is externally visible; and indeed he rarely cares for what is internal.

FOR THE FIRST TIME EVER, all the children, even down to Jim Bowie, were allowed to stay up to count the chimes of the clock at midnight on New Year's Eve, a wildly exciting event, at least in theory. It was also nerve-racking, as there had been talk by some religious societies that the world was going to end on the first day of the millennium. The newspapers reported that there were wild, bearded men parading the streets in Austin, dressed in long robes and carrying big signs that read REPENT, THE END IS NIGH. Father had pooh-poohed the men as a bunch of cranks, but Travis had taken it seriously and asked me after some thought, "Callie, is the world really going to end tonight?"

"No, silly. Granddaddy explained it to me. The century is merely the marking of the passage of time. Time is man-made and comes from England."

"But what if it does come to an end? Who will look after Jesse James? Who will feed Bunny?"

I could see only one way out of this discussion. "Don't worry, Travis. I will."

"Oh, okay. Thanks, Callie."

We went downstairs to an enormous dinner at six o'clock. The weather was dismal, but there were roaring fires in every room. Mother looked flushed and relaxed, and I noticed she was sipping bubbly wine that seemed to agree with her. Afterward, Father made several toasts and reassured us that the world was not coming to an end; that he was a fortunate man to be surrounded by his loving family, his own father, his own wife, his own children. There was a catch in his voice.

Then we all retired to our rooms to rest for the long evening ahead, to say our prayers and to consider our resolutions. Traditionally, we each had to stand up in turn and recite our resolutions, which Mother wrote down on a paper that she kept pressed in the family Bible until the next year, when the old ones were replaced with new ones.

I lay on my bed and stared out the window at the lowering sky. Part of me wanted our lives to go on as they always had, with all of us living together in our teeming old house. The other part of me yearned for desperate and dramatic change, to leave Fentress far behind. What good was it to have a hairy vetch "mootant" named after me, if my whole life was to be spent in Caldwell County, bounded by Lockhart and San Marcos, pecan trees and cotton fields? Granddaddy had told me I could make whatever I wished of my life. Some days I believed him, and other days I did not. This gloomy overcast afternoon, this last day of the dying century, was definitely turning into a "not" day. There were so many things I wanted to see and do in my lifetime, but how many of them were within my reach? I wrote a list of them on the last page of my Notebook. The red leather cover was creased and the deckled pages were getting grubby. My Notebook, my faithful friend for the past six months. I put it aside and fell asleep and dreamed that I was floating on a river. But it was not my own river. The water was pale green instead of blue, and, strangely, the riverbanks were covered in sand.

Viola sounded the gong at nine o'clock and woke me. We trooped downstairs to bowls of dangerously hot Apple Brown Betty that seared the mouth. We each were given a party cracker to pull, inside of which was a paper crown, a noise-maker, and a miniature tin toy. A brisk market in these favors emerged, with much trading and dealing. Then it was just a matter of sitting and waiting. The younger boys, who had never been up this late, responded to the generalized slackening of discipline by either tearing up and down the stairs or falling fast asleep on the parlor rug.

I ate half of my Christmas orange with ostentatious enjoyment, much to the annoyance of those who had already finished theirs. I saved the other half to eat in a different century. Would an 1899 orange taste different in 1900?

By ten o'clock, we were all exhausted and craving our beds but determined to make it to the magic hour. At eleven, it was time for the annual resolutions. Mother pulled our old resolutions out of the Bible and read them aloud to much laughter and then burned them in the fireplace. My last resolution had been to master darning and spinning. I had made it a lifetime ago, before the hot summer month when my grandfather and I had first recognized each other.

We tried to explain to J.B. what a resolution was, but he was too young to understand. Mother made a resolution for him, namely, that he would learn his ABCs in the coming year. Sul Ross made a resolution to finish his school assignments on time. Travis resolved to spend more time playing with Jesse James. This was impossible, as he toted the gangly cat with him everywhere, tucked into the bib of his overalls.

Then it was my turn. I stood up, pulled my Notebook from my pocket, and opened it to the last page.

"It's not so much a resolution. It's more like a list." I cleared my throat and read, "I want to see the following things before I die: the northern lights. Harry Houdini. The Pacific Ocean or the Atlantic Ocean. Any old ocean at all—it doesn't matter. Niagara Falls. Coney Island. A kangaroo. A platypus. The Eiffel Tower. The Grand Canyon. Snow."

I sat down to silence. Then Harry said, "Very good, pet," and started clapping. My other brothers joined in. Mother's and Father's applause was tepid. I felt vaguely melancholy.

Lamar said, "I resolve to do better in geometry." He spent hours each day running around the house measuring the angle of things with his new steel protractor.

Sam Houston said, "Lula Gates won't let me carry her books home from school, so I resolve to carry Effie Preston's, even if she doesn't want me to. I swear I'm going to do it." This got a good laugh.

Then it was Harry's turn, but he only smiled and said, "It's a secret." There was a general outcry of *that's not fair*.

I said, "You have to tell us, Harry. Otherwise it isn't a real resolution." Finally he relented to get us off his back. He glanced at Mother and said, somewhat weakly, I thought, "I resolve to study hard so I can get into the university next year."

Mother twinkled with pleasure at this, which of course was his intended result, but I could tell his heart wasn't in it, he was just throwing her a sop. The fact that he wouldn't tell us his real resolution made me suspect that it had something to do with Fern Spitty.

Mother's resolution was to make sure that every single one of her children made it to church at least twice a week. There was stirring in the ranks at this but no one had the courage to moan about it to her face.

Father's resolution was to give up dipping snuff. Since he was only allowed to dip at the gin, he'd decided that the agony of having to give it up at the front door every day when he came home outweighed the pleasure of partaking at work. Mother looked delighted and sipped her fizzy wine.

It took some badgering of Granddaddy, who took it jovially enough before he said, "It would be a sad commentary on my life if I were to have any resolutions left at my age. However . . . there is one thing. . . ."

Mystified, I searched my brain. Something to do with

the mutant? Or that he wanted to perfect his pecan spirits? I had no clue.

"I wish to go driving in an auto-mobile," he said. "I hear they have one in Austin."

"But they're dreadful machines!" said Mother. "And so unsafe! They say they're likely to explode without warning, and people are always breaking their arms at the crank."

"True." He smiled. There was a contented, faraway expression on his face. He looked to the world as if he were staring off into the distance; but I knew that he was gazing into the future.

Then there was nothing left to do but sit and wait for the next hour to pass. My parents talked quietly, Granddaddy smoked cigars and read his *National Geographic,* and my brothers and I took turns at fighting off sleep and failing miserably. Finally, *finally,* the clock struck midnight, and as the chimes died out, we heard a cacophony of pots and pans being beaten in the streets all over town. We clasped hands in a circle and sang "Auld Lang Syne." The words were incomprehensible, but the music was lovely. I looked around the circle of dear faces and considered all the gifts that had come to me over the past year. There were Mother and Father, holding hands and looking tired but happy. She had a few threads of gray at her temples, which I hadn't noticed before. There was Harry: proud, tall, handsome, his collar and tie immaculate, a young gentleman in the making. There were Sam Houston and Lamar; there was Travis with Jesse James in his arms; there was yawning Sul Ross. There was J.B., dead on his feet but gamely determined to see in the new year.

And there was my grandfather, adding his low baritone in sad, sweet harmony to the music, his long beard glinting in the firelight. We had been so close to missing each other, he and I. He had turned out to be the greatest gift of all.

Then the pots and pans died out, and the song ended. Everyone except for Mother and Father shuffled up to bed, leaving the two of them to sit up together awhile longer.

I put on my thickest red flannel nightie and dove into bed. Mercifully, SanJuanna had taken the chill off the sheets with a warming pan. I intended to lie there for a while and take stock of my life. That's what you do at the end of the century, don't you? But I think I actually fell asleep right away and only dreamed I was taking stock.

CHAPTER 28
1900

The action of climate seems at first sight to be quite independent of the struggle for existence; but in so far as climate chiefly acts in reducing food, it brings on the most severe struggle between the individuals. ...

I AWOKE IN A gasping panic. There was something terribly wrong with the world, and I knew in my marrow that something dreadful had happened during the night. It took me several seconds to figure out exactly what was wrong: There was such a deep, unnatural silence in the house and outside my window that it felt like the whole world had packed up and stolen away in the night. Had it happened? Had the world come to an end? Should I fall to my knees and pray?

And the light was all wrong. The light edging around my curtains seemed not so much like light as its absence. Every object in my room had taken on a flat, grayish aspect.

And then Ajax barked, just once. The sound was reassuring, even though it was muffled and as flat as the light. My panic was somewhat subdued by the realization that my bladder was about to burst. I felt desperate to use the chamber pot, but first I had to face the hideousness that awaited outside. I considered this. Well, if you did have to face the hideousness, it was a lot better to do so with an empty bladder. On the other hand, the china chamber pot would be awfully cold. I weighed these things, groped under the bed for the pot, and did a fair job of balancing above the icy rim.

That was better. Now to the business of facing hideousness.

I stood resolutely before the window and put my shoulders back in good military posture, took a deep breath, and yanked the curtain aside.

And there it was: a perfect blanket of white covering the lawn, the trees, the road, as far as I could see, all absolutely unbroken, untouched, and still. *Snow*. It had to be snow.

The world hadn't ended. It had just begun.

I looked around my room at my familiar things in the strange light: the hummingbird's nest in its glass box, my red Notebook, my framed butterflies.

I put on my rabbit slippers and pulled my wool dressing gown over my nightie. I edged around the noisy floorboard in the middle of the room and opened my door as quietly as I could, but it creaked loudly in the cold. I waited to see if anyone stirred, but to my relief there was no sound. I wanted to be alone. I wanted this just for me.

I tiptoed down the stairs out the front door and stood on the porch, clutching my gown around me. The temperature amazed me. How could the world be this cold? I inhaled deeply, and the air felt like a dagger in my chest. My exhaled breath formed clouds in the air that disappeared before I could catch them in my hands. There was no noise except for the *whoosh* of my breathing and the rushing of my own heartbeat. There were no birds in the silvery sky, no squirrels in the trees, no possums. Where had all the abounding life gone? The lack of living things made the landscape both beautiful and menacing.

As I looked out, a young coyote came slowly out of the trees, delicately lifting and shaking each paw before gingerly putting it down again in the snow. Step, flick, pause . . . step, flick, pause. . . . There was an expression on its face of such great disgust that I laughed. Startled, it looked up and saw me on the porch, and then I swear it sneered at me. It turned slowly on the spot and went back into the trees the way it had come, trying to step in its own tracks, still step-flick-pausing as it went.

Well, if the coyote could walk in that stuff, I could too. I walked down the steps into the snow. It was not solid like ice, but puffy. It was not silent either, but compressed under my foot with a squeaky crunch. My feet were chilled immediately, and I slipped and almost fell, but no matter. I picked my way down the front steps and looked over my shoulder at my own tracks, which rapidly turned into shallow foot-shaped puddles of water. Ahead of me lay perfection. Could I stand it? Could I bear to mar it with my presence?

I could. I had to have this gift of the moment—this great gift of the new century—to myself for one more minute, a few more precious seconds, before the bustle and shouts and tracks of the others shattered it forever. Gathering up my gown, I ran down the curved drive as fast as I could, lurching and slipping and filled with joy. I knew I looked crazed but I didn't care. I ran to the street, which was unmarked by any wagon wheel, then veered off and ran through the pristine brush toward the river. Here I came across a pecan tree downed by the snow, its raw, flesh-tinted core the only color in the otherwise black-and-white landscape.

I saw a few skittery tracks left by birds and other small creatures, no doubt as confused by this silent white world as I was. Of course they were confused; the last snow had been decades ago. If a finch lived for only two years, how could it pass along the idea of something it had never seen to the next generation? Did the word disappear from the finch language, from finch society? How could any species survive the snow if the word for it died out? The finch race, all the other races, would be unprepared. I would have to put out quantities of seed and suet, hay and ham, and in this way provide for all the links along the food chain.

My feet were turning into blocks of ice, and I realized I was exhausted. I turned and walked back toward the house. It was the first morning of the first day of the new century. Snow blanketed the ground. Anything was possible.

The house was beginning to show its usual signs of morning life. I saw my grandfather watching me from his upstairs window. He raised one hand to me in salute. I replied in kind. We stood that way for a moment. Then I ran for the warmth of our home.

ACKNOWLEDGMENTS

I have, for the sake of fiction, taken some small liberties with Texas history, and I apologize to any reader who spots those places where I have played fast and loose with the facts. Also for the sake of fiction, I have taken liberties with the blooming season of certain plants and the taxonomy of the *Vicia* genus. I beg forgiveness of those botanists and horticulturists who know better. Any errors concerning scientific matters are entirely my fault.

Thanks to the following entities for their encouragement and support along the way: *The Mississippi Review;* the Texas Commission for the Arts; the Writers' League of Texas; the Dallas Museum of Art.

Thanks to Barbara French of the Bat Conservancy, to Dr. Diana Sanchez-Bushong of Westlake United Methodist Church, and to Dr. Spencer Behmer of Texas A&M University for their expertise.

Special thanks to Lou Ann and Jim Bradley for the use of their cabin when I needed it; thanks to Professor Roberta Walker of the University of Texas at El Paso, who could teach a rock to write; to Lee K. Abbott and Grace Paley; to Shelley Williams Austin, Dr. Michael Glasscock, Karen Stolz, Roberta Preston Pazdral, Gerry Beckman, Robin Allen, and Katherine Tanney; thanks to Mike Robinson and his daughter Callie, and to Phil and Jeannie Tate for the name of our heroine. Thanks to the Fabulous Writers of Austin for their boundless support: Pansy Flick, Graciela Fleming, Nancy Gore, Gaylon Greer, Jim Haws, Cecilia Jones, Kim Kronzer, Laura van Landuyt, Diane Owens, and Lottie Shapiro. To Houston White, Dian Donnell, and Charlie Prichard for introducing me to the Old House; to the late John "Sandy" Lockett for the bat tale, which he swore actually happened to him at Scholz's Garden in Austin (an unlikely story, yes, but he never gave me any reason to doubt him). To my early readers, Joe Kulhavy, Wayne Price, Roxanne Hale Drolet, Carol Jarvis, and Noeleen Thompson for their encouragement, along with my *comadre*, Val Brown, who teaches piano with kindness and encouragement and in no way resembles Miss Brown. To my agent, Marcy Posner, for plucking me from the hopper. To Laura Godwin, Noa Wheeler, Ana Deboo, Marianne Cohen, and everyone at Holt for making this a better book.

And, of course, extra special thanks to Gwen Moore Erwin. After all these years.

DISCUSSION QUESTIONS

The author uses quotes from Darwin's *The Origin of Species* to introduce each chapter. What purpose do these introductions serve? Is the quote used for the first chapter relevant to Calpurnia's excitement about nature? How does Darwin's quote, "When a young naturalist commences the study of a group of organisms quite unknown to him, he is at first much perplexed to determine the differences to consider . . ." relate to Calpurnia?

The first time Calpurnia and Granddaddy go to the riverbank together, Calpurnia learns that she shares her name with "Pliny the Younger's fourth wife, the one he married for love. . . . There's also the natal acacia tree, genus *Calpurnia*, a useful laburnum mainly confined to the African continent. Then there's Julius Caesar's wife, mentioned in Shakespeare." Does the name "Calpurnia" suit her? Why or why not?

Much of the book's action is set in the heat of the summer. How might the weather affect the characters?

This novel is set in 1899. We learn a lot about Granddaddy through his war stories, but he never mentions the name or purpose of the war. Which war did he fight in? How do Granddaddy's experiences in that war affect his relationship with Viola? Is their relationship unusual for that time? How does Viola fit into the Tate family?

Calpurnia is the only daughter of six sons. She is expected to learn cooking, sewing, knitting, and other domestic skills to be a good wife and mother. In chapter eight, Granddaddy and Calpurnia examine a fuzzy, probably poisonous, caterpillar. When Calpurnia questions the "sting" of the caterpillar, Granddaddy replies, "I suppose you could touch him and find out. Which raises an interesting point: How far are you willing to go in the name of science?" How does this question relate to Calpurnia's struggle with her mother about a woman's role in the household?

Throughout the novel, Calpurnia is always claiming Granddaddy and Harry as "mine" and she is always nervous when other people come between her and them. Why does she react this way?

Viola calls Calpurnia "Miz" for the first time as she instructs her to mix the ingredients to make apple pie. As Calpurnia is introduced more and more into womanhood by her mother and other women in her life, how does her relationship with Viola change?

After trying his latest pecan alcohol experiment and claiming it to be unsuccessful, Granddaddy says, "The day the experiment succeeds is the day the experiment ends. And I inevitably find that the sadness of the ending outweighs the celebration of success." How does this comment relate to Granddaddy's reaction upon receiving the letter from the Smithsonian?

The year 1900 begins with a rare snowstorm. What does this symbolize for Calpurnia and her family? Does it seem like Calpurnia will continue her observations in science or is she more likely to become the woman her mother wants and expects her to be?

GO FISH

JACQUELINE KELLY

What did you want to be when you grew up?
I wanted to be a writer from the very beginning.

What's your first childhood memory?
Sitting with my father in a sunny garden and staring at goldfish in a pond. It was actually a beer garden. Am I allowed to say that?

What was your worst subject in school?
Algebra

What was your best subject in school?
English

What was your first job?
I started my vocational life as a babysitter, as so many do. Shortly after that I started teaching swimming. (I have a Water Safety Instructor badge, long expired.)

How did you celebrate publishing your first book?
My writing group threw me a wonderful party and we had a grand time. We drank champagne. Am I allowed to say that?

Where do you write your books?
I now write them at our Austin home in a spare room upstairs where I can look out into the oak trees. I wrote large parts of this book sitting on the front steps at our Fentress home.

Where do you find inspiration for your writing?
Inspiration is everywhere. In the faces of strangers at the airport, the grocery store, the beauty salon. In newspaper articles about funny or sad or ridiculous situations. In other books.

Which of your characters is most like you?
Oh, that's easy. Calpurnia, of course.

When you finish a book, who reads it first?
My writing group reads it as I go along. Once I have finished the whole thing, my husband and my agent read it.

Are you a morning person or a night owl?
Owl, definitely, although I would like to be one of those chipper, energetic morning people. I think the world belongs to them.

Which do you like better: cats or dogs?
I love them both, and we have two dogs and three cats. I secretly think that dogs are more rewarding (please don't tell the cats), but then they are also a lot more work. That's very much how life goes, isn't it?

What do you value most in your friends?
Wit, and the ability to make me laugh.

Where do you go for peace and quiet?
I curl up in bed with a good book and Callie, my calico cat. A little Mozart on the radio is soothing.

What's your favorite song?
"Ode to Joy" from Beethoven's Ninth Symphony, the most magnificent piece of music ever written. I have a silver bracelet inscribed with the opening notes.

What time of year do you like best?
If I lived anywhere other than Austin, I would say summer. But the summers are miserably hot here, so I suppose I must amend my answer to spring.

What's your favorite TV show?
When I started writing seriously, I essentially gave up on television. My husband and I rent videos fairly often. I think *30 Rock* is very well written and extremely clever, but I never remember when it's on. I only get to see it if my husband remembers and turns on the TV.

If you were stranded on a desert island, who would you want for company?
Tina Fey

What do you like best about yourself?
I am punctual. Rather a boring quality, really. But I can meet a deadline, or else die trying.

What is your worst habit?
I never clean my car, inside or out. I travel in a rolling pigsty.

What do you consider to be your greatest accomplishment?
Writing the book you are holding in your hands.

Where in the world do you feel most at home?
In a bookstore or at the library. I feel happy through and through when I enter a room full of books.

What do you wish you could do better?
Cook. And sew. I'd love to be able to design and sew my own clothes, but I'm hopeless.

What would your readers be most surprised to learn about you?
I got a motorcycle license before I got a car license. And I know how to drive a tractor.

Callie Vee, Travis, Granddaddy,
and the whole Tate clan are back
in this charming sequel!

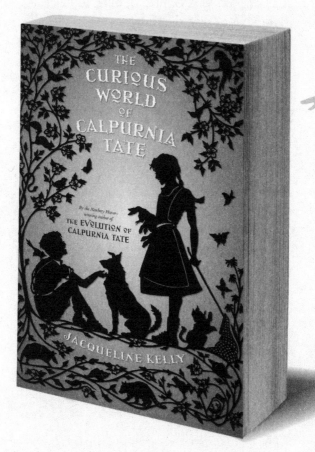

KEEP READING FOR A SNEAK PEEK!

CHAPTER 1

ARMAND VERSUS DILLY

One evening, when we were about ten miles from the Bay of San Blas, vast numbers of butterflies, in bands or flocks of countless myriads, extended as far as the eye could range. Even by the aid of a telescope it was not possible to see a space free from butterflies. The seamen cried out "it was snowing butterflies," and such in fact was the appearance.

TO MY GREAT ASTONISHMENT, I saw my first snowfall on New Year's Day of 1900. Now, you might not think much of this, but it is an exceedingly rare event in central Texas. Why, only the night before, I'd made the resolution to set eyes on snow just once before I died, doubting it would ever happen. My improbable wish had been granted within the space of hours, the snow transforming our ordinary town into a landscape of pristine beauty. I had run through the hushed woods at dawn clad only in my robe and slippers, marveling at the delicate mantle of snow, the pewter sky, and the trees laced with silver, before the cold drove me back to our house. And what with all the fuss and fizz and pomp of the great event, I figured I was poised on the brink of a splendid future in the new century, and that my thirteenth year would be magical.

But now here we were in spring, and somehow the months had slipped away from me, devolving into the usual humdrum round of schoolwork, housework, and piano lessons, the monotony punctuated by my six brothers (!) taking it in turn to drive me, the only girl (!), right around the bend. The New Year had duped me, sure enough.

My real name is Calpurnia Virginia Tate, but back in those days people mostly called me Callie Vee, except for Mother, when she was expressing disapproval, and Granddaddy, who would have no truck with nicknames.

The only solace came from my nature studies with Granddaddy, Captain Walter Tate, a man whom many in our town of Fentress mistook for a crotchety, unsociable old loon. He'd made his money in cotton and cattle, and fought for the Confederate States in the War before deciding to dedicate the last part of his life to the study of Nature and Science. I, his companion in this endeavor, lived for the few precious hours I could eke out in his company, trailing behind him with the butterfly net, a leather satchel, my Scientific Notebook, and a sharp pencil at hand to record our observations.

In inclement weather, we studied our specimens in the laboratory (really just an old shed that had once been part of the slave quarters) or read together in the library, where I slowly picked my way under his tutelage through Mr. Darwin's book *The Origin of Species*. In fine weather, we tramped across the fields to the San Marcos River, pushing our way through the scrub along one of the many deer trails. Our world might not have appeared all that exciting to the untrained eye but there was teeming life everywhere if you only knew where to look. And *how* to look, something Granddaddy taught me. Together we had discovered a brand-new species of hairy vetch now known to the world as *Vicia tateii*. (I confess I'd rather have discovered an unknown species of animal, animals being more interesting and all, but how many people of my age—or any age—had their name permanently attached to a living thing? Beat that if you can.)

I dreamed of following in Granddaddy's footsteps and becoming a Scientist. Mother, however, had other plans for me; namely, learning the domestic arts and coming out as a debutante at age eighteen, when it was hoped I'd be presentable enough to snag the eye of a prosperous young man of good family. (This was dubious for many reasons, including the fact that I loathed cooking and sewing, and could not exactly be described as the eye-snagging type.)

So here we were in spring, a season of celebration and some trepidation in our household on account of my softhearted brother Travis, one year younger than I. You see, spring is the season of burgeoning life, of fledgling birds, raccoon kits, fox cubs, baby squirrels, and many of those babies ended up orphaned or maimed or abandoned. And the more hopeless the case, the bleaker its prospects, the more impossible its future, the more likely was Travis to adopt the creature and lug it home to live with us. I found the parade of unlikely pets quite entertaining but our parents did not. There were stern talks from Mother, there were threatened punishments from Father, but everything went out the window when Travis stumbled across an animal in need. Some thrived and some failed miserably, but all found space in his susceptible heart.

On this particular morning in March, I got up very early and unexpectedly ran into Travis in the hall.

"Are you going to the river?" he said. "Can I come too?"

I generally preferred to go alone because it's so much easier to spy on unsuspecting wildlife that way. But of all my brothers, Travis came closest to sharing my interest in Nature. I let him come along, saying, "Only if you're quiet. I'm going to make my observations."

I led us along one of the deer trails to the river as dawn slowly warmed the eastern sky. Travis, ignoring my instructions, chattered the whole way. "Say, Callie, did you hear that Mrs. Holloway's rat terrier Maisie just had puppies? Do you think Mother and Father would let me have one?"

"I doubt it. Mother's always complaining about the fact that we have four dogs already. She thinks that's three too many."

"But there's nothing better in the world than a puppy! The first thing I'd do is teach it to fetch sticks. That's part of the trouble with Bunny. I love him, but he won't play fetch." Bunny was Travis's huge, fluffy, white prizewinning rabbit. My brother doted on him, feeding and brushing and playing with him every day. But training was a new development.

"Wait," I said, "you're . . . you're trying to teach Bunny to retrieve?"

"Yep. I try and try, but he just won't do it. I even tried him with a carrot stick, but he just ate it."

"Uh . . . Travis?"

"Hmm?"

"No rabbit in the history of the world has ever fetched a stick. So don't bother."

"Well, Bunny's awful smart."

"He may be smart for a rabbit, but that's not saying much."

"I think he just needs more practice."

"Sure, and then you can start piano lessons for the pig."

"Maybe Bunny would catch on faster if you helped us."

"Not so, Travis. It's a hopeless dream."

We continued our debate until we had nearly reached the river, when we suddenly spied some creature snuffling in the leaf mold at the base of a hollowed-out tree. It turned out to be a young *Dasypus novemcinctus*, a nine-banded armadillo, about the size of a small loaf of bread. Although they were becoming more common in Texas, I'd never seen one up close before. Anatomically speaking, it resembled the unhappy melding of an anteater (the face), a mule (the ears), and a tortoise (the carapace). I thought it overall an unlucky creature in the looks department, but Granddaddy once said that to apply a human definition of beauty to an animal that had managed to thrive for millions of years was both unscientific and foolish.

Travis crouched down and whispered, "What's it doing?"

"I think it's looking for breakfast," I said. "According to Granddaddy, they eat worms and grubs and such."

Travis said, "He's awfully cute, don't you think?"

"No, I don't."

But there was no use telling him that. The heedless armadillo then did the one surefire thing guaranteed to earn itself a new home with us: it wandered over to my brother and sniffed at his socks.

Uh-oh. We'd have to get out of there before Travis could say—

"Let's take it home."

Too late! "It's a wild animal, Travis. I don't think we should."

Ignoring me, he said, "I think I'll call him Armand, Armand the Armadillo. Or if it's a girl, I could call her Dilly. How d'you like the name? Dilly the Armadillo."

Drat, now it really was too late. Granddaddy always warned me not to name the objects of scientific study because then one could never be objective, or bring oneself to dissect them, or to stuff them and mount them, or dispatch them to the slaughter-house, or set them free—whatever the particulars of the case called for.

Travis went on, "Is it a boy or a girl, do you reckon?"

"I don't know." I pulled my Scientific Notebook from my pinafore pocket and wrote, Question: How do you tell an Armand from a Dilly?

Travis scooped up the armadillo and hugged it to his chest.

Armand (I had decided to refer to it as Armand for now) showed no sign of fear and proceeded to inspect Travis's collar with an avidly twitching snout. Travis smiled in delight. I sighed in aggravation. He crooned to his new friend while I rooted around with a stick to find it some food. I dug up an immense night crawler and gingerly presented it to Armand, who snatched it from me with his impressive claws and gobbled it down in two seconds flat, spraying messy bits of worm about. Not a pretty sight. No, not at all. Who knew armadillos had the world's worst table manners? But here I was doing it again, applying human sensibilities where they didn't belong.

Even Travis looked taken aback. "Eww," he said. I almost said the same thing, but unlike my brother, I had been annealed in the furnace of Scientific Thought. Scientists do not say such things aloud (although we may *think* them from time to time).

Armand licked shreds of worm off Travis's shirt. My brother said, "He's hungry, that's all. Boy, he doesn't smell so good."

It was true. As if his atrocious manners weren't enough, up close Armand emitted an unpleasant musky smell.

I said, "I think this is a bad idea. What's Mother going to say?"

"She doesn't have to know."

"She *always* knows." Exactly how she always knew was a matter of considerable interest to all seven of her children, who'd never been able to figure it out.

"I could keep him in the barn," Travis said. "She hardly ever goes out there."

I could see this was both a losing battle and not really mine to fight. We put Armand into my satchel, where he proceeded to scratch at the bag's interior all the way home. To my annoyance, I found several deep gouges in the leather when we finally unloaded him in an old rabbit hutch next to Bunny in the farthest corner of the barn. But first we weighed him on the scale used for rabbits and poultry (five pounds) and measured him from stem to stern (eleven inches, not including the tail). We debated for a minute whether to include the tail but decided that leaving it out was a better representation of his true dimensions.

Armand didn't seem to dislike this attention; on the other hand, he didn't seem to like it much either. He investigated the confines of his new home and then started scrabbling at the bottom of the hutch, ignoring us completely.

We didn't know it then, but this was going to be the extent of our relationship: scrabbling and ignoring, followed by more scrabbling and more ignoring. We watched him scrabbling and ignoring us until our maid, SanJuanna, rang the bell on the back porch to signal breakfast. We bolted into the kitchen and were met with the delightful fragrance of frying bacon and fresh cinnamon rolls.

"Warsh," commanded our cook, Viola, from the stove.

Travis and I took turns operating the pump and scrubbing our hands at the sink. A few slimy strings of Armand's breakfast still clung to my brother's shirt. I signaled to him and handed him a damp dish towel but he only smeared the stuff around and made things worse.

Viola looked up and said, "What's that smell?"

I said hastily, "Those rolls sure look good."

Travis said, "What smell?"

"That smell I smell on you, mister."

"It's just, uh, one of my rabbits. You know Bunny? The big white one? He needs a bath, that's all."

This surprised me. Travis was a notoriously bad liar on his feet, but here he was, making a pretty good job of it. In addition to my nature studies, I was making a project of building my vocabulary, and the word *facile* popped into my mind. I'd had no opportunity to use it before, but it certainly applied here: Travis, the *facile* fibber.

"Huh," said Viola. "Never heard of no rabbit needing a bath before."

"Oh, he's filthy," I chimed in. "You should see him."

"Huh," she said again. "I'll just bet."

She loaded a platter high with crispy bacon and then carried it through the swinging door into the dining room. We followed behind and took our assigned places at the table with my other brothers: Harry (the oldest, my favorite), Sam Houston (the quiet est), Lamar (a real pill), Sul Ross (the second quietest), and Jim Bowie (at age five, the youngest and the loudest).

I should say here that Harry was quickly sinking in his rating as Favorite Brother due to his stepping out with Fern Spitty. Even though he was eighteen and I'd finally resigned myself to his marrying one day, his courtship meant that he spent more and more time away from the house. Fern was pretty and sweet-tempered and fairly sensible in that she didn't recoil all that much when I walked through the house with some blobby specimen sloshing around in a jar. And even though I generally approved of her, the sad truth was that she would likely break up our family one day.

Father and Granddaddy came in and sat down, nodding to us all and solemnly proclaiming, "Good morning."

Granddaddy gave me a good morning of my own, and I smiled at him, warmed by the knowledge that I was *his* favorite.

Father said, "Your mother is having one of her sick headaches. She won't be joining us this morning."

This was something of a relief, as Mother could have spotted a wormy shirt at thirty paces. And if she rather than Viola had interrogated Travis, there was a good chance he'd have buckled and confessed all. I, on the other hand, had adopted the tactic of stout denial, no matter what. I had become so good, so *facile* at denial—even in the face of incontrovertible evidence—that Mother often didn't bother interrogating me at all. (So you see, being considered unreliable does have some use, although I don't encourage it in others.)

We bowed our heads while Father said the blessing, then SanJuanna passed the platters of food. Without Mother present, we were relieved of the burden of making the light and pleasant conversation that she required at mealtimes, and we pitched into our breakfast with a right good will. For several minutes there was only the scraping of forks and knives, muffled sounds of appreciation, and the occasional request to please pass the syrup.

* * *

AFTER SCHOOL, Travis and I ran to check on Armand and found him hunched in a corner of his cage, every now and then scrabbling halfheartedly at the wire. He looked sort of, well, depressed, but with an armadillo, how could you tell for sure?

"What's wrong with him?" said Travis. "He doesn't look too happy."

"It's because he's a wild animal and he's not supposed to be here. Maybe we should let him go."

But Travis was not ready to give up on his novel pet. "I'll bet he's hungry. D'you have any worms on you?"

"I'm fresh out." This wasn't exactly true. I had one giant worm left in my room, the biggest one I'd ever seen, but I was saving it for my first dissection. Granddaddy had suggested we start with an annelid and work our way up through the various phyla. I figured, the bigger the worm, the better to see its organs and the easier the dissection.

Nevertheless, I applied myself to the problem of Armand. He was a ground dweller and an omnivore, which meant he would eat all different kinds of animal and vegetable matter. I wasn't in the mood for digging grubs, and it would take forever to trap enough ants to make him a decent meal, so I said, "Let's go see what's in the pantry."

We ran to the back porch and into the kitchen, where Viola sat resting between meals, drinking a cup of coffee, Idabelle the Inside Cat keeping her company in her basket by the stove. Viola paged through one of Mother's ladies' magazines. She couldn't read or write but enjoyed looking at the latest fashionable hats. One of them had what appeared to be a stuffed bird of paradise perched in a nest of tulle, one wing swooping artfully over the wearer's brow. I thought the hat thoroughly ridiculous, along with being a terrible waste of a rare and wonderful specimen.

"What do you want?" Viola said, not looking up.

"Oh, we're just a little hungry," I said. "We thought we'd see what's in the pantry."

"All right, but don't you touch those pies. They're for supper, you hear?"

"We hear."

We grabbed the first thing at hand, a hard-boiled egg, and ran back to the barn.

Armand sniffed at the egg, rolled it around with his claws, and then cracked it open. He ate with messy enthusiasm, grunting all the while. When he'd finished, he retired to the far corner of his cage and resumed his hunched, miserable posture. I stared at him and thought about his environment. He lived in the ground. He was nocturnal. Which meant he liked to sleep in a burrow all day. But here he was in broad daylight without a burrow for protection. No wonder he looked unhappy.

I said, "I think he needs a hole in the ground, a burrow to sleep in."

"We don't have one."

"If you let him go," I said hopefully, "he could make himself one."

"I can't let him go. He's my Armand. We just have to make one for him."

I sighed. We cast about for materials and found a pile of old newspapers and a scrap of blanket used to wipe down the horses after their day's work. We put these items in the cage where Armand did his usual sniffing routine and then started industriously shredding the paper. He hauled it, along with his blanket, to the back corner of the hutch and, within minutes, had built himself a nest of sorts. He pulled the blanket over himself and thrashed this way and that. Then he grew still. Faint snores emanated from the mound.

"There," Travis whispered, "see how happy he is? You're so smart, Callie Vee. You know everything."

Well, of course this puffed me up quite a bit. Maybe it wasn't such a bad idea after all to keep Armand. (Or Dilly.)

JACQUELINE KELLY is the author of the Newbery Honor winner, *The Evolution of Calpurnia Tate*, its sequel, *The Curious World of Calpurnia Tate*, and *Return to the Willows*. Born in New Zealand, she now lives with her husband and too many cats and dogs in Austin, Texas.

jacquelinekelly.com